Billionaire Lumberjack's Bargain

Gwyn McNamee

BILLIONAIRE LUMBERJACK'S BARGAIN

© 2025 Gwyn McNamee

To everyone who has ever had to move through grief to find those little moments of joy.

Chapter One

DALTON

Vultures circling only mean one thing.

Death has come to the mountain.

Given the number of them filling the sky, gliding in effortless loops high above the forest, whatever died is *big*. Likely something that drew in an apex predator, and now, the scavengers are just waiting for it to abandon the carrion before they drop in for the scraps.

Dragging my gaze from them, I swing my axe again, slamming it into the log and sending the pieces flying off either side of the stump I use when chopping firewood.

Sweat trickles down my bare back, chest, and temples, and I swipe at it with my forearm to keep it from my eyes as I return to watching the ominous birds.

Everything dies.

It's part of life no one can run from or escape.

Especially here on the mountain.

Seeing the large, dark birds waiting to swoop in usually

doesn't bother me. Nothing more than a necessary cycle. One every animal plays a role in—humans included.

But something about their placement to the northwest of the homestead, just slightly down the mountain from us, makes unease crawl up my spine.

That's the Bower property...

Great-Uncle Tim's old place.

And the Bowers have a young child up there who can't be more than four, given how pregnant the wife was when they first rented from us.

By now, they could have more little ones.

Additional targets for any number of predators that lurk in the woods, waiting for something small and helpless to be unprotected.

A shudder rolls through me that I attempt to ignore.

It's probably nothing...

Gritting my jaw, I return to splitting wood, trying to focus on the task at hand. Doing my best to ignore both the slight ache in my back and that nagging feeling in the recesses of my mind that something might be wrong.

If it were, they would get word to us or someone in town. They would ask for help, and like always, the people of James Creek would offer any they could.

That knowledge settles my nerves long enough for me to break down half a cord of firewood to add to what's already in the shed in preparation for the coming winter.

This beautiful, unusually hot summer won't last long.

Soon enough, Mother Nature will flip the switch, and the icy-cold winds and snow will blanket the Adirondacks.

Anyone not ready for it will be in a very bad place—where I refuse to *ever* find myself. Even if it means working through the height of this heat and humidity, breaking down the firewood and getting it stored—and suffering for it later when it comes to my back.

By the time the sun reaches its peak in the sky and I step out of the shed, the vultures have either descended or given up and moved on. And I need to check in on Pops...

The old man has been left to his own devices for too long today.

God only knows what he's gotten into back at the cabin.

Throwing my axe over my shoulder, I duck between the shed and the barn, moving across the well-worn path back toward home.

Sunlight filters through the heavy foliage of the surrounding trees, but it won't be thick and green for long.

They'll be turning far too soon.

Which means I have a lot more work to do.

Pops isn't any help the way he is now...

The worry that's become such a familiar foe gnaws at my gut as I approach the cabin, knowing what I'll find—the same thing I have over the past few months.

A man I barely recognize some days. So unlike the one who raised me most of my life and has built a reputation for being an unbendable, unbreakable force of nature. Ruling over James Creek and all our various businesses alone for decades from up here on the mountain.

Always sharp.

Alert.

Completely on top of things.

Running everything like clockwork.

But lately, the lapses in his memory have left tasks undone...or done improperly.

And despite my best efforts, I don't know how to fix all of it.

The old man has made it damn near impossible when

3

he won't let me help with anything having to do with the business...

I rest my axe on the porch next to the door, push it open, and step into an eerie silence, bracing myself for what I might see. "Pops?"

This time of day, he's typically bustling around in the kitchen, making lunch, but the only sound is my own heavy footsteps across the hand-hewn wooden floorboards that have seen generations walk on them.

"Pops?"

I check the entire downstairs, including his office where he likes to hole up, but I don't find any sign of him.

Same with the second-floor bedrooms and bathroom.

My chest tightens as I descend the stairs and head toward the back porch, the only other place he could be, unless he left the house—which would pose a whole *other* set of problems. He could be *anywhere* on the mountain by now. "Pops?"

The back door stands slightly ajar, and I release a heavy, relieved breath as I nudge it open and step out to find him sipping a cup of coffee in his Adirondack chair, staring out at the beautiful vista.

His gaze stays locked on the peaks to the north.

"Pops...didn't you hear me calling for you?"

His head turns toward me slowly, and he raises one bushy white brow. "So, what if I did? Maybe I wanted to be left alone."

Smartass.

Huffing a laugh, I settle onto the arm of the matching chair next to his and run a hand through my sweat-dampened hair. "How long have you been out here?"

He returns his focus to the mountains. "A while."

"Did you see the vultures?"

4

Pops bobs his head and takes a sip. "Yep."

"Looked like they were near the Bower place."

"It did"—he glances my way—"but I'm sure the body is gone by now."

My back stiffens, goosebumps pebbling over my exposed skin.

Pops has been rambling more and has made a lot of statements that don't make sense over the last couple of months but nothing that has caused my blood to run cold like *that* just did.

"What do you mean, Pops?"

His brows rise as if he's surprised I'm not following. "You know...Dave's body."

It takes a moment for me to process the name of our nearest—and *only*—neighbor on the actual mountain.

"Dave Bower is dead?"

He presses his lips together in a firm line, shaking his head before he releases an exasperated sigh. "Of course, he's dead, Dalton. Has been a few months now."

A few months?

Not so long ago, I could trust anything that came out of this man's mouth. He was sharp as a tack, always on top of everything. But now, I watch him staring out at the trees as if he's searching for something he lost.

God knows what that might be—besides his memory.

This could all be nothing more than the ramblings of an old, confused man. I'd love to leave it at that without delving deeper, but something really big might be happening that I've been completely in the dark about. Questioning him further won't get me anywhere.

I reach out and squeeze his arm. "I'm going to make lunch. Are you hungry?"

He nods. "I could eat."

At least he still has his appetite, but whatever's causing the cognitive decline only seems to be getting worse. And he won't go into town to see Doc—despite my repeated insistence he needs to—nor will he let me radio him to come up here to try to figure out what's happening in his head.

Pops has always been a proud man; that pride might be what kills him.

I keep hoping things will get better, that whatever is going on with him will somehow correct itself. Because the thought of any other possibility makes bile crawl up my throat.

But I can only *hope* for so long.

At some point, I'm going to have to physically force him into the truck if I want any chance of getting him examined.

I swallow back my concern rather than push into another argument with him and move back into the house, directly to Pops' office.

He would lose his shit if he knew I was in here without him, making this call on the radio, but I won't be able to return to my work today without knowing what the hell he meant by that statement about Dave Bower.

Sliding into Pops' chair, I reach for the CB radio on the corner of his desk and listen to the familiar creak of the cracked leather as I sit back.

The room looks different from this side—bigger—but I don't take any time to dwell on it, not when the longer I'm gone, the more likely it becomes that Pops comes looking for me.

I adjust to the channel for the sheriff's office and press the button on the radio handset. "Sheriff Wilson, this is Dalton James."

It takes a few seconds before I get any response. *"Dal-*

ton, it's Betty. He's just coming in from a call. I'll grab him for you."

"Thanks."

I drum my fingers on the old wooden desk Great-Uncle Tim built before I was even born, waiting for the only person who might have any idea what Pops was talking about.

"Dalton?" Sheriff Wilson's familiar voice floats through the speakers. *"Everything all right?"*

As a James Creek native, Travis Wilson knows neither Pops nor I would radio unless there were an issue.

"I'm not entirely sure. Pops said something odd today." *And in the most casual way...* "He mentioned that Dave Bower may have died."

A brief silence looms before Sheriff Wilson responds. *"You didn't know?"*

"Shit." I wince and pinch the bridge of my nose with my free hand. "No..."

"I assumed your grandfather would have told you."

"It must have slipped his mind."

Just like everything else seems to lately.

There is no *way* he wouldn't have told me something like that immediately...if he *remembered* it. By the time he *did*, he probably assumed he already *had*.

"How long ago did it happen?"

"Um, going on maybe two months."

Fucking hell.

It's been *that* long, and Mrs. Bower and their child have been up there alone...

The apprehension I felt earlier at seeing the vultures rushes back even harder now. Not a wave. A goddamn tsunami of anxiety I haven't ever felt. A strange sense that something is very wrong.

"What happened?"

"Horse kicked him, apparently in the head. Died almost instantly, from what Camille told me."

Camille...

The wife.

A hazy memory of a dark-haired woman waving at me from behind a wall of falling rain and the slightly fogged truck window flashes through my head.

"She found him..." Sheriff Wilson sucks in a long breath, and knowing the man as well as I do, I can tell that whatever he saw when he went up there that day still burdens him. *"She's a nurse. Said there was nothing she could do when she found him."*

I might have only been four when Mom and Dad died, but I still remember that utter sense of helplessness and loss when they were suddenly gone. And once I was old enough to understand what really happened, another feeling settled into my chest and never left.

Guilt.

"I'm surprised your grandfather didn't tell you. I came up and spoke with him about it right after it happened. Asked him to check on her to see if she needed anything every once in a while—"

Shit.

My throat tightens. "Like I said, it must have just slipped his mind. I'm sure he's been dealing with it." *Lie.* "Just didn't let me know."

"Why didn't you ask him?"

Because everything is falling apart up here, and no one can know about it.

Ignoring his question, I try to shift the focus of the conversation away from Pops and his declining health. "I saw some vultures circling around their property earlier today."

"Well, damn." Concern makes his voice waver slightly. *"I hope Camille's all right."*

"They have a little one, right?"

"Yes. A son. I don't remember how old. You never met him?"

"No."

I run my hand through my hair and release a heavy sigh as I drop my head against the chairback. "You know how Pops is. He always takes care of collecting the rent and dealing with any business issues himself. I haven't seen the Bowers since they took over Uncle Tim's property, and I only met Dave once, when they first arrived and stopped by to talk about the homestead with Pops. Camille didn't even leave the truck to meet us formally because it was pouring rain and she was pregnant."

"I see..."

Though he tries to mask it, the uneasiness in his voice brought on by this conversation cuts through the radio feed.

Maybe it's for Camille and her son—or Pops.

Either way, I have to deal with it.

There isn't anyone else who can...

"I'll go up there and check on them."

Sheriff Wilson releases a little grunt of confirmation. "Let me know if I'm needed up there."

"Will do."

I return the handset to the cradle and stare at Pops' desk.

The normally immaculate, polished surface is cluttered with various papers in apparently no order, instead of properly filed away like they always have been within the drawers Pops always keeps locked.

That's changed, too.

A physical manifestation of whatever's happening in his head.

What's going on with you, Pops?

Besides chaos...

I release a heavy sigh and climb to my feet, pushing the chair back under the desk where it was. He may remember how he left it, and he can't know I was in here without him. Or he might not remember at all...

Which would be worse?

An ache blooms in my chest, and I rub at it as I step back into the living room, listening for any signs of him inside, but he hasn't moved from his spot on the porch.

I quickly throw together a sandwich for him and bring it out, setting it on the small table between the two chairs. "Here you go, Pops. I'm going to head over to the Bower property. Make sure everything's okay."

He raises his gaze to meet mine. "Why wouldn't it be?"

"The vultures..."

His brow furrows. "Oh, right." He nods slowly. "Good thinking."

"I'll be back, but it might not be before dinner."

Pops pats me on the arm. "Be careful, kid."

The same words he has said to me *every* day somehow hit differently today.

He's always worrying about me as if I'm still that little boy, and he seems completely oblivious to the fact that he should be worried about *himself*.

"I always am, Pops."

I squeeze his shoulder before I step down off the back porch and head out toward the barn. Apollo neighs from inside his stall when he sees me coming, his head bobbing in his excitement because I haven't been by since before the sun came up.

"Hey, buddy." I rub his neck, and he leans into my touch, eager for what he can already anticipate is coming. "Let's go for a ride."

He prances as I lead him out to saddle up for the ride to the Bower property.

It would be easier to take the truck and drive but far faster to take the direct route through the woods on horseback, which also allows me the opportunity to watch for any signs of what might have drawn the vultures in earlier today.

I mount and tug gently on the reins, directing him to head across the mountain in a northwesterly direction.

The closer I get to Uncle Tim's old place, the more a familiar scent lingers in the air underneath that of the smoke from the cabin the Bowers now live in.

Death.

I'd know it anywhere.

It comes for everyone and everything on the mountain.

I ease up on the reins as we reach the edge of the forest. "Whoa."

Apollo steps out from the protection of the tree-covered path and onto the property cautiously, as if he, too, can sense something is off.

Movement to my left immediately draws my head in that direction, and a little dark-haired boy pops out from around a tree, blue eyes wide, staring up at me in awe...

Maybe fear.

Or a combination of both.

"Hey, buddy." I slide off Apollo, keeping the reins in my hand as I examine the kid for any signs that he might be in trouble or alone out here. "Where's your mom?"

The answering sound of a shotgun being racked comes from behind me.

I freeze, turning my head slowly to glance over my shoulder without making any sudden moves.

Dark amber hair whips around her face in the afternoon breeze, the sunlight glinting off it, making the natural red tint shimmer. She stares me down with brilliant Caribbean-blue eyes filled with suspicion, the sight of the gun pointed directly at my back with an unwavering aim. "Right *here*."

———

CAMILLE

My heart thunders against my rib cage, every muscle in my body tenses with my gaze zeroed in on the stranger standing so close to Davey, but I somehow still manage to keep the shotgun leveled squarely on the threat.

With his back to me and head turned slightly, all I can see is his profile, a single green eye assessing me where I stand, only a hundred yards from him.

At this distance, I wouldn't miss if I pulled the trigger.

I risk glancing down at Davey a few feet to his left. "Come over here."

His focus darts between the man and me, as if he's debating his options. This is the first stranger he's seen on the property since Dave died, and he's bound to be curious. But the longer he stands there, the more queasy I become and the harder it is to hold this gun in position.

Inclining my head away from the trees, I encourage him back toward me and the safety of the cabin. "Come on."

Davey only hesitates a moment before he rushes over

and wraps his arm around my left leg, tucking his head behind my thigh shyly.

The man raises his hands, transferring the reins of his horse from one fist to the other as he turns to face me. A cut-off shirt hangs from muscular arms, unbuttoned in the front, exposing a chiseled chest and abs clearly honed by manual labor. From under thick sandy-blond hair, his soft evergreen eyes that match the trees surrounding us don't seem threatening, nor does his body language, but that doesn't mean anything.

Especially not up here.

Innocuous things can be deadly—something Dave taught me very early on when it came to off-grid home-steading on James Mountain.

The intruder watches me carefully, dipping his head slightly to put us more on the same level—a move likely designed to encourage me to let down my guard. "I'm Dalton James. My grandfather owns this property. We met once, sort of, when you and your husband first rented from us. You didn't get out of the truck..."

That rainy day almost five years ago comes back in bits and pieces.

A young man standing beside Edison James as he handed the keys over to Dave...

There isn't any reason to believe it isn't him, but that doesn't mean I'm going to lower this gun. Just because I know who he is doesn't mean he isn't a threat.

"What are you doing here?"

His gaze lifts to the clear summer sky. "I saw vultures circling the property earlier. I was concerned, especially when I found out about your husband."

My stomach twists violently, threatening to make me heave right out here in front of this man. Tears burn my eyes, but I can't wipe them away as they finally fall without lowering my only weapon.

"I'm sorry...I didn't know"—he glances down at Davey and seems to consider his words—"about what happened until today, or I would've come sooner to check on you, make sure you didn't need anything."

He sounds sincere, but if I learned one thing living up here, it's that letting down my guard can get me killed. Just like it did Dave.

"We're fine." I motion toward the path that leads through the forest to the James homestead. "You can go."

His gaze narrows on me, hands still raised. "I smelled it as soon as I got near the property. What died?"

Hell.

He is far *too observant.*

I swallow thickly, trying to ignore the very smell he's referring to that has done nothing to ease my nausea this morning. Breathing through my mouth, I manage to form a reply around the acidic taste on my tongue. "One of the cows. She gave birth this morning but didn't make it."

Dalton winces slightly. "I'm sorry. The calf?"

Davey squeezes my leg, peeking his head from around my thigh. "Rocky!"

I glance down at him, then back at Dalton. "Yes. Rocky. He's in the barn. Seems to be doing fine. We bottle fed him..."

"Where is *she*?"

Her body.

That's what he's asking without saying the words in front of Davey.

I incline my head toward the right to the fenced enclosure near the barn, where she collapsed shortly after giving birth.

He follows my gaze. "Inside or out?"

It isn't hard to see where he's going with this line of questioning.

"Out."

A muscle in his jaw tics, and he tightens his grip on the reins in his raised hand. "Has it drawn in any predators yet?"

My arms start to ache, and I adjust my stance, ensuring the gun stays squarely on him.

Besides you?

The words sit on the tip of my tongue. Because I know what people are capable of. I've seen it firsthand. It's the entire reason we moved up here in the first place. But the flash of black moving in the trees I saw early this morning, just after dawn, draws a vise tight around my ribs. "I think I saw a bear earlier, but I can't be sure... It didn't come onto the property, just along the edge."

Dalton winces. "The longer it stays here, the more danger you're going to be drawing right to you."

Like I don't know that already.

Biting back my annoyance, I consider my options.

There aren't many.

I'm in a shitty position, something I knew the moment Winny died.

Dalton raises a dark-blond brow at me. "Can I put my hands down?"

I nod, but I don't lower the gun.

Not yet...

Dalton lets his hands fall, relaxing at his sides, reins still clutched in white knuckles. "I imagine it's hard to get much done up here alone with this little guy." He motions toward Davey. "What's his name?"

I feel Davey pop his head out from behind my leg. "Davey!"

His sweet little voice carries across the space between us, and the ease with which he so readily gave Dalton the information instantly tightens my shoulders.

I peer down at him. "Shh. Don't talk to strangers."

He glances up at me. "Sorry, Mama."

"Davey..."

Hearing his name from Dalton sends a little shiver through me. It's soft, kind, and I haven't heard anyone else say his name like that since Dave died.

"Have you been helping your mom?"

Davey nods vigorously, shifting around to my side slightly.

Dalton grins at him, the curl of his lips making him seem even more relaxed and approachable before his gaze returns to me. "I can help you take care of it. You can't leave it sitting out there."

"I've got it handled."

His brows rise slowly. "I can see you're quite capable of taking care of yourself, but I imagine she probably weighs at least 1,000 pounds, and you need to get her buried quickly. Do you have a backhoe?"

It's like this man can see straight through me. Spot every weakness and mistake I've made since Dave died. All the ways I've failed laid bare the same way I feel under Dalton's assessing gaze.

"I do, but it stopped firing up last week. I don't know what's wrong with it."

His lips press into a firm line. "So, you were going to dig by hand?"

It isn't said with any malice, but a tinge of disbelief taints his deep voice. With a hint of something else thrown in there. Almost like he's impressed that I thought I *could.*

"Everything happened so quickly this morning, helping with the birth, then knowing she wasn't going to make it, and having to focus on the calf. I haven't had much time to figure anything out."

But he's right.

The longer the decaying body sits out in the middle of the livestock enclosure, the more of a danger it becomes. Once predators know there's something for them on our property, they'll keep coming back, even when the carcass is long gone.

Dalton's gaze softens. "I know you don't have any reason to, but you need to trust me, Camille."

I flinch at the use of my name, the ease with which he uses it. Like we're friends even though we've just met—and I'm still holding a gun on him.

"You can't do it on your own." His eyes drift down to Davey clinging to my leg. "Especially with this little man here being so inquisitive."

Shit. Shit. Shit.

I press my lips together, biting back the desire to tell him I'm fine, that I can handle it...that natural instinct to *want* to take care of things myself and not let anyone in.

Because I *can't.*

I'm only going to be risking Davey and myself if I don't accept his help.

We're completely exposed here. Alone on the homestead with nothing but this shotgun to defend us against *any* type of predators that might wander onto our land.

If I can't trust Dalton James, who can I trust?

No one.

There isn't anyone else *to* trust up here.

My heart clenches, all the struggles of the last few months weighing so heavily on me now that I can't hold the gun up any longer and slowly lower the barrel to the packed dirt beneath my feet.

Dalton offers me a half-smile that makes him look even younger than he must be—maybe mid-twenties. "I'm going to go tie up the horse, then we'll figure it out. Okay?"

I give him a little nod, but I can't manage to respond otherwise without letting a sob slip out.

This entire day has been a clusterfuck of epic proportions.

And now I have to put this in the hands of this man I just met and trust that he's going to solve a problem that has been threatening to crush me all morning.

He moves over to the fence post and ties his horse to it, leaning in to whisper something to him and pat his neck gently a few times.

The animal nudges him affectionately.

A good sign.

If the horse likes him, he can't be all bad...

Dalton advances toward me slowly—cautiously closing the distance that existed between us only moments ago.

My back immediately stiffens, one hand tightening around the gun and the other on Davey's head, where he still clings to me.

The younger James stops a few feet in front of me, and this close, I can see the tiny little flecks of gold in his green eyes. He smiles, and this time, it reaches them fully as he squats. "Hi, Davey. I'm Dalton."

He holds out his palm, and Davey glances up at me for permission. I nod, and he reaches forward and gives Dalton a high five with a giggle that helps relieve a little of my concern.

"It's nice to meet you." Dalton grins up at me in a way most women would melt over. "You, too, formally. Though I wish it were under better circumstances."

Some of the tension in my shoulders relaxes slightly. "Same."

When we moved up here, everyone told us the James family controlled everything, owned most of the town named after them and all the mountain range visible in the area, but they also said that Dalton's grandfather was a kind man, one who could be trusted.

In my limited contacts with him since we arrived, that's proven true.

I just hope his grandson is cut from the same cloth.

He pushes to his feet and glances back toward the paddock. "How long has she been out?"

"Hours. Maybe six."

His jaw tightens. "Then I need to move quickly."

"What are you going to do?"

He surveys the area around the small clearing the cabin and barn sit in. "Hey, Davey, I see some buttercups over there. Why don't you go pick some for your mom and me? I bet they'd look really pretty in the house."

Davey smiles and looks up at me.

I nod. "Go ahead."

He rushes toward them, happy to have a reason to dig in the dirt.

Dalton steps closer to me, cautiously checking Davey's progress to ensure he's not in earshot. "I'm going to have to break down the body." He looks toward the barn. "It's been sitting out too long to save any of the meat that might have been usable, and she's likely too big to carry her whole, even with the backhoe."

I squeeze my eyes closed as my stomach roils violently.

No matter how often it happens, the taste in the back of my throat threatens to overwhelm me.

Breathe.

Inhaling deeply, I hold the air in my lungs for a few seconds, pressing my hand over my stomach.

One.

Two.

Three.

I release it and open my eyes to meet Dalton's concerned ones.

His gaze darts down and widens slightly. "Are you—"

"Yes."

What can only be pity flashes across the green, and his jaw tenses. "Then you probably don't want to be out here to see this"—his attention darts to Davey—"and he shouldn't be, either. Tell me where everything is."

"The barn storage room and behind it, near the woodshed."

"Do you have someplace I can bury her?"

Oh, God.

There goes my stomach again.

I swallow the bile. "West side of the property. There's a clearing. It should be easy to get in and out of it with the backhoe."

If he can't, he'd have to dig by hand, and that could take *days.* But we need it as far away from the house as we can get it, as quickly as possible.

"This might take all afternoon, maybe even into the evening." Now it's Dalton's turn to look queasy. "It'll be messy."

That's a massive understatement.

He's trying to downplay what he's about to do and make

me feel better about this entire situation he's been brought into.

His gaze softens the longer it takes me to say anything, but I can't seem to find the words for what he's doing for us. "I really am sorry about your husband. I didn't know him since my grandfather was always the one coming up here, but..."

He trails off, seemingly as lost as I am when it comes to finding the right thing to say.

Swallowing through the emotion clogging my throat, I blink away the threatening tears. "Thank you."

Dalton rubs the back of his neck, making the thickly roped muscles in his arms and chest shift under his open shirt. "You've been up here alone since he passed?"

His question claws at my chest, threatening to rip me open, and I start to lose the battle with the telltale burn in my eyes.

He scans the property.

Probably seeing all the ways I've failed since Dave died.

The overgrown brush surrounding the clearing the house sits in.

Weeds growing up the haphazardly patched livestock fences.

All the damage the last storm did to the cabin and greenhouse that I haven't fixed.

The chickens running wild when they should be contained—if I could manage to catch them.

It's a mess.

But he doesn't say anything about any of that.

"I'm going to get to work. I would call down to town and have people come help me, but—"

I nod slowly. "But it would take them several hours to get up here, and by then, it'll be dark."

His brow softens. "You know you could have always radioed us if you needed something, if you needed help."

That tightness in my sternum returns, but I don't bother responding or explaining to him why I didn't, why I couldn't.

And thank God, he doesn't press me.

Because I am *this close* to completely losing it.

Dalton turns and stalks toward the barn, and I release a heavy breath as Davey returns with a fistful of flowers, holding them up to me.

"Here, Mama."

I squat and accept them. "Thank you, Bubs. They're beautiful."

The bright yellow blurs as my tears finally fall.

"Where's Dalton?"

His wide eyes search the clearing.

"He's going to take care of some things for me. You and I are going to play in the house today." Far away from what Dalton is going to have to do. "Maybe we could bake some cookies or something."

Davey's blue eyes that match mine light up, and he darts back toward the cabin.

I push to my feet, my focus drifting toward the retreating back of the young man who just came to my rescue, even though I didn't ask for it or want it.

You needed it.

That little voice inside my head screams loudly enough to break through that last bit of fight I have left in me, and for the first time in two months, I feel like I can actually take a deep breath.

Chapter Two

DALTON

She's pregnant.

From the moment she went so pale and subtly shifted her hand over her stomach, I knew it without even asking. Her confirmation made my heart break even more at the situation Camille Bower has found herself in.

Alone on this homestead with a four-year-old and another one coming...

And what I've observed over the last several hours as I've worked to get rid of the remains of her cow has only made my apprehension for her grow.

She isn't ready for the coming winter—not by a *long* shot.

This property where Great-Uncle Tim once lived is in disarray.

The stunningly beautiful woman with a thankfully steady trigger finger has obviously attempted to keep things going since her husband's death. But it would be impossible for almost anyone to handle a property this large by themselves—not to mention with a child that age clinging to her twenty-four-seven.

Just moving the livestock feed alone must be a tremendous physical effort for her. Yet, she has somehow managed to keep their handful of animals alive and thriving, from what I've seen.

That will change once the temperatures plummet and the snow hits.

It won't be possible.

That nagging voice won't stop reminding me how truly perilous her position is or that I'm likely the only person who knows anything about it.

The strong set of her shoulders, the hard press of her perfectly pink lips, and the high tilt of her chin when I offered to assist were enough to make it crystal clear that Camille doesn't easily admit weakness or need for a helping hand from anyone.

It seemed almost physically painful for her to even allow me to get this cleaned up for her—something she *knows* is necessary to keep away not only the predators but also any number of diseases the carcass would have brought.

That kind of stubbornness is necessary to survive out here.

It could also mean disaster.

Like *this* could have.

I toss another shovelful of dirt onto the grave I dug with the small backhoe once I got the engine running again with some new spark plugs. The machine made this job easier, but in order to ensure nothing tries to dig up the carcass, I have to ensure it's well camouflaged and the lime and cayenne I spread over the body covers the entire area.

The sun dips below the tree line, and the temperature begins to drop.

A welcome reprieve from the hot rays that have been beating down on me all afternoon while I've worked—probably too hard. My back screams each time I use the shovel.

Too much bending. Too much lifting. Too much...everything today after already spending the entire morning chopping wood.

And now that night is falling, Pops is probably wondering where I am...

If he even remembers I left.

That incessant pain in my stomach returns, and acid climbs my throat. It has nothing to do with the fact that I skipped lunch and dinner to come here to hack up the carcass with the axe I found in the shed.

What if I hadn't?

Camille wouldn't have asked for help.

That tenacious woman would have tried to do this very sweaty, bloody, messy, disgusting job herself—with Davey underfoot.

Anyone who comes up here, who chooses to live the way we do, usually wants to be left alone to live their lives as they please, without interference from society or the unwanted complications that come with it. But Camille is a single mother now, on the side of a mountain, with us as her only real neighbors...and she didn't even come to us for help when her husband died.

Shit...

Or maybe she did and Pops forgot to tell me, then promptly forgot about it himself...

Which would explain part of the welcome she gave me.

If she asked and feels like we abandoned her, she has every reason to mistrust Pops and me.

I need to talk to her again. To find out more about her situation so I can lend any assistance possible—any I can convince her to *take*. Because she and that little boy won't make it through winter like this.

There isn't enough feed.

Their garden is a weed-infested mess with almost nothing edible growing in it.

The greenhouse is half-collapsed.

And I would wager a guess that her freezers are empty, too.

Even if she has the skills, Camille can't hunt when she has a child to care for. Which means she's likely felt as hopeless the last few months as I have, watching Pops decline day by day.

And I've been away from him too long as it is today.

The sun continues to drop behind the trees as I finish leveling the clearing, hopefully fully concealing the burial spot.

I swipe the back of my hand over the sweat trickling down my temples and forehead as the last vestiges of daylight disappear, leaving the orangey-pink sky above the trees the only illumination.

There's only one thing left to do—head back to the cabin and have a very uncomfortable conversation with her before I try to go home in the darkness.

Light from a single bulb attached to the side of the barn leads me through the heavy trees until I finally step out next to the livestock pens—the woefully inadequate ones.

She's been patching them, doing her best to keep the animals contained, but the roaming chickens are as much a draw for a predator like a bear or a coyote as that cow was.

I grind my teeth together, trying to fight back the rising anger that this woman has been here alone all this time.

Is she so stubborn that she couldn't ask for help, or has Pops' memory issue finally put someone's life in jeopardy?

Neither is good.

No one can survive up here like this without people to rely on and trust, without neighbors who will come to your aid, something I'm seeing more and more as I look around her property, even in the darkness.

I return the shovel to its place and make my way up to the house, the porch lit by another single bulb. The smell of whatever she's cooking reaches me, making my stomach rumble.

But I can't even *think* about eating until I speak with Camille and figure out...*something*.

The tears that formed in her beautiful blue eyes when she spoke earlier were enough to cement my resolve that I'm not leaving here without at least a glimmer of a plan of how to save this for her.

I step up and knock on the door.

Muffled words she must be speaking to Davey reach me before it opens hesitantly. She cracks it and peeks out, keeping the door closed as much as she can.

Still doesn't trust me.

Got it.

It's not a bad thing, really.

I'm almost proud of the way she held that shotgun on me earlier and the wariness she still has in her sharp gaze now.

I offer her what I hope is a reassuring smile to try to assuage some of her unease. "I'm all finished."

Some of the tension releases from her dark brow. "Thank you."

I try to glance behind her into the house to ensure

Davey isn't close enough to hear anything, but she blocks my view protectively.

Can't say I blame her.

I'm a stranger to her—nothing more than a man she met once through a car window years ago.

Why should she trust me when I know she's alone up here? When there are people in this world who would take advantage of that in a heartbeat?

I hold up my hands before she reaches for that shotgun again. "There are some things we need to talk about, things I don't think you're going to want your son to hear."

Her jaw tightens, and her beautiful Caribbean gaze narrows on me. "If you're all right with it, can you step out so we can have a conversation?"

She glances back, her fingers tightening on the wood jamb. "He's occupied with his blocks right now, but we can't leave the porch."

I give her a tight nod. "Of course, I understand."

The door opens enough for her to slip out, her hand immediately falling to her barely visible expanding belly, though in other clothing, it may be more noticeable. The heavy sweater she now wears seems an odd choice for as warm as it still is, but maybe it's intentional, protecting what lies underneath.

"I don't think you're going to have any other trouble, but I suggest you keep that shotgun of yours loaded and ready in case anything comes looking for that cow...or one of the chickens."

She bobs her head gently.

"And though I appreciate your desire not to scare your son, if there is something here, you need to fire. You need to scare it away from the property. The longer they're here and think they have free rein, the more dangerous it is because they'll just keep coming back."

Her gaze hardens again, but there's a determination in it that wasn't there only a moment ago.

This woman will do *anything* to protect her son.

Even fire that gun if she has to.

I run a hand back through my sweaty hair and release a heavy sigh. The last thing I want to do is ask this, but I have to know—for her sake and my own. "I need to ask you something that might be uncomfortable."

She glances away, her eyes darting across the darkening property, as if she can somehow avoid whatever I'm about to ask by simply not looking at me.

"When your husband died, did you talk to my grandfather?"

Her gaze snaps back to me, her brows rising. "What?"

Apparently, not what she was expecting...

"Did you radio my grandfather when your husband died? Did he come up here and speak with you after?"

She wraps her arms around herself and shakes her head, sending a chunk of dark hair falling against her cheek. "No, I radioed the sheriff. He took care of everything with—" She swallows thickly, her eyes glazing over with unshed tears that make my throat tighten. "You know."

I give her a nod. "So, he hasn't been up here at all?"

"No."

Shit.

"Has he been collecting the rent?"

Pink crawls up her neck and across her pale cheeks as she averts her gaze again, chewing on her bottom lip. "I haven't seen your grandfather since well before Dave died."

Fucking hell.

———

CAMILLE

Dalton runs a hand over the light stubble on his jaw, his emerald gaze holding mine with an intensity that makes me squirm. "I want to apologize again for not being up here earlier, for not checking on you. My grandfather has been a little..."—he trails off, his jaw tightening—"forgetful lately. He never mentioned to me that your husband died, and I didn't know that he hadn't been up here himself to check on you."

The pure emotion in his voice tells me he's being candid, and it carries a waver when he talks about his grandfather, but something about his final words rankles me.

They stir that part of me that has always striven to survive on my own, to do everything I can not to be reliant on anyone else. Even after seven years with Dave, I fought when he tried to help me with things I might have struggled with. He always called it my "stubborn streak" and joked it would get me in trouble one day.

Maybe that's now.

I pull my shoulders back and stand straighter, like that might somehow change my small stature or the fact that I *am* limited in what I can do in my condition with Davey running around underfoot all the time. "I don't need anyone to check on me."

My words come out with more of a bite than I intend them, but I have to hand it to the young man in front of me —he barely reacts to the incredulousness in my tone.

If anything, he looks sympathetic to my plight and resistance.

"I understand your reluctance, Camille. You don't know

me." His lips press into a tight smile that doesn't quite reach his eyes. "And I'm going to tell you something you're probably not going to want to hear."

My shoulders tense as I brace for what I know is coming —for what I've known for the past two months as I've struggled relentlessly to keep things going here.

The animals alive and healthy.

The garden growing during the only months I have any hope of actually harvesting what could get us through the winter.

The memory of Dave alive for his son who is so young I'm afraid he won't remember him...

Dalton scans the darkness around us, as if he's picturing it how it appeared in the daylight when he arrived. "I didn't have a lot of time to examine the homestead, but from what I did see, I can tell you're in trouble."

I grit my teeth, trying to breathe through my nose. "We're fine. Davey and I are *fine*."

Tears sting my eyes as I say the words I know aren't true.

But I want them to be so badly.

I want to be able to care for him on my own, to give him the life up here Dave and I always planned for him. I want him to see me being strong, resilient, not caving under the weight of what's been thrust upon my shoulders.

Yet none of that seems possible, and that realization slams into me full force as I stare at the handsome young man who came to my rescue today, even when I didn't want it.

He offers me a kind smile, one that seems entirely genuine and softens his eyes. "I know you're doing the best you can. I can't imagine what you must have to do every day to keep him occupied and safe and also try to manage everything you need to here." He spreads his hands wide. "This would be a lot for anyone, but for a single mother..."—his eyes drift down to my stomach, and I immediately drop my hand there protectively—"who is expecting another one... There's no way you can do this on your own."

Firey indignation ignites deep in my veins, but he holds up a hand before I can argue.

"And that isn't meant as an insult to your capabilities. Obviously, you're more than capable. It's just a statement of fact. I've lived on this mountain my entire life, and it's hard enough for me to maintain our property, even with my grandfather still helping where he can. You *can't* do it alone."

His words cut to the very core of the agonizing despair that keeps me up every night.

I didn't want to hear anyone else say it.

It was one of the reasons I never asked for help—not just because I was too proud, but because it might mean leaving here.

This place that Dave loved so much.

That *I* do.

The only home Davey has ever known, above the town where his father is buried.

And I can't bear the thought of that.

Every time I consider the possibility of leaving James Mountain, I can't bring myself to reach for that radio or to tell anyone in town what's happening when we drive down for supplies or my doctor's appointments.

That we don't have money for anymore...

Dalton watches me for a few moments as I try to gather my wits and some sort of response, but I can't come up with any way to answer the truth he's laid out very blatantly at my feet.

I just stare at the determined young man who showed up out of the blue to save my ass and who is now calling me out on the one thing I wish I didn't have to admit.

"You need help, Mrs. Bower, and I know how hard it is to admit that for people like us, believe me. I'm going to come back tomorrow, and I'm going to walk the property with you and examine everything. Figure out what needs to be done and where you stand. Winter will be here faster than you think, and it could be a very hard one if you're not prepared..."

He trails off, and my throat constricts.

If I'm not prepared, I'm not just putting myself at risk but Davey and this baby, too.

It's the awful truth I've known since the moment I found Dave and realized our perfect little life here was over.

A fresh wave of anguish engulfs me.

Just as hot and raw as that fateful day.

Tears flood my eyes, blurring Dalton's face.

He waits for me to respond in some way, but all I manage is a little nod as I swipe at the drops before they can fall.

Dalton smiles—a true, genuine offering from a stranger, who I have a feeling won't be one for very long. "Again, I am sorry I wasn't here sooner. Radio us if anything comes up tonight, but I'll be here at first light. Keep your gun close."

I nod and suck in a long, slow breath to try to contain my sob as Dalton stalks over toward the barn, unties and mounts his horse, and takes off through the dark woods.

It doesn't take long before he completely disappears, swallowed up whole by the night and the trees, leaving me alone here with Davey and my own guilt and twisted emotions I can't seem to get a grip on...

Dave was never one to accept charity, and the thought

of doing so makes a part of me want to rebel. But as soon as I slip back into the house, my gaze lands on the reason I have to put that aside.

I have to.

Davey sits on the floor with his blocks piled up around him, happily stacking them almost as tall as he is. Whatever he's building topples, and he bursts into tears, looking up at me with so much distress that it renews my own.

"It's okay, buddy. We can rebuild it."

But as soon as I say the words, I have to swallow back my own sob because I can't ever rebuild what I had here with Dave.

He's gone.

So is the dream we once had of our life here together.

Free from all the bullshit life below the mountain contains.

All the anguish and turmoil.

The way the entire world seems to be burning.

Now, it's *my* world that seems to have been set aflame.

All of our plans gone in an instant.

The look on his face when I found him flashes through my head, and I bite down to stop another strangled sound from slipping through my lips.

He didn't stand a chance, and there was no way I could have saved him, no matter how much I wanted to. I accepted that truth the very day he died, but it doesn't make it any easier.

Two months later, I still wonder what would have happened if I had been out in the barn with him that morning...

I pull Davey onto my lap and hold him tightly, both of us allowing our tears to fall. His for his block creation; mine for his father and the lives we could have had.

"Is Daddy coming home soon?"

His question slices at my chest with the force of a driving axe.

He hasn't been asking as often as he used to, but I don't know if I should be happy about that or not.

I don't want him to forget his father, but a part of me feels like if he understands he's not coming back, it'll be easier on him in the long run. "No baby, Daddy's not coming back. Remember, Daddy went to Heaven?"

Blue eyes lift to me, with tears streaming down his puffy little cheeks. "Is that where Winny went?"

This time, my smile is genuine as I stare down at him and brush the hair back from his forehead. "Yes, that's where she went."

His tiny brow furrows. "Dalton helped her?"

It's such a simple question based on what he pieced together from the very little portions of our interaction he was privy to today.

He's so observant for his age.

In many ways, being raised on the mountain has made him grow up faster than he would have down in the city. And he knows enough to understand what Dalton did without even seeing it.

"Yes, Dalton helped her, and he's going to help us, too."

As much as I may want to fight it, we need it, or he's right; we won't survive the winter.

Chapter Three

DALTON

B y the time I finally make it back home, get Apollo settled, and step back into the cabin, night has fully descended, and my body aches *everywhere*. Not that it isn't used to hard, manual labor every day, but what I had to do for Camille is something entirely different. If we lost an animal here, I would have had access to better equipment, and Pops would have assisted me with disposal, making the task far easier to accomplish in far less time.

Doing *that* alone isn't anything I ever want to repeat.

My back screams its displeasure with how I spent my afternoon and evening, and I rub at it and gently close the door behind me as quietly as possible so I don't wake Pops in case he turned in early.

I need to get his advice on how to handle the situation at Camille's, but given how I'm feeling at the moment, all I want to do is shower with scalding-hot water and then get horizontal.

"Dalton?" His gruff voice cuts through the quiet, still air of the cabin. "That you?"

Shit.

Guess the old man is still awake.

I bend down to untie my boots, wincing at the sharp bite of agony that travels through the lower half of my body with the movement.

Fuck.

It's been a while since it's been this bad, and I know I'll pay for it tomorrow. No amount of sleep will ease what can't be fixed, and I doubt I'll be getting much anyway, with the jumble of problems rattling around so violently in my head.

How the hell am I going to help Camille when I can't even help Pops?

It feels like an impossible feat at the moment. Especially when the simple act of kicking off my boots is enough to make me grit my teeth against a wave of pain that threatens to double me over. I have to take a minute and grip the door handle before I regain enough control over myself to push off it and slowly make my way back to Pops' office.

He sits at his desk, the papers now more organized than they were the last time I was in here, and he glances up at me with his glasses perched low on his nose. "Where were you this late?"

Hell.

Pops doesn't even recall the conversation we had earlier today.

Any flicker of hope I had that he was having a *good* night disappears instantly.

"Remember, I told you I was going to check on Camille Bower?"

His weathered forehead crinkles for a moment, his eyes

glazing slightly before he nods. "Oh, right, right. How is she?"

"Not great, Pops."

He raises a single white brow. "Really?"

"Really." I cautiously lower myself into one of the chairs that faces the desk, trying to gauge how much he remembers while concealing my discomfort—something he is far too adept at noticing. The mostly cleaned-up papers suggest he had at least a moment of semi-clarity, but that doesn't mean it lasted. "Do you remember why I went up there, Pops?"

He scowls at me as he glances down at a document in his hand. "Of course, I do. The vultures."

I let out a long, slow breath, releasing my death grip on the arms of the chair and leaning forward slightly to take some pressure off my back.

At least he remembers that...

Maybe he will actually be able to help me formulate a plan of attack for the Bower property before I head over there in the morning.

"One of her cows died after calving."

"Oh." He peers up at me over the rim of his glasses. "Calf survive?"

I nodded. "Yes, but..."

Pops sets down the paper, actually focusing on me with the clearest eyes I've seen on him in weeks. "But what?"

Shit.

Having this conversation with him a few months ago would've been easy. He would've known exactly what to do. He would've jumped on it and put together a detailed, well-structured plan to bring her homestead back from the brink, and he would have ensured we could accomplish it in the short amount of time we have before winter hits the mountain.

But now?

Nothing is certain when it comes to Pops, except that everything is *uncertain.*

Which means treading lightly.

"You know her husband died..."

He nods slowly. "Of course."

So casual.

Pops has no idea he's forgetting things or that the consequences of it could be catastrophic—not just for us but for everyone on the mountain and in James Creek.

The town relies on all the businesses we own that Pops runs from his throne up here. Without him pulling the strings and controlling the supply of goods and services we provide, it won't be able to keep running. Just like Camille couldn't keep up what she was doing forever alone, Pops can't continue like this for much longer.

"She's been alone at the homestead since then with their four-year-old...and she's pregnant."

His brows fly up, and I continue because there isn't any point in beating around the bush when he probably won't even remember this conversation tomorrow.

"No one's been to check on her."

"What?" His forehead furrows again, and his gaze drops to the desk as if he's trying to recall something and might be able to find it by staring at the papers stacked on it or in the swirling wood grain. "I could have sworn I was just up there to collect the rent a few weeks ago."

That familiar agony hits my chest at seeing his confusion.

"No, Pops. You haven't been up there. I don't think you've seen her at all since her husband died." I shift forward, resting my elbows on my knees, and the pull at my tense back with the change of position makes me wince. "Pops?"

His eyes meet mine, annoyance sharpening them. "What?"

"I need to see the books. I need to make sure everything has been taken care of."

He glowers, and I can almost see the steam starting to build behind his green eyes as they darken. "I don't know what you mean."

Antagonizing him won't get me anywhere.

Not when he's like this.

He's ornery when he's at his best, and he certainly isn't that right now. But I also can't keep walking on eggshells around him. If something doesn't change *fast*, the James legacy built over two and a half centuries on this land will vanish before we have a chance to move to save it.

"Pops, you know how important it is that we keep everything running smoothly. What's going on at the general store, the feed shop, the coffee shop, the bakery..."

I don't bother listing the rest of the businesses we own in James Creek, which amount to about ninety percent of the town. The Bowers' rent is literally a drop in the bucket that isn't going to make or break us, financially speaking. But if he forgot about Camille, that means he may have forgotten about something *else* he's supposed to be doing.

That stubborn jaw of his locks. "You know I handle all that, Dalton."

I rest my hands flat on the desk as I shift closer to him, trying to keep my voice level. "I know, Pops, and you've been very good at it. But it's time I learned the business, don't you think, should anything happen to you?"

He snorts with the confidence only age can bring. "I'm going to live forever, kiddo."

A smile tugs at my lips despite the tension still pulling at my muscles and nerves. "I wish that were true, Pops, but you forgot to get the Bower rent. Have all the bills been getting paid for the various businesses? Have the deposits been made properly at the bank by all the managers? Pops, please. I need to see the books."

He pushes up from his chair, glaring at me, and despite his age, his large, broad shoulders and heavy frame still show that he's spent every day of his life working this property on this mountain. This is the type of man no one wants to cross, yet that's exactly what I'm doing.

"You sure have some balls on you, kiddo. After everything I've done for you..."

Recoiling at his comment, I suck in a sharp breath. "Pops, please. This isn't about ambition. I don't care about the money. I don't want *everything* the family has built to be lost, and I'm terrified we *will* lose it."

I'm terrified I'm going to lose him.

He presses his palms flat against the desk and leans across it toward me, and I know that look in his eye. It's the same one he would give me when I wouldn't finish my chores on the property as a child.

Not anger.

More *concern*.

That hurts more than if he were pissed.

His shoulders sag slightly. "You don't trust me."

Shit.

"It isn't that, Pops."

"Oh, really? Then what is it?"

"You're seventy-five years old, and maybe you *will* live forever, but what if you don't? What happened to Dave Bower could happen to you tomorrow." I spread my hands across the desk and the various stacks of papers. "How am I supposed to make sense of any of this when you won't even let me see any of it, when you don't let me know what needs to happen every day to keep everything running? How?"

His jaw tenses, and a muscle there tics.

I want to believe that his reluctance has nothing to do with his not believing I can do it and everything to do with whatever has been messing with his memory lately. That it isn't because he doesn't trust me or thinks I'm incapable.

"I'll teach you when you can prove to me that you're not a child any longer."

I clench my jaw and rise to my feet, matching his height now. "I'm twenty-three years old, Pops. I'm not a child, and I've lived every moment of my life on this mountain, proving that."

"Not every moment."

I wince at his comment, squeezing my eyes closed, and that ache in my back intensifies, the scars flaring and burning as hot as the memory. It isn't like him to bring it up. I certainly don't need the reminder of the car accident that took Mom and Dad from me or the fact that I was the reason we were off the mountain the day it happened.

It's something Pops would never use as a weapon against me.

Not if he were in his right mind.

Which only proves to me that he *isn't.*

I open my eyes and meet his—ones that match my own and look so much like Mom's. For some reason, that's one thing I can always remember when other memories of her and Dad have faded over the last two decades. Maybe because I see them when I look in the mirror or at Pops. Or maybe because I chose one thing to cling to and never let go.

"This conversation is over, Dalton." He points toward the door. "Get out of my office."

Hell.

This certainly didn't go as planned.

I had intended to address the issue at Camille's homestead.

Even if I could walk away from a woman and child in peril—which I *couldn't* under any circumstances—considering we own that land, that cabin, and all the other buildings on that property, it's in our best interest to ensure it remains in good condition.

He should be as worried about it as I am, but I wasn't even given the chance to delve into what I saw today because the conversation went off the rails so damn fast.

I reluctantly back away from the desk and step out of his space because I won't get anywhere with him tonight.

Maybe in the light of a new day, I can make some progress—both on getting him to admit there *is* a problem and opening up to me about the business and ways to help Camille.

God willing.

I'm too wound up to head upstairs to my room, though. I tug open the front door and stalk out across the porch and down the few steps that lead to the gravel drive in front of the cabin.

There's only one place I can go right now to try to find some clarity in the chaos—the barn and Apollo.

He's been with me for almost fifteen years, become my priest and my confidant. Though his advice leaves something to be desired, he's a damn good listener and maybe the only one I'm going to have soon.

Because despite Pops' insistence, he is not going to live forever. And the way he's been deteriorating, I fear that day is coming sooner rather than later.

There's nothing I can do to stop what's coming, but I have to try.

For him and the Bowers.

———

CAMILLE

Tires crunching over gravel cut through the almost silent, still morning air, and I look up from bottle-feeding Rocky in the livestock pen as a red truck pulls through the trees and onto the property.

My first instinct is to dive for the shotgun leaning against the side of the barn only a few feet from me, but Dalton opens the driver's side and steps down, his already familiar form visible in the early light that's just barely starting to trickle over the horizon.

He glances up at the cabin, then over at the barn, and his eyes finally find mine.

Just like yesterday, the deep-green gaze rakes over me, assessing me in a way that makes me squirm slightly.

I'm not used to having anyone look at me so intently. Like he's trying to unravel everything I have wound up inside me and break through all the walls I've had to put up to protect us while up here alone.

The longer it lingers on me, the harder it becomes not to react, not to avert my gaze or shift restlessly.

I don't think he intends it to be sexual, but the close perusal finally forces me to look away, back at the tiny calf whose birth caused this man to come barreling into our lives so unexpectedly.

And I am not ready to have him inserting himself into our world.

I am *so* not ready for *him*.

But it's impossible to ignore his presence, either.

I cast furtive glances his way as I keep working. He starts toward me in a pair of worn jeans, work boots, and an open plaid shirt with the sleeves cut off that shows off his lean, muscular body, honed by years of endless work on their homestead.

This man is strong.

And he knows what he's doing.

Accepting his help may not be instinctual, but it's necessary if I want to be able to stay here.

He stops at the edge of the fence and leans against it. "Where's Davey?"

I incline my head toward the cabin. "Still sleeping."

A sandy-blond brow rises. "Aren't you worried he'll wake up and you won't be there?"

Rocky nudges me, asking for more when his breakfast runs dry. "Yes, but I don't have much of a choice, do I?" I point to the back pocket of my jeans with my free hand. "Baby monitor. It covers almost the entire property so I can listen for him while he's sleeping in the early mornings or evenings or napping during the day. It's the only time I really can get anything done around here."

The corners of his lips twitch, and he seems more relaxed today, despite what I know we need to discuss. "That's smart." He scans the yard, his gaze landing on Rocky, who still presses against my hand, seeking more. "Is this Rocky?"

I nod. "Yes."

"He seems to be doing well."

"He is, so far."

Dalton watches me as I move to stand in front of him on

the opposite side of the fence. "That's part of what I wanted to talk to you about."

My back stiffens at his carefully chosen words.

His eyes roam over me, like he's memorizing every feature, taking stock, and I glance away, tucking a stray strand of hair that fell out of my ponytail behind my ear. "I know I mentioned it last night, that I would help you around the property..."

I bite my tongue to stop the objection that I know won't get me anywhere.

Dalton locks his gaze with mine. "...but I need something in return."

Unease settles low in my stomach, churning it more than the damn hormones did when I first woke this morning and spent twenty minutes with my head in the toilet, dry heaving.

Maybe I was wrong about him and his intentions...

I narrow my eyes on him. "And what's that?"

He releases a long, heavy sigh. "This has to stay between us."

This doesn't sound good.

A million different possibilities immediately flicker through my mind, and I don't want any of them to be true because I actually think I *like* and *trust* Dalton James and don't want to have to repaint the picture of who he is in my head that has formed since yesterday afternoon.

"Okay..."

One of his hands moves through his hair in a rough, frustrated shove. "My grandfather isn't well. He's been..."—he shakes his head, glancing off into the distance—"not himself for the last several months."

My medical training immediately kicks in, the potential

causes for an older man to be unwell coming in a never-ending list. "What's wrong?"

"I don't know." His gaze meets mine again, this time filled with panic I haven't seen from him before—even when he knew there might be a bear wandering around the property while he was breaking apart what would amount to a very nice meal for it. "I'm hoping you can tell me that. You're a nurse, right?"

"How did you know that?"

"The sheriff told me."

"Oh..." The fact that he's been discussing me with Sheriff Wilson causes me to shift nervously under yet another intense assessment. "I *am*, but it's been years since I've been part of any medical practice."

He drums his fingers along the top of the fence. "What sort of nursing did you do?"

"Before I moved up here, I was an ER nurse."

A sigh filled with audible relief floats through his lips. "My grandfather has been forgetting things. His memory is worsening. And he won't go into town. He hasn't for years, not since—" He cuts himself off, his jaw tensing. "It's been a long time. So, he won't go see a doctor or let me call Doc up to the cabin, and anytime I try to bring up that I think something's wrong, he gets defensive."

"Has he been violent?"

He shakes his head, and I chew on my lip, wracking my brain for anything that might cause memory issues. If he had mentioned violent outbursts, my first thought would be Alzheimer's or dementia. I can't rule them out even without them, but there are dozens of conditions that can cause memory issues in someone his age—including just *normal* aging.

"Does he have any other symptoms?"

Dalton crosses his arms over his muscular chest, making his biceps bulge, though he seems completely unaware as he stares off into space, seemingly contemplating the question. "A little unsteady on his feet at times. But some days, he almost seems normal." He lets out a heavy breath, and it carries the weight of his concern for the man he's obviously close to. "I don't want to think the worst, but..."

I tighten my hands around the top rung of the fence, waiting for him to figure out whatever he needs to say.

His eyes finally meet mine again, and the despair they hold is so easily recognizable that it makes my own rise to the surface again. "I want you to meet him, spend some time with him, try to see if you can figure out what's wrong."

"Without any medical testing?"

He nods.

"Shit, Dalton, that's—"

"I understand it isn't ideal, but I don't know what else to do. If anyone finds out, it could be disastrous for us, for the businesses, and all of James Creek. If he gets worse. If he can't keep up with the demands of everything he runs, it's going to be catastrophic for a lot of people."

I see the pain in his eyes, the worry.

He loves his grandfather—that much is certain.

"So, you want me to try to diagnose him and treat him if I can?"

He nods. "And in exchange, I'll help you get your property ready for winter, ensure that you and Davey will be safe, as much as I can."

It seems like a fair deal, but making a bargain like this with a billionaire who owns the property I live on feels like it has some unspoken expectation that I'm not seeing. Some conditions that will pop up out of nowhere to blindside me the same way Dave's death did.

"And that's it?" I search his face. "Nothing else will be expected of me?"

His eyes widen slightly. "No, I just need to make sure he's okay, and I couldn't live with myself if I didn't know that you and your son were, too. Even if you don't want to do this, I'll still help you..."

My chest warms with his promise and the realization that this offer of a bargain is as much for me as it is for him. Because he could see I was reluctant to accept his help. This offer allows me to help *him* in return, and that was likely his intent—to allow me to feel useful and like I'm not taking charity.

He understood exactly what I needed to feel more comfortable with this situation, and the fact that it might help his grandfather is secondary. It's an act of desperation on his part to try to help someone he loves when he saw the opportunity to do so, not because he actually expects it or needs something in return to do the right thing.

Dalton James is exactly who I thought he was when I lay awake last night, going over his arrival and his insistence that he'd be back to help.

All that makes my answer so much easier. "Okay."

He offers me a relieved smile that's still far too tight. "Let's walk the property and figure out what needs to be done. Then tomorrow morning, you and Davey can come to meet Pops."

"Is that what you call him?"

His head bobs gently, sending his sandy-blond hair flopping over his forehead. "He raised me after my parents died, so he was like a father to me."

Tears sting my eyes at the thought that Davey is going to grow up without *his* father, but I blink them away as I unlatch the gate to allow Dalton to enter the animal pens.

"That's very sweet of him. How old is he now?"

Dalton sighs as he examines what's laid out in front of him. "Seventy-five." He glances over at me with a half-smirk as Rocky approaches him and nudges his hand. "And I'm twenty-three, in case you were wondering."

I laugh lightly, the sound so foreign to me after so long without it. "I wasn't."

The corners of his lips curl up slightly as he pets Davey's new best friend. "Sure, you weren't. I know how young I look, but I've been working this land for decades. And I remember meeting you, sort of, when you moved up here."

I lead him into the barn with our spotted friend following closely behind until I manage to corral him into his stall. "I was almost eight months pregnant already when we finally rented from your grandfather."

"Did you give birth up here?"

The concern in his tone makes warmth bloom in my chest in a way I haven't felt in so long. I never realized what being alone up here with Davey had done to me. How not having friends or anyone to talk to for weeks at a time unless I went to town would affect me mentally. And having someone actually *care* feels far better than it probably should. "Yes."

He glances down at my stomach, still barely visible under Dave's shirt I wore to work in today. "Is that your plan with this one?"

Instinctively, I place my hands across it. "I haven't gotten that far yet. Too many other things to worry about."

A look of pure compassion crosses his face, softening his features. "Well, hopefully, we can take care of some of those things so you can concentrate on what's important."

Any lingering reservations I've held onto about trusting

this man, about putting my life in his hands, evaporate with his words.

The sincerity lacing them.

It's the same I heard when he was talking about his grandfather.

Dalton feels and loves deeply, and he isn't doing this because of some ulterior motives. He's doing it because he *cares*. Even when he doesn't know us. Even when he should be preparing *his* homestead for winter instead of spending time here trying to resurrect ours.

He stalks through the rest of the barn, examining each stall and all the animal pens on either side. "Where do you get your feed?"

"The general store."

"Good." He examines the current woefully inadequate stock for the two cows, one horse, three goats, and half a dozen chickens I currently have. "We own that, so it won't be a problem for me to get enough sent up here to last you through the winter."

"I can't—" I swallow thickly, embarrassment heating my cheeks. "I can't pay for that."

His soft eyes meet mine, a knowing in them that makes my tears burn anew. "I understand that, Camille. I'm not worried about the money. I'm worried about you and Davey and your animals making it through winter."

That's *thousands* of dollars of feed he's offering me, in addition to his physical help, and he says it like it's *nothing*. Like he doesn't even have to *think* about it.

He walks past me before I can say anything, making his way across the exterior pens and out the gate toward the greenhouse that has seen better days. The door hangs cock-eyed off broken hinges, and half the roof panels lie in pieces where there should be additional food we could be canning and storing beyond what the garden could produce if I had time for it.

"When was the last time you had anything growing in here?"

"March. When that big storm came through, it destroyed it. Dave was going to fix it up in time for me to plant a winter crop, but..."

I can't bring myself to say it, and thankfully, Dalton doesn't turn back and look at me—almost like he knows what he'll find and wants to give me a moment to compose myself.

He stares up at the damage and tugs open the door the rest of the way to peer inside. "I can get this fixed up in a few days once I get the supplies ordered and delivered."

My chest tightens, and I step around him and into the door frame, effectively blocking him from entering. "You can't spend that much time or money on this. You have your own property to take care of...and your grandfather."

Dalton steps forward and places his hand on my forearm, squeezing it gently. Warmth spreads from where his calloused fingers brush against my sensitive skin, rushing up my arm. "We'll be fine." A steeliness fills his emerald gaze. It's more than determination. It's a sheer force of will I haven't seen before—from anyone. "And I don't care what it takes; I'm going to ensure that you will be, too."

Chapter Four

CAMILLE

Pulling onto the James homestead, my stomach knots violently, and I will the churning bile to stay down. I already had to delay leaving to come here by an hour due to the morning sickness that seems intent on making waking up an awful experience, and it wouldn't make a very good first impression with Dalton's grandfather if I puked all over him or his cabin.

I glance into the back at Davey bouncing in his car seat, clapping his hands excitedly as he takes in their two-story cabin and the land surrounding it. "Are you excited, Bub?"

He nods.

"Remember what I told you. We have to be on our best behavior while we're here. Dalton's grandfather is older, and I don't know how he'll react to having you running around wild in their house, okay?"

Davey bobs his head again. "Okay, Mama."

Hopefully, I brought enough things to occupy him while we're here.

I glance at the bag on the passenger seat filled with a few toys and snacks.

No matter how good he normally is, his energy needs to be channeled. And I can't help but worry about how an unwell old man will react to having a rambunctious little one invading his personal space while I try to pry into his medical situation.

I pull up near the steps leading to the porch, throw the truck into park, and turn off the engine. Almost immediately, the cabin door swings open, and Dalton appears with a broad smile that makes those gold flecks in his eyes sparkle in the early morning light.

That relief I've felt over the last two days since he appeared as our savior floods back through me, releasing the tension I felt the entire drive here.

He actually looks *happy* to see us as he crosses the small porch and heads down two steps to where we're parked. Before I can even move to do it, Dalton opens the door for me, the muscles in his bare arms flexing as he leans against it casually in what appears to be his favorite apparel—another unbuttoned, cut-off plaid shirt. "You made it."

My lips pull into a smile I actually feel for the first time in months at the welcome reception. I nod, trying to avert my gaze from all the hard, exposed flesh that's impossible *not* to see. "We did. Sorry we're a little later than I had planned. How's your grandfather this morning?"

His body goes rigid, his jaw locking as he glances up at the home that's probably stood here for over a hundred years, given his family's history with the area. Maybe longer. "Better than he has been..."

The pain in his expression is all too familiar.

It's the same look I saw on the faces of so many families waiting anxiously for updates on my patients over the years when I was working in the ER. It's the kind of anguish we were trying to get away from when we moved up here by separating ourselves from the disease and violence and all-around ugliness of the world, but I should have known it would follow us. There is no escaping the things life can do to you, whether you're in the city or up on a mountain.

I slide out of the truck, only a sliver of space between us now, and I rest my hand on his shoulder, squeezing it gently. "I'll do what I can. I promise."

Dalton gives me a tight smile, then steps back, giving me room to get out. He opens the rear door and reaches in for Davey. "Hey, buddy." After unbuckling him, he easily lifts him and settles him on his hip. "You want to meet my grandpa?"

Davey enthusiastically bobs his dark head, the morning sun glinting off the amber undertones the same way it does mine.

I give Dalton a wary look. "Are you sure your grandfather is going to be okay with him?"

Dalton offers a smile that doesn't quite reach his eyes. "I told him you were coming by because you needed a little social interaction after being alone for so long. It's the only excuse I could think of for why you'd be here today. If he's not okay with this little guy being around, Davey can help me on the property today while you deal with Pops. It'll be all right."

That isn't the most comforting statement.

Edison James is well known for his isolation on the mountain, and I'm about to bring a tiny bull into his proverbial china shop.

· · ·

I close my door, grab my bag from the passenger seat, and follow them up the steps.

Dalton pushes open the door, ushering me in before he closes the door and sets Davey on his feet on beautiful hand-hewn oak floors. "Hey, Pops?"

His voice carries across the lofted living room.

"Wow..." I scan the place, my eyes trying to take in everything at once, which is nearly impossible given the size of the cabin.

A two-story fireplace occupies the center of the main wall of the living room, towering up beside a second-floor landing that must house the bedrooms. The kitchen lies just beyond the stone hearth through a large opening that allows me to see partially in, and two other doors stand closed on either side of the large room.

The door on the left opens, and an old man appears, with hair as white as the snow that will be falling in a few short months, eyebrows to match. They rise over a pair of reading glasses, and he takes an unsteady step forward, grabbing the doorjamb to keep himself upright. "Who is this?"

Dalton approaches him while Davey clings to my leg, peering around at yet another stranger who has popped into his life so unexpectedly. "Pops, remember I told you this morning that Camille and her son Davey were going to come over for a bit today."

He narrows his wise gaze on us, and I immediately squirm under his perusal.

Davey apparently doesn't have the same discomfort with him as he steps out and waves and smiles. "Hi."

Edison's gaze lowers to him, but instead of an irritated scowl I expect to come, his lips curl into a bright smile, and he squats slowly, a motion that shows how unsteady he really is. "Well, hello there, little man. Come here so I can have a look at you."

I toss Dalton a questioning look, but he just gives me a half grin. Like this is exactly what he expected to happen, despite what he said outside.

Davey rushes over to Pops and stares at him with wide eyes.

"How old are you, son?"

"Four...and a *half.*"

The added detail makes me hide a laugh.

Pops grins and pats him on the head with a shaky, weathered hand. "I bet you're causing a lot of trouble for your mama, aren't you?" He glances over at me with a smirk as he pushes upright, gripping the jamb again to get to his feet. Once he's steady, he motions for us to come in farther. "I was just about to make some coffee."

Dalton starts to follow him toward the kitchen. "I already did that, Pops."

"Oh"—Edison stops and looks over at his grandson—"I guess you did, didn't you?"

"And you had a cup."

"Oh..." His brow furrows deeply. "Well, I guess I'll have another one, then. Would you like one, Camille?"

I nod and move to join him as I mentally catalog the symptoms I'm observing. "Sure."

Unsteady on his feet, just like Dalton said.

Clear memory issues, even about something that just happened this morning.

Davey trails Pops into the kitchen, and Dalton pauses and grabs my elbow, stopping me from following them. A little shock trickles through my arm at the contact, and his warm, rough palm encircles me carefully, easing me away from the opening more.

"That unsteadiness..." He presses his lips together firmly, his worry making lines crinkle around his soft eyes. "The man was always sure-footed and did just as much on this property as I did until a few months ago, but lately..."

The way he draws in a long breath makes my heart ache for him again. He's spent months watching his grandfather decline, feeling like he can't do anything about it, and now, he's terrified of what I might actually find.

I wait for his gaze to meet mine so he can see how determined I am. "I know how worried you are, and I promise, I'll do everything I can to figure this out."

He nods, then glances into the kitchen, where Pops is showing something to Davey near the counter. "Try to do it delicately. He isn't going to want to answer any medical questions and doesn't like people prying."

That isn't anything new.

Most of my elderly patients didn't want to be in the hospital, and many were reluctant to share what was going on with them openly. They take a special touch—delicate but also *firm*.

"I can handle your grandfather. Don't worry."

The corner of his lips curls, lifting some of the darkness clouding his face. "I know you can. Are you okay with me going out on the property? I won't go too far. You'll be able to call for me, and I'll hear you if you need something."

I peek into the kitchen again and find Pops helping Davey onto a chair at the table. "He seems okay with him now."

Dalton grins, but it falls away quickly, as if he just realized something that took any of the initial joy from the moment. "That's the age I was when my parents died. He probably thinks it's me."

Any humor or positivity I was feeling toward unraveling this mystery fades, too. "You think he's that far gone?"

He shakes his head. "I don't know."

The pain in his voice matches the same I felt for months.

I lost Dave, but he's been slowly losing the sole parent figure he really ever had. Apparently, the only family he has left.

"I'll take care of him. I'll call for you if I need something."

He nods and releases my arm, my skin instantly pebbling with goosebumps at the loss of contact. "Help yourself to anything in the kitchen. I think some of my old toys are still in the spare bedroom upstairs, last door on the left, if Davey wants to go exploring to see if there's anything fun."

"I appreciate that."

Dalton stalks to the door, opens it, and turns back to me. "Camille..."

"Yes?"

"Thank you for doing this." Another tight smile pulls at his lips. "I realize it's asking a lot."

It's almost like he's *apologizing* for needing my help, which is absurd, considering what he's done for us over the last two days.

I shake my head. "It isn't, not with what you're doing for me."

Another true smile appears, despite the heaviness that's settled over him. "I'm glad we could help each other."

"Me, too."

I just hope I'm able to figure out what's wrong with Pops and can do whatever he needs to get better.

Dalton slips out the door, closing it behind him, and I set down my bag and head into the kitchen.

Two mugs of coffee sit waiting on the table, and Pops slides another one in front of Davey.

"Whoa, what's that?"

He looks up at me, brows raised. "Hot chocolate, is that okay?"

I release a relieved breath. "Of course. That's very sweet of you."

A grin pulls at his lined mouth, and he takes his seat next to Davey. I take mine on the other side, sticking my finger into the cocoa to test the temperature, but it's perfect.

The old man knew exactly what to do.

I watch him as he takes a sip of his coffee, gnarled hands wrapped around the mug shaking slightly. My gaze immediately drifts to the slightly blue tint to his nails that wasn't visible from across the living room.

No...

Could it really be that simple?

Hope floods my chest in a tidal wave that threatens to bring tears, but I try to force my voice to stay level. "Mr. James, can I ask you a question?"

He swallows and sets down his mug. "Please, call me Pops. Everyone does."

I smile and nod, taking a sip of my own coffee even though I don't drink it anymore since finding out I was pregnant again. "Do you have any feeling of pins and needles in your hands and feet at all?"

His astute gaze narrows on me. "Why do you ask?"

Be delicate...

"I noticed you were a little unsteady coming out of the other room. Sometimes that happens when you have that feeling in your feet."

Pops rubs his stubbled jaw, looking up at the wood ceiling beams. "Now that you mention it, I do have that feeling sometimes." He releases a little chuckle. "Don't tell Dalton, but I'm getting old."

I laugh and take another sip of the coffee I don't intend to finish. "I won't. It'll be our little secret."

Davey grins with chocolate across his face. "Can I be part of the secret?"

That draws both of our attention his way, and I exchange a knowing look with Pops.

A four-year-old is the *last* person to trust with anything you want kept confidential.

Pops chuckles low. "Guess I shouldn't have said that in front of the kid..." He grins over his mug before he takes another sip. "Why did Dalton bring you down here, anyway? To help clean up the place?"

I glance around at the immaculate kitchen and out to the clean living room I saw when I came in. "Doesn't seem like you need any help in that regard."

He waves a dismissive hand. "Dalton always fusses about taking care of everything."

"From what I hear, you're busy with the businesses."

Pops nods. "That does take up most of my time."

For the briefest moment, I almost consider mentioning our inability to pay the rent. It's been months since he came to collect, and even if he *had* shown up, I wouldn't have had it to give him. Dave always kept things running so smoothly on the homestead, including taking in horses to train—which he was so damn good at —to ensure we had an income. With him gone, I don't have any way to replace that or ensure I can stay on their land.

But what Dalton said about his grandfather getting

upset whenever he mentions the slipping memory leads me to bite my tongue instead.

"We stopped by because Davey needed to see some-place new. We've been up at our property alone for a while..."

Pops grins and ruffles Davey's hair as he happily sips his cocoa. "Well, I'm sure we can find some things to entertain him today."

As much as I may have wanted to do this all on my own, knowing Dalton is here, offering anything we need, and seeing Pops interact with Davey has renewed that bloom of hope.

There might actually be a chance I can stay in the only place Davey has ever known as home, and I might actually be able to help Pops and Dalton the way they are us.

———

DALTON

By the time I return to the cabin as the sun goes down, even walking up the two treads to the porch sends so much pain shooting through my back and legs that I have to grit my teeth and force myself to take the final few steps to reach the front door.

Shit.

I drop my forehead against the worn wood panel and take a long, deep inhale, trying to push the agony to that space in the back of my mind I usually manage to place it and lock it away there.

But this is different.

It can't so easily be brushed aside the way most of my daily aches and pains can.

It isn't something I could keep working through, even though I wanted to do at least another hour at the Bower property cataloging all the projects I need to tackle before winter.

I pushed too hard.

Did too much.

I shouldn't have gone there this afternoon.

Now, I'm paying the price for overexerting myself and pushing myself past the limits I never want to admit are there.

I should have waited for tomorrow, after a good night's sleep and the rest I know my body needs, but the state of Camille's place has left me more panicked than I will admit to her.

There's so much to do in so little time, especially when I'm splitting working hours between here and there.

Pops isn't much help these days, and I have to ensure *we're* ready as much as Camille is, so I didn't want to waste any daylight. But now my body is protesting, and so is my stomach, since I only managed to snag a quick sandwich to eat on my drive over there earlier.

It growls as the scent of something meaty and rich reaches me through the closed door. My mouth waters, and I drag my head back and open the heavy wooden slab, worn by years of rain, wind, snow, and use, stepping into a sight that stops me in my tracks.

Pops sits on the floor with Davey, pushing a faded red fire truck that I recognize all too well.

A vise constricts around my ribcage so tightly that it robs me of my breath and ability to speak.

They both look up at me, and Pops smiles and lifts the old toy. "Look what I found."

I swallow thickly and force myself to move, nudging the door closed behind me until I hear the click securing it.

Davey's excited blue eyes widen even more. "Fire truck!"

"Yep, that was mine..."

The memories it brings only aggravate the pain still coursing through me, making all the broken things flare angrily.

Pops bringing it to the hospital for me...

Trying to distract me from the agony and all the surgeries that seemed never-ending...

And for some reason, seeing the little boy on the floor with it takes me back to those awful days with shocking clarity—as if it happened yesterday instead of almost two decades ago. Or maybe it's the throbbing, searing torture that's engulfing me now that's doing strange things to my mind and making me relive the worst moment of my life.

After the last few days, getting the cow taken care of, exploring the property with Camille yesterday and examining the damage to the infrastructure, and today, handling everything on our homestead and then spending extra hours up at hers, I've reached my breaking point.

If I don't get horizontal soon, I won't be able to stand much longer.

I bend down to unlace my boots, biting back a groan as the movement sends another fiery shock up my spine. My hands shake, but I manage to untie them, pull them off, and set them next to the door.

When I return to fully standing with far more effort than it should take, Pops watches me with narrowed eyes, seeing far too much. "You okay?"

Far from it.

But the last thing I need to do is give Pops a reason to worry about me.

It's why I've done my best to keep *this* from happening up until now. I've kept the pain in control. Moderated myself. Ensuring I wasn't doing too much too fast.

That plan went out the window the moment my eyes met Camille's terrified ones.

There isn't time for carefully controlled progress. At this point, it's nothing more than a mad dash to secure *two* properties before the snow finally falls. And up here, that could be as early as October, if we're unlucky.

I grit my teeth, refusing to let Pops see how uncomfortable I am. "Yep, I'm good."

Camille appears from the kitchen, her dark brow raised as she wipes her hands on the apron over her jeans and gray T-shirt. "Oh, you're back."

"I am."

It comes out a little clipped, and I instantly regret the tone I let filter into my words. I'm not used to having to interact with anyone other than Pops, and even when I do go into town, I've never felt like *this*. Where my legs shake and it takes every ounce of strength I possess to stay upright.

Either she doesn't notice, or she chooses to ignore it, motioning over her shoulder. "I just finished dinner, if you're hungry."

"I'm definitely that."

And for the first time since I've met the woman, the smile that appears on her perfect pink lips lights her up entirely, her blue eyes shimmering like Caribbean waters, her high cheekbones and heart-shaped face framed by several strands of dark amber hair that have fallen away from the messy bun she tied at the back of her head.

My heart stutters, and I swallow again, trying to force

the air I draw in through my suddenly dry throat. "Let me just go...uh, wash up."

Because if I don't splash some cold water onto my face and other parts of my body, I might start thinking about horizontal things with the very beautiful widow who absolutely should *not* be entering my mind.

Ever.

She motions for Davey and Pops. "Let's go, boys. Time to eat."

Pops grabs the edge of the couch to pull himself to his feet, and Davey rushes past his mother with the old man lumbering after him.

Rather than following them into the kitchen, Camille pauses in the archway and turns back to me. "You and I need to talk privately after dinner."

Instantly, my stomach plummets, my appetite and that frighteningly strong guttural reaction to this woman gone in an instant, replaced by a foreboding sense of dread. "What's wrong?"

"After dinner."

I shake my head and close the distance between us, not even caring that I probably reek like sweat and everything I've been doing all day out in the hot sun. "Do you know what's wrong with him?"

She purses her lips and glances over her shoulder to ensure Pops and Davey are occupied at the table before she motions me away from the kitchen toward the closed door of his office. "I'm ninety percent sure I know what's going on."

A mixture of relief and trepidation flows through me, replacing the physical pain I've been nearly drowning in.

"Is it..." I can't even think the word, but I manage to force it out. "Is it Alzheimer's?"

Her gaze softens, and she shakes her head. "I don't think so."

The rush of air that pours from my lungs surprises even me, and I scrub my hand through my sweaty hair. "Thank God."

"I actually think it's something that could be relatively easy to correct."

"What do you mean?"

She checks the kitchen again. "I've been watching him all day, asking questions when I can in ways that hopefully won't upset him."

"That can be difficult."

Her answering tight smile demonstrates she has witnessed Pops' stubborn streak herself today. "He seems like he can be a difficult man at times, but he's so good with Davey. He's been incredible with him, showing him all around the cabin, playing games with him. He even took him out to meet all your animals after you went to our place." She does another peek at them. "And I managed to get enough information from him to know that it's not just his memory and the unsteadiness. He's dizzy at times, and he says he gets tingling in his hands and feet."

"And that means something?"

She nods, those thick, dark strands drifting across her soft cheeks with the movement. "It does, especially coupled with his fingernails."

"His nails?"

"They have a bluish tint. You haven't noticed?"

I shake my head, wracking my brain to try to remember seeing anything like that. "No. I likely assumed they were just dirty. He still works in the garden and greenhouse a lot, since that doesn't require a lot of physical exertion on his part."

"Well, they're pretty classic signs of B12 deficiency."

B12?

All the homeschooling Pops spent so much time and energy on while I was growing up doesn't seem to mean much because I don't have a clue what she's talking about.

"What's that?"

"A vitamin we all need to keep our brains functioning properly." She twists her hands in the apron. "It's actually a very common deficiency, especially in the elderly."

"Is it curable?"

She nods, shifting restlessly like she's worried Pops will stick his head out at anytime and catch us talking about him, and a light scent of orange blossom hits me. "He can take oral B12 supplements, but that will take a lot longer to really see any effect, and some people have trouble absorbing them properly. If I can get B12 shots, we should see improvement relatively quickly and know if I'm right or not."

"Jesus..."

I rest my shoulder against the wall, and some of the weight I've been carrying for months finally eases from my shoulders as hopefulness washes over me. "Like how quickly?"

"Within a couple of days, he should show *some* sort of improvement, and if it isn't that..."—she gives me a sympathetic look—"then we'll deal with it. We'll figure it out. But I think I'm right. It's like reading a medical textbook. I only saw it a few times when I worked in the ER, and it was years ago, but I'm pretty confident." Her gaze searches mine. "You don't look happy."

I force a smile and scrub my dirty hands over my face. "I'm relieved. I'm just angry at myself that I didn't figure it out sooner or force him to go to town."

"He doesn't seem like the type of man who will let anyone *force* him to do anything."

She has no idea.

I snort. "That's exactly the problem. He hasn't left this mountain in almost twenty years."

"Ever?"

Shaking my head, I shift slightly to take the weight off my right leg that always seems to aggravate me the most. "He manages all the properties in town from here, and if something needs to be brought back and forth, he sends me or has somebody from town bring it to him."

"Geez." She brushes the loose strands of her hair behind her ears. "I had no idea since he came up and talked to Dave every month."

Except the last few...

"Could this have caused any permanent damage? It's been months of him like this..."

She bristles slightly, pulling her bottom lip between her teeth. "My understanding is that some people who only have mild deficiencies usually don't have any lingering effects, but for someone who has had a severe deficiency, recovery can take a long time. Months or years. And some people have permanent issues with balance and memory."

"Shit..."

Guilt carves a new space, mingling with the pain threatening to drop me to my knees.

Camille watches me carefully. "Can you get B12 shots?"

I nod slowly, rubbing the back of my neck. "I'll radio into town to the clinic and talk to Doc. He can probably get them for us, and I'll pick them up as soon as they're ready."

Pops sticks his head out from the kitchen and narrows

his eyes on us. "What are you two doing out here? I thought we were eating."

Hopefully, he didn't catch any of that.

Forcing a smile, I incline my head toward her. "I was just updating Camille on some of the things over at her property."

"Oh"—his eyes widen slightly—"well, food's probably getting cold. Get your ass in here."

Camille fights a smirk as he steps back into the kitchen. "I hate to say it, but I kind of like the old man."

"Yeah, me too."

And he's all I have left.

"Thank you again for all your help."

She offers a soft smile. "You're the one helping me."

I push off the wall and grit my teeth at the sharp jolt across my lower back. My right leg almost gives out under me, but Camille's hand whips out against my side and steadies me.

Blue eyes search mine. "Are you all right?"

Managing a tight smile, I lock my knees, keeping myself upright. "Yeah, just overworked it a little today."

She narrows her gaze on me, and I can see the wheels churning in her head as she conducts her medical analysis. "I don't want you burning yourself out trying to help us. Maybe this is a bad idea. Maybe Davey and I should just go—"

An iciness slides across my chest, freezing my lungs. "Leave the property?"

Camille chews on her lower lip again, peeking back at her son. "I've considered it."

"Where would you go?"

Her eyes dart up to meet mine. "I don't have any family left, and Dave was never close with his. There are a few friends from before we got married, but I haven't stayed in touch with them since we moved up here. I would have to renew my nurse's license, try to find somewhere for us to stay..."

I can see the panic starting to well inside of her as she shifts nervously, and without even thinking about it, I reach up and slide my hands to her shoulders, squeezing gently. "Camille, you don't have to go anywhere. Do you want to stay on the property?"

Tears shimmer in her eyes. "Yes. It's the only place I've ever really felt at home."

I sympathize with that so deeply that it might as well be *me* saying those words. "The mountain has that pull, doesn't it?"

"I want Davey to grow up there, the way Dave and I intended." She finally pulls her hand away from my side and rests it across her stomach. "And I want that for *this* baby."

My gaze drops to her hand. "When are you due?"

She swallows thickly. "End of October."

While it's not the dead of winter, it isn't the ideal time to be giving birth, especially when you're living alone in a place like this with another child to take care of.

But I'm not about to get into that with her now.

That's a problem to address months down the road.

"I know you can't pay the rent, Camille, and I understand it seems bleak right now, but I'm not going to abandon you and Davey. Pops won't, either. We'll make it work."

She gives me a nod, swiping away at the tears that trickle from the corners of her eyes with shaky hands. "Okay. Just please don't hurt yourself trying to help us."

"Trust me. The damage was done long before you came around."

Chapter Five

ONE WEEK LATER

DALTON

The bell above the door on the building housing the James Creek Medical Clinic and pharmacy jingles, and Ted lifts his head from where it's buried in a book next to the register and smiles. "Dalton, it's good to see you."

"You, too."

Though it would have been better if he had been out grabbing a cup of coffee or taking an early lunch instead of manning the pharmacy desk right now. Less risk of him overhearing any of the meeting I need to have with Doc.

I let the door close behind me and step in, scanning to ensure no one else is inside, lurking between the aisles of products and OTC medications. "Is Doc available?"

He nods, placing his book face down to save his page. "I'll grab him for you."

"Thanks."

Ted hustles into the clinic area behind the pharmacy,

and Dr. Baker appears behind him on his return and motions for me to come back.

Doc doesn't say anything until I've followed him into his private office and closed the door behind me. He reaches into a drawer in his desk and pulls out a large, unmarked paper bag, pushing it across to me. "I assume you're here for this."

I nod, eying the innocuous bag that could hold the key to helping Pops. "I am."

"How is he doing?"

Even though only the two of us are in here, and I know no one will be able to hear us openly discussing Pops, it still makes the back of my neck tingle. "The initial shot you gave us last week seems to have helped slightly, so that's good, I guess."

He motions for me to take a seat. "I know we didn't have a lot of time to discuss this when you stopped in before, but depending on how severe the deficiency is, it could take months or even a year for him to fully recover, if he does. Some people have lingering effects."

I nod slowly. "That's what Camille said."

The corners of his lips tip slightly. "I'm glad she's assisting you. I know your grandfather never would've come down here, and I really don't feel like making that trek up the mountain to give him shots once a week until you can back off on the dosing schedule."

The battle that ensued last week when I returned from my supply run with that first dose where Camille and I had to wrangle Pops and convince him to let her inject him replays in my head like some slapstick comedy movie.

Only Camille's "nurse voice" and insistence that he comply "if he knew what was good for him" got him to stop fussing long enough for her to give him the shot.

I laugh and rub the back of my neck, relaxing into the chair. "She's good with him, doesn't let him boss her around or rattle her. And she tolerates his moods far better than I do."

Doc chuckles low. "I don't know her very well, but it certainly is nice to know she's around, should anything else ever arise."

Should anything else ever arise.

His words bring that fear that's been lingering in the back of my head since the moment I met Camille to the forefront again.

"She's pregnant."

Doc doesn't react to my statement, just reclines and props one foot up on his desk.

Shit, maybe I shouldn't be discussing somebody else's medical conditions when I'm sitting here worried about Pops' private information getting out.

"I only tell you this because..." I take a long breath and let it out slowly. "I'm concerned. She's due at the end of October, and she's alone at the homestead with Davey."

He nods slowly. "Well, thankfully, she's a nurse, so she can monitor herself during the pregnancy and knows what will need to happen when the time comes for delivery."

"Has she been to see you?"

Rocking in his chair, he shakes his head. "You know I can't tell you that, Dalton."

"Shit." I run a hand over the scruff growing on my cheek. "I know. I'm sorry for even asking."

It isn't any of my business what her plans are for the delivery of her baby. She's an adult. A *nurse*. And she's done this before on the mountain. But I can't turn off this protective instinct that has bloomed since I met the Bowers. This need to ensure both Camille and Davey are safe drives my actions every day I step onto their property and push myself beyond what I should.

I push out of the chair. "I'm just not sure what I can do to help her when the time comes."

He offers me a knowing grin. "It'll all work out, I'm sure. She'll ask for assistance, if she needs it."

"Yeah..."

Easy for him to say.

He likely hasn't had a shotgun pointed at him for wanting to help.

I want to believe she's not planning on delivering the baby at the homestead. If there were any complications, especially that time of year, getting down here to the clinic for any sort of medical intervention would take half the day, if it isn't impossible altogether with the state the roads end up in during a snowstorm.

A million worst-case scenarios race through my head, but I try to push them away and do what I told myself I would—leave tomorrow's concerns there. Right now, I need to concentrate on getting Pops well and triaging Camille's homestead.

I snatch the bag and hold it up. "Thank you."

"Anytime. You keep me updated on his progress, please. And let me know if I need to come up there. As I said last week, I can draw blood, confirm the diagnosis, and check for anything else unusual—"

I shake my head. "No. He already put up a fight when I told him he needed a shot. I almost had to restrain him to give it to him the other day. Camille only managed to get him to calm down by combining her expert nursing skills with bribing him with a German chocolate cake. If you come up there talking about blood draws..."

He laughs and drops his feet to the floor, standing

behind his desk and leaning casually against it as I approach the door. "I've treated your grandfather and the rest of your family for almost forty years; I'm well aware of how ornery he can get. I can only imagine how it has been amplified by his current condition. Hopefully, that will be resolved soon."

I open the door, then turn back to him to remind him how important it is that no one knows about Pops' condition, but he narrows his eyes on me.

"Dalton, I would never say a word to anyone, even if I *could*, ethically."

Damn, is the man a mind reader?

Or is my worry just that obvious?

Neither is a particularly appealing idea, considering what else I've been hiding from Pops and Camille.

"What about you, son? How have you been feeling? Have you reconsidered—"

I snap my head up to meet his gaze. "No. I haven't. I'm fine."

The tight smile he gives me tells me he doesn't quite believe that. Given his knowledge of what a mess I am, he shouldn't. If anyone in James Creek knows the kind of pain I live with day in and day out, it's Doc Baker.

He's also smart enough not to push me about it. "Just take care of yourself."

I incline my head by way of goodbye and close the door behind me. My boots squeak on the linoleum as I make my way up through the pharmacy and past Ted. "See you around."

He tosses me a wave and quickly returns to his book as I step out onto the sidewalk. The fresh summer mountain air fills my lungs, replacing the antiseptic scents inside.

I pause to take in the quiet of Main Street. A few people

mill about the sidewalks, making their way from shop to shop, but most of the three hundred people who live around James Creek and call it home are still in theirs.

And I only have a few more stops for supplies before I can head back up the mountain where Camille is waiting.

A warmth spreads through my chest, imagining the way her face lights up now when I pull into their drive or meet her on the porch in the mornings she comes to our place to spend time with Pops after taking care of the animals on her property.

The wariness and fear that soaked her gaze when I met her and she held that shotgun on me with trembling hands seems to have disappeared or at least abated somewhat.

I might not be able to fix all her problems.

I may not have any idea what we're going to do once winter hits and it's going to be nearly impossible to move between the homesteads safely.

And God knows I don't have a fucking *clue* what we'll do when she goes into labor and has that baby.

But those are problems for *future* me.

Current me needs to forget the way my heart has started to do that stupid stuttering thing every time I'm around her and the fact that my cock seems to come to life with just a simple, appreciative look from her.

I'm not doing *any* of this because of my attraction to Camille Bower. She's just a friend who needs a hand—and that's all she can ever be.

If only I can convince my traitorous body of that.

I head back toward the truck to drop off the bag, and the door to a black sedan parked in front of me at the curb opens. A man steps out in a sleek, dark-blue suit that belongs in a boardroom or a courtroom, not up here. He nudges the door closed behind him and steps toward me in shoes that look just as out of place here as he does in James Creek.

Instantly, my hackles rise. I scan him from his glossy, sleeked-back black hair to the practiced smile on his face, but I don't recognize him.

"Dalton James, correct?"

I bristle slightly, narrowing my gaze on him. "Yes, and you are?"

He holds out a hand. "Crosby Gallo, I represent certain interested parties—"

And I was right to be wary.

"We're not interested in selling."

Pops may have done his best to keep me insulated from any of the business dealings, but as I've grown older and more aware of just what we actually own, it doesn't take a huge leap to know why someone would want a piece of the mountain.

I move to take a step away from him, but he places a hand on my shoulder.

My initial reaction is to lash out at him for having the balls to confront me like this, but that won't do any good. Especially when I have a feeling Pops has been fighting these types of assholes for decades.

As this area of the Adirondacks grows more popular with tourists, the land becomes increasingly valuable. And we have a fuckload of it, just sitting here, undisturbed and as pristine as it was the day my ancestors settled on it.

The city slicker forces another cold smile. "You haven't even heard my offer, Mr. James."

"Don't need to. Not interested. And even if I were, I'm not the one who makes those decisions; my grandfather is."

He raises dark brows in a sinister way that makes my hand tighten around the bag. "Is he? Your grandfather is aging, Dalton. At what point do you become the one making those decisions?"

I grit my jaw.

It isn't that he doesn't have a point.

I just don't need to be reminded how fragile Pops is. How easily what's going on with him could be something more serious. How quickly I could find myself in a position I'm not ready to be in—alone and in charge of all *this*.

He removes his hand from my shoulder, holding both up with his palms out toward me. "Just give me five minutes to say my piece, and then I'll let you go on your way."

I scowl at him. "You have thirty seconds, not because I'm actually interested in what you have to say, but because people are starting to watch."

It's impossible not to notice someone who stands out so much in James Creek, someone who so clearly doesn't belong. And the gossip mill will be turning very soon, drawing folks out of the various stores and shops along Main Street, which will make our conversation very public.

"Fair enough. As I said, I represent certain interested parties and would like open discussions about purchasing some of your land."

I raise a brow at him. "Is that it? That's your pitch? As I said, we're not interested."

"The people I represent are willing to pay obscene amounts of money, Mr. James. I don't think you quite realize what you sit on."

He glances up behind me toward the mountain, the range we own nearly all of, as far as the eye can see from here.

"I'm well aware."

Gallo huffs indignantly. "If you were, your family

wouldn't have squandered it by letting it sit unused all these years."

"We live there, other people do..."

The man gives a dirty smirk that only makes him look more unsavory. "And you could be making billions, hand over fist, if you sold to us. For doing literally nothing but signing a piece of paper."

"So what? You can turn it into some resort so rich fucks from New York City can come up here with their friends to ski in the winter and swim in the summer?"

"Something like that."

"Fuck you." I turn to fully face him, until my chest almost brushes his. "My family has been here for 250 years, and we're not going anywhere."

His jaw hardens, and he leans in as several people step out from the bakery to my left and the bookstore across the street. "We'll see about that. I came to you in good faith, Mr. James, because getting a hold of your grandfather has proven difficult."

"Yeah? Or did he just flat out reject you, so you thought I'd be an easier target because I'm young and you thought that would make me greedy and pliant?"

He offers another little smirk that tells me I'm probably right. "If you don't take the offer, we'll have to take other action."

I raise a brow at him and snort. "Good luck with that."

Before he can utter another word, I stalk to the truck, tug open the door, and climb in, my other errands forgotten.

The supplies can wait.

I need to get back to the cabin.

I need to talk to Pops.

CAMILLE

Dalton's heavy footsteps on the porch draw me away from the game of Uno I'm trying to help Davey win against Pops on the kitchen table, and the knock on the door comes far harder and more urgently than I would've anticipated, considering we're expecting him.

Davey glances up with an excited smile. "Dalton?"

"I'm sure it is, Davey." Though, given the urgency in his arrival, I don't necessarily want him opening the door in case there's something wrong. "Why don't you let me go see while you play with Pops?"

Pops peers up from his hand over the rim of his glass, a smug grin pulling at his lips. "You are just running away because you know I've already won this game."

Davey pouts, his bottom lip quivering as if he's about to cry.

Rolling my eyes at the old man, I make my way to the door. "Gee. Thanks for that."

His mouth hangs open slightly, like he's completely innocent in causing that look on Davey's face. "What?"

I make it to the door and tug it open, ready to ask where the fire is, just as Dalton raises his hand to knock again. The wild look in his evergreen eyes and the set of his jaw make my spine stiffen instantly and eliminate any joke I might have made about his insistence.

Dalton is usually so laid back. He doesn't get worked up easily, and his calm, measured approach to everything that has to get done has somehow made it feel less daunting. His presence over the last week and a half has brought an almost peacefulness to what had been chaos such a short time ago.

But this isn't *that* Dalton.

"What's wrong?"

He holds out the bag to me with a quick jerk of his hand. "Nothing you need to worry about. I assume my grandfather's here with you, since I stopped at our place and he wasn't there?"

I nod and motion for him to come in, keeping an eye on them at the kitchen table. "Yes. He said he wouldn't mind coming back with me this afternoon and staying with Davey so I could work on some of the smaller repairs in the barn that I can do myself. I thought that would be helpful..."

His gaze softens slightly, appreciation flashing through it and allowing those golden flecks to shine. "It is." He leans in, until his woodsy scent—of freshly cut pine and crisp, clean mountain air—reaches me. "And the fact that you trust him with your son means more to me than I can ever express."

The heat of his body and the scent clinging to him that has become so familiar over the last several days draws me closer, and the true emotion in his words shows me that Dalton James is every bit the man he portrays himself as to the world. Something very rare in this day and age. And that's all because of Pops.

"Of course, I do, Dalton. He raised *you* right." I give him a little half smile, and it manages to make his lips twitch, but the amusement doesn't quite reach his eyes. "Are you going to tell me what's wrong?"

He shakes his head. "Really, nothing you need to worry about. Family stuff."

I raise a brow at him, but before I can press, he motions toward the kitchen, where we can partially see the continuing game.

"How is he today? I only spoke to him briefly before I headed down to town."

"He seems better than yesterday. It's only slight

improvements. Better recall about things that have happened since we met and little things like that. But I think it means I was right."

Dalton nods slowly, watching them surreptitiously. "I spoke with Doc, and he confirmed essentially the same thing. He also said he would come up if he needed to."

I shake my head. "I don't think that's necessary. I mean, ideally, we could get Pops down for a battery of tests to be sure. But other than physical therapy to address some of the balance issues and memory therapy to address those lingering problems—which I have been trying to accomplish with him when he cooperates—there's not much you can do for somebody who has had a B12 deficiency other than let their body recover."

A long, drawn-out sigh slips from Dalton's lips, and his hands tighten into fists at his sides. It isn't anything I haven't told him before or that Doc hasn't confirmed during our radio calls with him since I first tried to diagnose Pops.

But the frustration radiates off Dalton.

And I don't think it has anything to do with his grandfather's medical situation.

"I need to talk to him."

"All right." I throw my thumb over my shoulder in the direction of the small kitchen. "We're in the middle of a game of Uno."

His gaze darts to mine, and he offers a half-smirk. "That man is a card shark. Don't ever play anything involving a deck with him. Even a child's game. Because he's also competitive as hell and will not lose to save anyone's feelings—including Davey's."

He glances over my shoulder at Pops and Davey, who seem to be having a heated discussion about a card that was played. Though Davey understands the basic concept of the game, his full knowledge isn't quite there yet, which means Pops is probably taking advantage of it.

I don't know if I should be annoyed that he's beating the snot out of my son in a simple child's game or happy his memory seems good enough that he *can*.

"Hey, Pops!"

The cunning old man looks up at Dalton, and his grandson inclines his head toward the front porch.

"We need to talk."

White brows draw low in annoyance. "Can't you see I'm in the middle of something?"

"Your game can wait. This can't."

His head jerks up fully, catching on to Dalton's tone. "Davey, I'm going to let your mom take over my hand." He pushes back from the table, approaching us slowly as Davey continues to stare at the cards like they might change the longer he does. "What's wrong? Are you two going to jab me full of needles again?"

I smile and plant a kiss on his cheek. "It's for your own good, old man. Stop complaining about it."

He grumbles something unintelligible under his breath, and I lift the bag.

"And I have dozens of needles to jab you with now."

Dalton tips his head toward the porch again. "But that isn't what we need to talk about, Pops, so follow me."

Pops steps out into the afternoon heat, and I start to follow them, but Dalton turns in the door frame and shakes his head.

"Family business."

My shoulders tense at the rejection. "Sorry. I didn't mean to intrude."

I shouldn't have assumed he wanted me involved in whatever they wanted to discuss. Of course, they have things going on beyond this property and the burden I've become for them.

A lot of things.

Given the amount of time they've been spending with Davey and me, neither of them can be addressing those *other things* the way they should.

"It's not that, Camille. You're not intruding. It's just..."—he releases a heavy sigh, searching for an explanation—"nothing you need to worry about."

Despite him repeating those very words to me multiple times, something tells me it *is* something I need to worry about, or he wouldn't be hiding it.

If it were about me or about some complication I've created, would he really discuss it in front of me?

I know the answer deep in my soul.

Dalton would try to protect me from whatever is happening, the same way he's bent over backward since the moment he appeared on the homestead to do anything and everything necessary to ensure Davey and I can stay here.

And I can't force him to tell me.

As much as I may want to know what's about to be said out there, I am not in *any* position to demand or even *request* anything from the man who is already sacrificing so much for us.

"I understand."

I don't.

He slips out the door and closes it behind him, and through the window to my right, I see Pops lean against the rail, staring at what is still *their* property, even if I've been living on it and trying to make it my own.

It's already starting to look better in only the week or so Dalton has been coming up to help me. Not quite back to the way Dave and I had it before that last winter storm surged through and destroyed so many things he never got a chance to fix, things that only got worse after he was taken from me.

Despite my best efforts *not* to think about him, the memories of turning this place into our dream home bubble to the surface.

I have to fight them back, or I know I'll end up crying like I do at night when I can't escape that one *particular* memory.

"What's going on, Dalton? You seem rattled."

Pops' question comes surprisingly clear through the window I had cracked to allow in the breeze, dragging me from wandering down that road that always leads to more tears.

Should I stay and listen?

I check on Davey, who has apparently given up on the game they were playing and is now randomly stacking cards and talking to himself. That won't last long, but maybe long enough to find out what's going on.

Dalton didn't want you to hear this...

That should be enough to make me move away, but the need to ensure I'm not causing problems for the James men wins out. My hand tightens on the bag with Pops' medication, and I inch closer to the window and flatten my back against the wall so they won't see me if they happen to glance in from the porch.

"Do you know a douchebag suit named Gallo?"

I freeze at the cold tone and harsh words that are so unusual coming from Dalton. He has never struck me as the type to speak ill of *anyone*, but whoever Gallo is, he seems to have gotten under his skin.

"That fucker's still barking around?"

Apparently, Pops feels the same way...

Dalton releases a long, audible sigh filled with annoyance. *"He cornered me on the street outside the pharmacy."*

Pops lets out a low whistle. *"Did he now?"*

"He did."

"What did he want?"

A flash of movement in the window makes me freeze, and I hold my breath, casting another quick glance at Davey, who still seems unaware of what's happening. He stacks the cards by color, saying each number as it comes up with a proud smile.

Dalton passes by the window, pacing the length of the porch with his hands laced at the back of his neck. *"For me to talk you into selling."*

Selling?

Selling what?

Panic churns my stomach, and I place my free hand over it to keep my breakfast from coming back up. It's hard enough battling the ongoing morning sickness, but now the stress and uncertainty of whatever is happening out on that porch might force me to dash to the bathroom before I can ever figure out what's actually going on.

Does he mean selling this *property?*

It would be logical.

A good business decision.

Selling—or even *renting*—to someone else would make far more sense than having Dalton put so much work and effort into making it livable for us, especially when I'm offering them absolutely *nothing* in return. Not even able to pay the rent we agreed to when we moved up here.

They don't really need me to take care of Pops—Dalton can handle the simple balance and memory exercises I've been doing with him.

They don't need me to cook for them, since they've

been doing it on their own for decades before I came along and seemed to be handling things just fine.

They certainly don't need my young child constantly underfoot—or this new baby coming.

They don't need me here for *anything.*

I'm a liability.

Only making things more difficult in an already difficult place.

Pops snorts and makes a disgusted noise. *"That'll never happen."*

The determination in his voice, the absolute, steadfast stance he's taking, is enough to allow my stomach to settle finally and me to take a full breath again. But now, I also understand why Dalton didn't want me to hear any of this.

Someone is trying *to get them to sell something.*

Which explains why Dalton has been so worried about Pops' memory, beyond what any normal person would be for someone they love.

Their business doesn't run without Pops, and if he's not all *there,* Dalton would be left in a position of making these decisions and potentially fighting someone who could come at them with something more than an *offer.*

Dalton sighs, leaning back against the cabin right next to the open window, close enough to have me holding my breath again. *"That's what I told him, but he made it sound like there may be something in the works if we don't."*

Pops harrumphs. *"And what would that be?"*

"I'm not entirely sure. But he said they have other ways of getting what they want. I assume he meant eminent domain. But would they really take the mountain so they can build some fucking resort?"

I gasp, then slap my hand over my mouth.

Take the entire mountain?

The more I overhear, the worse the queasiness returns, and I have to fight back the bile crawling up my throat.

Pops lets out a long sigh. *"He isn't the first person to show up with an offer someone thinks I can't refuse because, if you haven't noticed, I'm getting older."*

Dalton lets out a barked laugh from right beside the window that has me inching away from it slightly. *"You don't say."*

"They will never get it."

Pops' stern response settles over me like a soft, warm blanket.

It's unwavering.

Just like Dalton's was when he said he would make sure we were safe and could stay on this homestead.

These men don't quit.

They don't back down from a fight or fail on a promise.

"How can you be so sure, Pops?"

"Because our family was the first to settle on this mountain. Our blood is in it. They can't take that."

Dalton pushes off the house. *"But they can, Pops. They can take whatever they want. Offer us whatever the fuck they determine is fair market value and kick us off the mountain if they get government support."*

"I'd like to see them try."

The frustrated breath Dalton releases in response echoes my own sentiments. *"I appreciate your confidence, Pops. But we can't stick our heads in the sand about this. And honestly, you keeping me in the dark about all the business stuff doesn't fucking help, either."*

I wince—for Dalton *and* Pops.

They're trying to protect each other, but they're doing it in ways that only seem to cause tension and frustration that's finally boiling over.

"What's that supposed to mean, kid?"

"Pops..." The sound of Dalton's footsteps crossing the porch slip through the cracked window, and I have to lean toward it to hear as he moves closer to Pops. *"You haven't collected the rent from Camille in months. I have no idea what's happening in town with any of the businesses. You didn't even tell me that Camille's husband died...or that she was up here alone with a four-year-old. I had no idea that they might need help. I had no idea that there was this threat lingering out here, one this big. You can't keep me in the dark forever. This conversation is the most you've told me about the business in my entire life."*

Pops lowers his voice. *"I didn't want to burden you with any of it. Not when I have it handled. And I do have it handled, kid. You need to trust me."*

"Bullshit. You don't trust me."

The true pain in his accusation cuts through me as if it's my own.

I may not have known Dalton very long, but from what he's shown me of himself since he arrived as our savior, I can understand his hurt and frustration.

He's young—over a decade younger than *me*, even—and Pops has controlled the James empire alone for a long time. He isn't used to sharing information or workload beyond what happens on the homestead. Something that clearly needs to happen if Dalton is ever going to take over for him.

I peek out the window to find both men leaning against the railing with their backs to me.

Pops reaches over and wraps his arm around Dalton's shoulders. *"I trust you more than I trust myself, Dalton. You've helped me keep our place running so that I could concentrate on the businesses. You've done more work than anyone your age should ever have had to, even as a child, and especially with your limitations."*

Limitations?

The way he wobbled the other day flashes through my head.

I thought he was just tired from all the work he had taken on, but maybe there was more to it than I could see.

"Mama, what are you doing?"

Shit.

I whip my head away from the window and push off the wall as Davey rushes over to me.

My heart thunders against my ribcage as I scoop him up and move away from the front of the house before they can hear us—if they didn't already figure out that I was eavesdropping when I *definitely* shouldn't have been.

It was stupid.

Rude.

But Dalton seemed so rattled, and if this had anything to do with us, if I was somehow causing a problem...I needed to know.

Now, a million questions flood my head, and the dread and panic that had disappeared once Dalton stepped in to help us return with a vengeance.

Could someone really come take the mountain from them?

And what's wrong with Dalton that he is keeping hidden?

Chapter Six

THREE WEEKS LATER

DALTON

A light drizzle falls from the darkening sky, pelting the plexiglass roof of the greenhouse, creating a soft, soothing song that fills the otherwise nearly silent space.

Other than the sounds of Camille and me moving the small seedling plants from plastic containers into the newly built planter boxes and the scrape of Davey's plastic shovel along the bottom of the one we're letting him play in to keep him occupied, the companionable silence that settled over us a while ago had gone unbroken.

And somehow, it *hasn't* been awkward.

After almost a month of being here and having Camille and Davey come to our place daily, we've settled into a comfortable routine and found normalcy that I didn't think would be so easy, given the way things started out—at gunpoint.

Mornings working our homestead as much as I can.

Caring for the animals.

Making regular repairs and conducting maintenance on the hundreds of little things that wear down constantly.

Doing what I can to ensure Pops and I are prepared for the coming winter by stockpiling wood, hunting, trapping, and fishing—often before the sun even comes up.

Camille and Davey arriving to work with Pops on his exercises and to keep the old man company as he continues to get better day by day.

Afternoons spent here, trying my damnedest to keep Camille afloat by fixing and improving what I can on the property with the last remaining hours of daylight and energy I have left as we reach the height of summer.

Which isn't much some days.

The pain has become unbearable at times, and I've had to dial back my workload or grin and bear it in order to keep Pops or Camille from worrying.

But it's worth it.

Because the woman who has become so much more than just a neighbor no longer has to agonize over what will happen when the snow—and her baby—come.

She'll have a warm, safe home for her children, and her animals will be well-protected from the elements. Along with this greenhouse we've been working on for days in order to get it ready for planting, the meat and fish I've started stocking in her freezer and the new chickens I've added to her now-contained flock mean she won't have to worry about where her food is coming from, either.

There are still things to do—far too many for my liking. But there's an end in sight. One that doesn't result in her leaving the mountain with Davey.

Every time I consider that possibility, a renewed panic sets in.

She doesn't feel the same way I do—doesn't *want* what I

do—but even if I can't have that part of her, I can't imagine not having them here and in my life.

I glance over my shoulder to check on her and Davey. Both are still intently working, but Camille's brow holds that deep furrow I often find there.

She's worried.

But it isn't about what we still need to accomplish here. Not with the finish line in sight.

This is something new, something that has lingered in her gaze as she watches me since the night I confronted Pops about the threat that skeezy lawyer made.

I suspected she was listening, but it wasn't until I heard Davey's voice through the cracked window that I knew for sure she had overheard at least part of our conversation.

How much?

Enough that she's kept a watch on me like she expects the other shoe to drop.

Like she's wary and waiting for it.

Maybe she should be.

Despite how well things have gone here, a sense of dread has clung to me since my confrontation with that asshole. Nothing Pops has said to try to quell my concern has done anything more than make it worse.

The old man seems to have his head in the sand.

He thinks there's nothing anyone can do—but the world has changed since he was born on this mountain.

Things aren't so simple anymore.

And I can't share his blind confidence that whatever his "secret plan" is will be enough to protect our backs from anything that might be coming for us.

I'd give anything to be able to wipe away those creases from her soft skin, to touch her and tell her everything will be okay while *truly* believing it. But I don't dare allow myself to dream of that being a possibility.

My dreams are already filled with her blue eyes and gentle touch, my days haunted by wondering what she's thinking when I catch her gaze from across the yard and she smiles.

I have to shake my head now to clear away those thoughts, or they'll end up leading down the dead-end path of wanting anything *more* from Camille.

And I can't work like this anymore.

Not in these tight confines with her, feeling her eyes on me every few minutes, when her orange blossom scent permeates the humid air, and I'm insanely aware of every move she makes.

I push to my feet, biting back a groan at the tension in my back from having been bent over for so long, working in the planter bed, and Camille looks up from her spot farther down the line.

Her eyes rake over me, as if she's searching for something in particular more than actually taking in how I look in my jeans and open shirt. "How are things coming?"

I scan up and down the row that runs along the middle of the newly updated greenhouse. "Good. I think we're almost done with this portion."

Which only leaves two more sets of beds to plant.

It should be relatively quick work.

Much easier than rebuilding the broken structure and constructing the new beds that can hold far more than the old ones and will be watered with an automated drip line from the fresh water coming in from the well.

But I narrow my gaze on Camille sitting on the dirt floor, her belly now even bigger, and that same worry creeps in that I've been trying to keep at bay for months.

That I'm pushing her too hard.

That I'm making her do too much when she's in this condition.

That I still don't know what the hell her plan is when the baby comes.

And I've been too afraid to ask.

Too afraid to further insert myself into her life when she just wants to have her dream here with Davey and the baby. A dream I am not a part of.

She may need Pops and me to get back to where she would have been had Dave not died, but this was never meant to be anything more than one neighbor helping another.

It isn't my place to take that protector role, to agonize so much about what her future holds, but I can't help myself. Not when I see her like this.

"How are you doing? It's been a long day..."

She glances down and presses a dirt-covered hand against the apron covering her belly. "I'm good."

I raise a brow, looking for any signs of discomfort. "Sitting on the ground and bending over isn't too hard on you?"

Her lips press together tightly, like she's getting ready to launch into the same debate we've had numerous times in the past month when it comes to her helping with any sort of manual labor. "I'm *okay*. It isn't any harder on me than it is on *you*."

I instantly regret even mentioning it—and not just because her final comment makes me think she heard *too* much that night. The last thing I want is for Camille to know how much pain I'm in or how much worse it's become since more than doubling my workload.

Plus, I know damn well how much Camille likes to believe she's invincible, how tough it is to get her to admit any weakness. Even *implying* she might not be capable or shouldn't be doing something is enough to be a direct insult to her.

Which is the last thing I want to do.

I pull off my gardening gloves and run a hand back through my hair, stepping over to where Davey digs in the dirt, getting more of it on the ground around him than actually in any of the buckets we gave him. Squatting, I ignore that pull in my back, and I ruffle his hair. "How you doing, buddy?"

His eyes that match his mother's light up. "Look what I did."

The pride in his voice warms my chest as I glance down at the single spinach sprout he has lopsidedly placed in the planter bed and grin at him. "That looks amazing. You're really good at this. You're a great helper."

He nods and goes back to it, happily moving dirt back and forth between the bed and buckets, seemingly with no rhyme or reason.

I push to my feet and turn to find Camille watching me carefully, her eyes holding that dewy softness that always makes my heart skip a little beat, even though it shouldn't.

Shouldn't.

Yet it's impossible to ignore how beautiful she is, how her sadness and tender nature call to me in a way I didn't even know was possible. How badly I want her to start living again instead of constantly dwelling in the past and being afraid of what's coming next.

The rain starts falling heavier, the sound now almost like thunder echoing around us in the greenhouse, and I glance up, staring through the almost clear top to the darkened sky.

No lightning.

No *actual* thunder.

Just a nice warm summer rain.

A grin pulls at my lips, and I turn back to Davey. "Hey, Davey." He glances up, and I point toward the semi-transparent roof. "The rain is coming down pretty hard."

He nods, clearly more interested in his mess than my weather observations.

"I bet you there are some great puddles out there."

Little brows furrow as if he's not following me or understanding what I'm getting at. I can't help but chuckle at how sweet and innocent he is as I turn back to Camille to find her fighting a smile.

I scoop him up easily, and he protests slightly, his plastic spade slipping from his hand. Setting him on my hip, I ignore the twinge in my lower back and lean in to whisper conspiratorially. "Don't you want to go play in some puddles?"

His eyes widen slightly and immediately dart over to his mom, who gives me her nod of approval, without me even having to explain my intentions.

He finally smiles and bounces in my arms, clapping wildly. "Let's go!"

I carry him past Camille, who gives me an appreciative look, before I push open the greenhouse door and step out into the rain, inhaling the crisp, clean smell that always comes with it.

Instantly, the memories flood back of another time I stood out in a summer downpour, a time before everything was taken from me because I wanted something I shouldn't have.

I refuse to do that with Camille.

To make that same mistake.

Stepping out farther onto the property, I search for the

perfect spot and locate the low-lying area along the edge of the grass near the gravel drive. I set Davey on his feet and point it out. "That looks like a pretty good puddle right there."

He glances up at me, as if to ask my permission, and I run toward it and jump, landing right in the middle and sending a giant wave of water up and out.

Davey squeals and claps, then rushes over after me and leaps in just like I used to with Dad, helping dull the ache of that memory by giving me this incredible new one.

———

CAMILLE

Davey's peal of laughter makes my heart clench violently. I try to drag in a breath, but it gets stuck in my suddenly clogged throat. A boulder seems to sit there, something heavy and laden with emotions I'm not willing to examine if I want to maintain any of my sanity.

Through the semi-transparent greenhouse, I can just make out their shapes moving through the downpour.

Dalton, so much bigger, and Davey so tiny, chasing after him across the yard and jumping up and down, making himself a bigger mess than he already was after "helping" us with the planting all afternoon.

But none of that matters.

Not how dirty or wet he might get or how stained his clothes may end up.

Not when he sounds so damn happy.

Hot tears track down my cheeks, and I wipe them away on my forearm, my hands too dirty to do the job without leaving evidence across my face. And I do not want Davey or Dalton to see me come undone like this.

I've fought too hard to hold it together in front of Davey. To be strong for him so he doesn't become a hollow shell of himself the way I sometimes feel. At least, when I'm alone.

It's easier when Dalton's around.

To see that hope.

To be something other than a miserable, hormonal mess.

Listening to him out there with Davey, how carefree they sound doing something as simple as playing in the rain, makes me even more thankful he's come into our lives and for everything he's brought with him.

His calm, reassuring presence.

His physical strength as well as the emotional support he's given both of us when we had no one else to lean on.

And most of all, the glimmer of hope that's always trailed along in his easy smile.

He found a way to draw something out of Davey I don't think I could have today.

It's incredible how resilient children are, how quickly they can bounce back from the kind of pain that should crush them, and how easily they can find joy in such simple things. To me, it still feels like my world is incomplete, like a part of me is missing and has been since the moment Dave died.

I force myself onto my feet and brush my hands off on my apron, annoyed I didn't wear my gardening gloves today. Drawn to the sound of their laughter and indistinguishable words, I push open the greenhouse door and watch them from the protection of the jamb.

The sound of the pouring rain stampedes on the roof as it falls in an almost solid sheet only inches in front of me, just like it did the first time I saw Dalton.

Back then, he was barely eighteen, but watching him now, I can't deny that he has become one of the strongest men I've ever met.

This life demands it.

And the role model he had in Pops ensured that his strength isn't just physical but also of character, too.

He leaps, slamming his booted feet down into the massive puddle they stand in and sending water flying and splashing up over Davey, who just grins and tries to do the same to the man who has somehow become so important to us in such a short amount of time.

Dalton has truly become our friend.

He's more than just our savior.

He's somebody we look forward to seeing every day, spending time with, someone who can draw a smile from either of us, even at a time when I didn't think that would ever be possible again.

I rest my hand across my belly as the renewed agony of knowing this baby is never going to meet his or her father washes over me.

Will Davey even remember him?

Dalton looks up from where they're playing and grins, motioning for me to come over and join them, but I quickly shake my head. If I get anywhere near him, he'll see what a wreck I am, how I'm completely falling apart over something so trivial as watching them play in the rain.

But all I can picture is Dave doing this with his son.

What should have been, if not for that freak accident...

Dalton's brow furrows as he watches me, and he bends down and whispers something to Davey. Davey glances my way, then races over through the rain, slamming his feet through the smaller puddles forming across the property until he reaches me.

He stares up, drenched from head to foot, with the biggest grin I may have ever seen on his face, and grabs my hand. "Come on, Mama."

I shake my head and squeeze his tiny fingers. "No, Bub. You go have fun with Dalton. I'm going to stay dry right here."

His bottom lip pops out in a pout, and he tugs at my arm. "Come *on*, Mom."

Dalton chuckles, the sound carrying across the yard to me along with this positive energy. "Yeah, come *on,* Mom."

The sing-song way he mimics Davey draws a grin across my face, and I allow the tiny hand to tug me out of the protection of the edge of the greenhouse and into the rain.

Warm rain drenches me almost instantly but somehow helps temper the humidity that's been almost suffocating the last week. It's likely the end of the season, the last summer rain we'll get before fall starts to work its way onto the mountain.

And this is exactly what Davey should be doing: enjoying the weather, the property, and just loving life being out here surrounded by all this pristine beauty.

This is why Dave and I chose James Mountain in the first place.

For moments like this.

I just never could have anticipated that the man having them with Davey wouldn't be *him*.

Swallowing back the despair threatening to choke me, and thankful the rain will hide the tears that I can't stop from falling, we finally reach Dalton. He flashes me that easy grin of his and takes my other hand, tugging me toward the puddle, with Davey doing the same on my opposite side.

Dalton nods toward the pooling water. "Come on, Mommy, give us one good splash."

I try to give him an annoyed look, but I can't fight the smile that naturally pulls at my lips as I lock gazes with him and see the amusement dancing in his green eyes.

Before I can do or say anything, Dalton jumps and comes down, spraying muddy water across both Davey and me. I gasp at the sensation, even though it isn't cold, while Davey just squeals in delight again, drops my hand, and flails his legs up, kicking wildly and creating an inescapable spiral.

Scowling at Dalton, I swipe my face clean on my sleeve as best I can, only for it to get instantly soaked again. "You did that on purpose."

He raises a shoulder and lets it fall, completely unapologetic and looking every bit his age with the playful smirk, even though the lean, rippling muscles on his chest and stomach certainly show the opposite. "Don't be a party pooper."

I bark out a laugh that echoes off the trees and gets swallowed by the sound of the rain hitting the greenhouse and pooling water all around us. "I didn't know you were also four."

He squeezes my hand still in his. "Just because we're adults doesn't mean we have to always act like it."

"I'm thirty-six, Dalton..."

Another muscled shoulder rises and falls, as if the thirteen-year age difference between us means absolutely nothing, and without warning, he jumps up again.

This time, I manage to turn away before I get sprayed directly in the face.

When I turn back, it's with determination. I release Dalton's hand and jump up, stomping my boots into the puddle as hard as I can when I come down.

It sprays both of them with a violent flood of murky water that *almost* rivals the one Dalton sent my way.

Dalton tips his head back and laughs, the sound so full of warmth I almost forget for a second that there's a gaping, icy hole in my chest, and Davey races around us in a circle, churning up the water with his little booted feet and spraying us both.

I scoop him up, and he giggles as I dangle him over the water, pressing my lips to his wet cheek. "Are you having fun?"

He nods, and I kiss him again, wishing there were a way to capture this exact second when he looks like this and hold on to it forever.

"Good. That looks like a pretty awesome puddle over there."

He follows my gaze and sees the one directly across from us that has formed since the rain started more heavily. His eyes light up, and he tugs out of my hold and races across to it to take a giant leap.

Dalton shifts behind me, then moves to my side, glancing over at me with a half-smirk. I watch Davey rushing from puddle to puddle, trying to see how big a splash he can make in each one, then look up at the man who has managed to make him so happy today.

"Thank you."

He raises a wet brow, his blond hair darkened and matted to his head, curling slightly at his forehead. "For what?"

I incline my head toward Davey. "For this. It isn't easy for him to not have his father here. He's so young..."

The rest of the words I intended to say get caught in my throat, and Dalton steps in front of me, dipping his head to catch my gaze.

"I've been where he is, Camille. I know how important it is for him to do normal things and to have moments like this. I had them with my dad before he died, and I wish..."—he swallows, his Adam's apple moving slowly—"I wish my grandfather and I could have kept doing it."

It's on the tip of my tongue to ask why they didn't, but the conversation I overheard several weeks ago rushes right back.

His limitations...

The old man's words ring in my ears, mixing with the rain and Davey's giggles from across the yard.

Looking at Dalton now, I can't imagine him having any.

He's been nothing but a goddamn living, breathing Superman since the moment I met him.

Bending over backward to do anything we need.

To be everything we need him to be.

Dalton reaches out and tips my chin up, forcing me to look at him. His calloused fingertips graze over my skin, sending a shiver of awareness through me. "You need to know that it's okay for you, too."

Staring into his eyes, the gold in them practically glowing in the reflected sunlight now filtering through the breaking clouds and rain, I struggle to breathe. "Wh-what is?"

"To have fun, Camille. To be *happy*. I know what grief feels like. I may not have lost a partner the way you did, but I understand what Davey is going through. And I know that the only way to survive it is to move *through* it. To find moments of pure joy like *this* in every day, if you can."

He barely speaks the words before a rainbow appears over the trees behind him, arching across the entire property like a damn neon sign telling me that he's absolutely right.

Chapter Seven

ONE MONTH LATER

CAMILLE

Davey runs from the barn and toward me as I carefully climb from the truck a little slower than I used to and slam the door behind me. Pops ambles out after him, taking careful steps, though he seems far more stable than he has any other time over the last few months.

The shots and our continued rehab work are definitely helping.

Slowly but surely, I'm starting to fully see the Edison James who raised such an amazing man like Dalton, who helped build up the James empire and who bends over backward to help anyone in James Creek who needs anything, even now when they're busy preparing both their place and mine for the harshest time of the year on the mountain.

We've made tremendous progress in resolving *that* issue, and now that the weather is starting to cool and fall is on the horizon, it feels like a miracle how close the homestead is to being ready for it. There are still things to do, but they seem manageable compared to where we were only a few months ago.

The chilly breeze wraps around me as I wait for them to reach me.

Davey runs as fast as his little legs will carry him, and Dalton's words from that very rainy day last month still echo in my head and heart.

The only way to survive it is to move through *it. To find moments of pure joy like* this *in every day, if you can...*

He made it sound so simple.

And I've been trying my best to do just that.

To see the way Davey lights up whenever he's around Pops and Dalton.

How he enjoys every single moment of life on this property.

Like he clearly has been all morning since I've been gone, given the massive grin on his face. Davey practically throws himself at me, latching on as I lift him and settle him on my hip the best I can with my expanding stomach.

"Mama, did you see the baby?"

I grin at him, his bursting excitement infectious. "I did. Do you want to see?"

He nods, so I set him down and reach into my purse to pull out the sonogram picture sheet. Turning it toward him so he can see it, I watch that light and awe in his eyes as they widen.

"That's my brother?"

I shake my head and let him hold the picture. "No. The baby was finally in a good position for them to tell me it's a girl. You're having a baby sister."

Pops finally makes it over to us with a half grin and a half-hearted groan. "Damn, that kid is fast." He leans against the truck, crossing his arms over his chest and giving me an exaggerated huff. "Everything good?"

I snag the photo from Davey and nod. "Yes, Doc says everything's fine."

"Good." He scowls slightly, taking on that gruff, fatherly, disapproving look he often gives me over trivial things. "Though I wish you had let Dalton take you into town. Neither of us like you driving that road yourself."

Pursing my lips, I give him a look that would probably wither anyone except him, since he's seemingly become immune to it over the last couple of months. "Like I told Dalton this morning, while I appreciate your concern, I'm perfectly capable of driving into town myself. Plus, he has enough to take care of here without having to waste half a day to chauffer me up and down a mountain for an appointment."

Pops opens his mouth to argue again, but I press my hand against his chest and tap gently over his heart. "Really, I do appreciate it, old man."

And I actually mean it.

Pops has become almost like a second father to me, and nearly twenty years after I lost my own, the knowledge of how much he cares truly does warm my heart as much as it annoys me to have him and Dalton constantly hovering over me.

Davey comes over and clings to Pops' leg. "It's a *girl!*"

I can't tell if he's excited or disgusted by the proposition. Maybe because even *he* doesn't know at this age. But the smile Pops offers tells me he's thrilled.

He doesn't often talk about Dalton's mother, but when he does, it's clear she was a daddy's girl and the absolute greatest joy in his life, especially after Dalton's grandmother passed away.

His eyes mist over, and he pushes off the truck, clearing his throat. "A girl. That's great. You should tell Dalton. He'll want to know you're back safely."

I scan what I can see of the property from here near the cabin, but I don't see any sign of him.

Dammit.

The way my heart sinks slightly when I can't immediately spot him is stupid.

It's only been a few hours since I drove away down the mountain.

Yet, on the drive back up, all I could think about was seeing Davey, Pops, and *him* to share the news about the baby.

Stupid and dangerous.

I can't let these stupid pregnancy hormones get the best of me...

Pops motions over his shoulder. "He's in the south clearing, felling some trees and working on the firewood stock."

It's going to be one of the biggest issues come winter, ensuring we have enough wood, getting it moved from outside and into the shed, and then from there into the house once there are feet of snow. It's also one of the most time-consuming and physically draining things Dalton has to accomplish.

"Go. He's worried." Pops grabs Davey's hand. "I got him."

"All right."

Pops grins at Davey. "Maybe we'll go play a card game."

I toss him a disapproving look. "Be nice. He's just a child, Pops."

He shrugs and winks. "Kid's got to learn. He's not always going to win in life."

It isn't the *worst* lesson he could teach Davey because

he's right that it's important for children to be taught it's realistic to win *and* lose. But the way the old man goes about it often leaves something to be desired.

I give him an exasperated sigh before I start out across the property in the direction Pops sent me.

The chilly early fall breeze blows across me now that the cabin no longer blocks most of it, and it carries the smell of the fire burning in the fireplace, leaves just starting to change color, and all the other familiar scents of the mountain.

Inhaling deeply, I hold it in my lungs for a moment, considering the fact that only a few short months ago, I thought I would have to leave this place. I believed I'd never experience fall on the homestead again, that Davey would never play in the golden and red leaf piles or watch the first winter snow from his bedroom window another time.

I'm happy to be rid of the scalding heat of the summer, especially now that I'm into my third trimester and feel like a bloated whale waddling everywhere, but the further we slip into autumn, the closer we get to this baby coming and the more aware I become that we're not ready.

Not by a long shot.

The seemingly never-ending list of tasks—big and small —haunts me every night. Though it's better than the night-mare that used to come every night.

Always the same.

A single moment in time.

The one that changed everything.

Replayed in my mind on an endless loop whenever I closed my eyes.

I can't even remember when it started to dissipate. I just know that slowly, over the last few months, it became less and less frequent, until I only wake in a cold sweat and sobbing every once in a while instead of every single night.

Maybe the sense of security the James men have offered us has helped me put that memory into the vault where it belongs, but seeing our little girl on that monitor today brought it roaring back with such clarity that Doc was concerned I was losing it.

He wasn't far off.

I shouldn't have gone to the appointment alone.

That stubborn streak Dave always accused me of having certainly didn't go away when he did. If anything, it comes back more frequently, as a defense mechanism whenever Dalton gets too close or says something that reminds me how badly I want him with me at times, like lying on that clinic bed today.

Which isn't fair.

Not to Dave.

And certainly not to Dalton.

Even now, as I make my way down the narrow path through the woods toward the large clearing Dave always used when he was cutting wood where Dalton has also set up shop, I half expect to find a different man there.

The one who asked me out from an ER bed after he came in with his head split open by a construction site accident before he even knew my name.

Who got down on one knee after only a dozen dates because he said he just *knew* I was "it" for him.

My hand drifts over where the baby kicks, and I rub at the spot, fighting the tears that want to fall. "Your daddy loves you so damn much, little girl."

The sound of the axe whacking against logs echoes off all the tree trunks around me, a steady rhythm that starts to vibrate in my chest the closer I move toward it, until

Dalton finally comes into view across the clearing from me.

Bright sun beats down on him, his chest glistening slightly with sweat as he raises the blade and slams it down on another log, splitting it in half. Pieces pile up on either side of the giant stump he uses as a base, and he grabs another one, sets it on its side, and swings the weapon in the practiced motion that seems almost second nature to him.

He catches me moving toward him out of the corner of his eye and sets down the axe, a grin pulling at his lips as I approach. "You're back."

I nod as I stop a few feet from him, staring at the massive piles of firewood that are all going to have to be moved into storage. "I am."

His chest heaves, his breathing struggling to return to normal after what must have been an insane amount of felling and splitting all morning. "Is everything all right?"

I nod, forcing myself to keep my eyes on his instead of drifting down his shiny torso. "Perfect."

Relief relaxes his features and shoulders, as if he's been carrying that tension since the moment I left this morning. Maybe he has been. "Good."

"I found out the sex of the baby..."

His eyes widen, the excitement practically pouring off him the same way it did Davey. "And? Don't leave me hanging."

"It's a girl."

Dalton sucks in a sharp breath, then whistles in a way so similar to Pops that I can't help but laugh. "Damn. That's amazing. A girl... congratulations, Camille."

"Thank you." I give him a worried smile. "Honestly, I'm a little nervous. I feel like I was prepared for a boy after having Davey."

A slow grin curls Dalton's mouth, and he runs the back of his hand over his forehead, wiping away the sweat there. "I am one hundred percent confident you are going to be an amazing girl mom."

"I'm glad someone thinks so."

He chuckles as he lets the axe fall and turns away from me to grab his shirt off the ground. "You need to give yourself more credit, Camille. You're an incredible mother..."

My breath catches in my throat, and I can't tear my eyes from his skin.

Scars track across his lower and middle back, up the length of his spine and out across the top of his hips.

Clean.

Meticulous.

Definitely surgical...

What the hell happened to him?

In all the time we've spent together, I've never seen his back exposed like this. Whether that was intentional on his part or not, he's always kept his shirt on around me or worn one open in the front only on really hot days.

Was he trying to hide this?

He tugs on his shirt and turns to face me. His eyes meet mine, and his entire demeanor shifts in an instant. The relaxed posture he had only a second ago morphs as his body goes rigid.

Apparently, I'm doing a shitty job covering my shock at what I've seen.

I never did have a good poker face.

Even in the ER, I had a hard time concealing my reaction to truly catastrophic cases and often had to leave the room for a moment when I could to gather myself and prepare for what I was going to walk back into.

Knowing the pain they were in...

How much they were suffering...

It was impossible not to feel for them, not to want to ease their agony any way I could...

And whatever happened to Dalton was clearly catastrophic and agonizing.

No one has scars like that from anything other than a life-altering injury.

He clears his throat and steps around me. "I'm going to move all this tomorrow. Let's head back to the house so I can get cleaned up before we tackle dinner."

His avoidance of what I've seen, of the questions I undoubtedly have, doesn't go unnoticed, but I'm not about to push him about something he clearly doesn't want to discuss with me.

Just like he never does about Dave.

Which I appreciate more than he could ever know.

For as close as Dalton and I have become over the last few months, there are still so many things we haven't said, and maybe we never will. And that's probably for the best. For both of us.

———

DALTON

The steam from my quick shower still fills the bathroom as I tug up my clean jeans and grab a T-shirt from the bag I've started bringing with me to Camille's house every afternoon so I won't stink while we all sit around the dinner table together at night.

Something that has become so routine it would feel odd *not* to do it.

But before I put it on, I swipe away the condensation

coating the mirror and turn around, peering over my shoulder to see what Camille did earlier today out in the clearing.

Shit.

It's so rare that I actually look at the scars, that I allow myself to view the very *real* evidence and reminder of the worst day of my life. I can handle the pain. I've learned ways to cope with it as a constant companion, but I will *never* get used to the way other people react when they see these or the cascade of violent, agonizing memories that come when I do.

They barrel down on me now.

Starting with so much love and laughter.

Then squealing tires.

Skidding across the road.

The crunch of metal and shatter of glass.

And nothing but sheer anguish.

I turn back to face the mirror, squeezing my eyes closed against the onslaught of visions and feelings from that day and the ones that followed.

How could you let her see them?

Because I've become so accustomed to having her around that I completely forgot to cover the evidence of my greatest weakness.

There's a *reason* I keep them hidden, that I never remove my shirt while I'm working, even in the worst of the summer heat. I shouldn't have taken it off today, regardless of how uncomfortable I was by the time Camille showed up.

She'll have questions...

Ones that will be far too painful for me to answer.

Fucking hell.

I was just so happy to see her back, to know that she returned safely and that everything with the baby is okay...

It made me let my guard down.

But I was already so rattled by her refusal to allow me to take her to the appointment. The rejection hurt far more than I ever let on to Pops or her. I know I don't have any right to be there with her, but to be able to hold her hand and celebrate with her when she found out she was having a girl...

Somehow, it feels like I missed something magical that I so desperately wanted to be a part of. And every minute she was gone, I worried. I wondered. I obsessed over what was happening without me there.

"Shit..."

I slam my palms against the countertop, shaking my head to try to clear away all these feelings I *can't* be having about Camille and *her* children.

My place is set in stone.

I'm a *friend*.

Someone she can lean on during the worst time of her life.

I *cannot* want anything more.

So, stop!

I scrub my hands over my face and back through my damp hair.

The smell of whatever she's making for dinner wafts through the crack under the bathroom door, reminding me I can't hide out in here forever when they're all waiting for me to eat. But I just need another minute to try to calm myself down, to try to forget that look in her eyes—of sympathy, of pity, of whatever else it was when she saw how damaged I am.

Easier said than done.

Since the moment I realized what a dire situation Camille was in, I've wanted nothing more than to fix it for her—for *them*. To make it *right*. To give her the security she should have had if Dave hadn't been ripped away from her.

I never wanted anything in return.

Never expected it.

But the friendship that's grown between us has given me more than I ever could have anticipated.

And I'd be lying to myself if I said what I'm feeling for the beautiful dark-haired woman isn't more than friendship.

These feelings are *dangerous* in a way I never saw coming, that I never could have anticipated when I first met her and had that shotgun barrel pointed at me.

Which is precisely why I can't ever act on them.

I push away from the counter and force myself to turn the door handle and walk out, down the short hallway of the small cabin Great-Uncle Tim built and lived in, toward the living room.

No matter how many times I'm in here, I'm still struck by the personal touches Pops' older brother left on the cabin he built. They're still everywhere, including his initials carved into the beam running over my head.

I reach up and rest my hand over it—something I do every time I'm inside to let him know I haven't forgotten about him, even though I was barely ten when he died.

His memory will live on through this space he put so much time, love, and effort into, that's become a home for Camille and Davey.

Laughter floats from the kitchen, and I grin, despite the tension my shower didn't relieve. I step in and find Pops at the table with Davey. Camille's blue gaze finds mine, and she moves a pot of something from the stove onto a potholder in the center of the small round table Great-Uncle Tim built that has remained the center of his cabin.

He was always a better woodworker than Pops. And I certainly don't come anywhere near what he could do with a slice of lumber and the right tools.

His pieces will last forever, just like the memories created around this table will.

I head to the empty chair across from Davey, still trying to shake off the thoughts that followed me from the bathroom.

Pops raises a brow at me from my left. "You good?"

I nod, but as I sit, the sharp pain in my back makes me wince.

Even the hot shower and letting the spray hit me for as long as I dared stay in didn't help loosen it, and knowing I'm going to have to move all those logs into the firewood shed tomorrow makes the throb even more incessant—like my body is anticipating what's coming and objecting already.

I may do my best to hide it, but there is no way Pops doesn't suspect how bad it gets on days like this.

I'm not about to let Camille know, though.

She may have seen the scars, but that doesn't mean I'm about to allow everything I keep so tightly locked away out into the open.

"I'm good."

Pops gives me a look that tells me he doesn't quite believe it, but he lets it go, returning to whatever conversation he was having with Davey—apparently about fishing.

The little boy chatters excitedly, motioning with his hands, mimicking a casting motion that makes Pops grin proudly. He leans into Camille's son and whispers conspiratorially with him.

I catch Camille's smile watching them, and she brings over bowls, keeping her eye on the duo.

She sets one in front of me, pursing her lips. "They're up to something..."

I raise a brow at her. "Oh, yeah?"

Her head bobs, and she leans down, sending a chunk of her hair falling over her cheek. "They've been whispering like that ever since I got back."

"Knowing Pops as well as I do, he's probably up to no good."

Her mouth twists into a grimace. "That's my worry."

If I didn't know she was half joking, I might feel the need to convince her that Pops would never do anything to put Davey in danger—a promise I can make now that he's back to his old self. But Camille understands who Pops is, and she trusts him as much as I do.

So, I don't have to.

Still, I can't stop myself from reaching out and sliding my hand across her lower back. "They'll be fine." Her eyes cut from them over to me, a spark of something in them that I can't quite place. "Dinner smells amazing, by the way."

She shakes her head slightly and smiles. "Oh, thank you."

"What did you make?"

I had every intention of coming in, cleaning up, and helping her with dinner, as has become part of our nightly ritual. The two of us moving around the kitchen easily, like we belong here together. But tonight, I couldn't bring myself to face her right away after what she saw.

Now, with her standing beside me, looking so beautiful with her hair twisted up at the back of her head and that single strand that never seems to want to stay put hanging across her cheek, I realize it's probably a good thing we weren't in this kitchen together.

My inability to keep from touching her, even as simply as I do now with my hand resting gently on her back, is leading me down a road that will only end with me even more broken than I am now.

Camille clears her throat. "Um...ratatouille."

"Ratatouille?"

She nods with a tilted smile. "My grandmother on my mom's side was French and used to make it for my mom. Then, my mom made it for me growing up. It was kind of like what chicken soup is for other people, I guess. One of our comfort foods, and when I saw they had eggplant at the store today while I was in town, I had the strongest craving for it."

I recline slightly in my chair to look up at her easier, my hand still pressed lightly against her in a way I know it shouldn't be. "You don't talk about your family much."

Her back stiffens under my palm, and she slides away from me, heading to the counter where a loaf of bread sits, waiting to be cut.

Pops turns an ear, clearly listening to the conversation even while he tries to still pay attention to Davey, who is now talking about Rocky, the young calf who has become his "best friend."

In all the time we've known each other, I don't think I've ever heard Camille mention her family other than to say they were all gone. Given her reaction to my observation, it seems it's a sore subject I maybe shouldn't have brought up.

I start to think she's not going to respond, but then she gives me a sad look over her shoulder. "I never knew my dad. My mom died when I was twenty-two."

No matter how much time has passed, I can still sense the pain saying those words causes her. "I'm sorry."

She offers a shrug, as if it isn't a big deal. And that is *so* like Camille to try to downplay her own feelings to make everyone else more comfortable. "She didn't take very good care of herself. It was one of the things that always drove me to want to be a nurse, actually. She had high blood pressure, diabetes, and a handful of other issues, but no matter what I did, I just couldn't get her to understand how important it was to follow doctor's orders and stay vigilant."

I cross my arms over my chest and glare at Pops. "I understand the feeling."

He turns his head slowly to meet my gaze and offers me an annoyed huff. "I'm as healthy as a horse."

Camille snorts a laugh and steps between us, sliding the bread onto the table. "While I can attest to the fact that you have decent blood pressure and strong general vitals, without actually *seeing* Doc, there are very few things I can actually test you for or monitor, old man."

Pops leans back in his chair, puffing out his chest. "I'm fine. Whatever you two are shooting me up with seems to be working."

She pats him on the shoulder. "B12. When you say, 'what we're shooting you up with,' it makes it sound like we're giving you heroin."

He snorts incredulously. "How do I know you're not?"

I share a look with Camille before staring him down. "You'd be feeling a *lot* better and then a *lot* worse."

Pops chuckles low. "True."

Davey's gaze bounces between all of us, his forehead wrinkling. "What's hair-oh-in?"

Shit.

I ruffle his mop of dark hair. "Nothing you need to

worry about, buddy." I drum my fingers on the table as Camille gathers the last few things from the fridge and heads over to us. "You really should see Doc, though, Pops. It's been a few years since he's been up to examine you—"

"That's because, as I just stated, I'm healthy as a horse."

"Well, I'd like to keep you that way rather than have to send you off to the glue factory."

Camille sits to my right, directly across from him, fighting a smile at my comment.

Pops inclines his head toward her. "That's what I have *her* for now."

"I'm not a doctor, Pops. You know that." She grabs a ladle and points it at him. "And I don't have any of the equipment the clinic does to actually, you know, run tests..."

"Test, schmests." He reaches out and pinches Davey's cheek playfully. "I'm going to live forever. Aren't I, kid?"

Davey nods, the sweet innocence of a child who has no concept that what was just said is far from the truth. He reaches out a tiny hand and snags a piece of bread, shoving it into his mouth and chewing on it while my focus shifts to Camille.

He may not understand the statement, but I catch the pained expression on her face.

Davey has already lost his father, and before too long, he's going to lose Pops, the man he seems to have bonded with so tightly over the last several months.

Hopefully, that's not for many years down the line, but death is as inevitable as the sun rising and setting.

I'm certainly not ready to think about it coming for him any more than I was when I thought he was declining due to something a lot more serious than a vitamin deficiency.

And Camille isn't, either.

She quickly pulls the lid off the pot. "Let's dig in."

My stomach growls at the scents coming from the cast-iron crock. "I'm starved..."

Camille dishes it out, starting with Davey and Pops, then placing a heaping pile of the stew into my bowl. "I imagine you are. You were working hard today." It's said as a casual observation, but I catch the hint of concern in her tone. "Does that ever bother you?"

I dig in and take a bite, releasing a little groan at the delicious flavors that melt in my mouth. "God, this is good."

Camille gives me a tight smile. "Thank you, but you didn't answer my question."

Intentionally.

But I should have known she wasn't going to let this go so easily.

I feign ignorance and inhale another bite before raising a brow. "What was it again?"

She narrows her eyes on me. "You know exactly what I asked."

Pops takes a bite and waves his fork at her. "Don't bother, sweetheart. The day you get Dalton to admit any sort of weakness is the day Hell freezes over."

"Pops—" I issue him a warning, then glance over at Camille to gauge her reaction to his *completely* uncalled-for comment.

Her blue gaze stays locked on me, as if she can see the answer to her own question if she looks hard enough. "I believe that."

The accusation in her tone makes my back stiffen.

I've been nothing but open and honest with her since the day we met, yet it doesn't seem to be enough for her. She wants me to hand over that part of me I've never shared with anyone when she is the worst offender at keeping things locked away and refusing to accept her own weaknesses.

"I could say the same for you..."

She recoils slightly, squeezing her eyes closed.

Icy regret hits me instantly.

We're both proud people, probably far too much, and though my weakness might be physical, hers is far deeper, far more painful, and I've just rubbed salt into the wound.

Chapter Eight

DALTON

Camille's soft voice floats over me, rising and falling as she does different characters in the story she's reading to Davey, like she's performing a one-woman play.

I lean against the wall just outside his open bedroom door, listening to every word. Letting the love laden in every syllable sink deep into my skin and warm me when I've felt nothing but cold since the moment I saw that look on her face at the table.

God knows I sure as hell shouldn't be here.

After the tension I created settled over the table and all of us during what should have been a happy meal, I should have made Pops leave the moment we could duck out without another awkward moment with Camille.

But almost as if he could tell that we needed to talk, Pops just settled into the chair in front of the fireplace with a book after dinner, leaving me to play with blocks on the floor with Davey while Camille cleaned the kitchen—

insisting I *not* help her in a way that made it very clear she wanted me nowhere near her.

Can't say I blame her for that.

So, I definitely shouldn't be eavesdropping on this sweet, loving moment she's sharing with her son, and I shouldn't be waiting to ambush her the moment she walks out.

Shouldn't...

That doesn't make me leave, though. Not when the thought of her being so hurt by my words won't let me get any sleep tonight, anyway. Knowing I caused her that kind of pain is worse than the one still attacking my back and legs despite trying to rest my weight on the wall.

"Good night, Bub." Her soft steps move toward the door, the old floors creaking the closer she comes to me, and she eases the wooden panel closed and turns, jerking backward when she sees me. "What are you doing out here?"

"Waiting for you."

She scowls and moves to walk past me in the narrow hallway, but I push off the wall and block her escape.

"Please, Camille..."

Her gaze plastered squarely at my chest in front of her, she tightens her hands into fists at her sides. "You don't have to say anything."

"I do."

Those Caribbean-blue eyes I have found myself lost in far too many times to count dart up to meet mine. The anger and pain in them make me shift away from her slightly, but I refuse to back down before I've said my piece. "Maybe I don't want to hear it, Dalton."

"That's completely fair."

And if I had any self-preservation instinct, I might walk away.

But I can't, knowing I put that look on her face with one insensitive comment.

"I am sorry I said that..."

Camille presses her lips together tightly, crossing her arms over her chest, above her growing belly, like she needs to protect herself from me. As if I could *ever* hurt her.

She doesn't say anything, but she doesn't try to move past me again, either.

She just waits.

Apparently, for the explanation I came here to give, but that somehow seems so hard to say in the moment.

"I was deflecting."

Her brows rise. "You think?"

I release a sigh and shake my head, running a hand through my hair that just flops right back over my forehead. "What Pops said is true. I don't like admitting any sort of weakness. I get that from him—clearly. And I don't like anyone pointing it out. That's even worse."

Closing the distance between us, I dip my head to ensure our voices don't carry into Davey's room or out into the living room where Pops sits near the fire. And this close, that orange blossom scent that always seems to cling to her is so strong I can almost taste it on my tongue. "But what I said is true, too, Camille. Whether you want to admit it or not. You are a strong, stubborn, proud woman..."

Her mouth gapes open, and I reach out and tip her jaw up to close it, holding her there, forcing her to meet my gaze and really hear what I'm about to say.

Because it's stupid and dangerous.

But I'm going to say it anyway.

"But those are all the things I find so fucking fascinating about you. All the reasons I'm so impressed by you and in awe of everything you do every day. All of *that* is why I still think about you every moment I'm not with you."

Her eyes start to glaze over with tears, and I'm not even *close* to done.

"You kept this place going without any help for months—"

"I failed."

Her bottom lip quivers, and I brush my thumb across it.

"You didn't fail. You just didn't have the resources to do it, no matter how hard you worked, no matter how hard you tried. You were brave and strong and also stupid. And you *know* it. I can't apologize enough for the fact that Pops and I weren't here to help you from the beginning, but you should have *asked* for it, from us, from someone else in town. That's *not* failing."

She clears her throat, stepping back out of my hold. "That's easy for you to say. You don't fail at anything."

I chuckle low, stepping even closer to her until only the baby growing inside her separates us. "That's where you're wrong. I have failed miserably over the last few months since I met you."

And being this close to her in this hallway, touching her like that, makes it all the more evident to me how badly.

"How did you fail?"

"I failed to be a good friend to you. I failed to keep my distance from you and Davey. I failed to close myself off to caring the way I always have, the way Pops taught me to."

Camille stares up at me with her soft eyes searching mine. "What do you mean?"

Of course, I'm not making any sense.

I never intended to tell her any of this when I came up here.

I shouldn't.

But now that the floodgates have opened, I feel like I can't close them.

"It's always just been the two of us up here since my parents died, and he wanted to keep it that way. I never had friends. I never had a life beyond the homestead, save for occasional visits with people from town who needed to see him. He was my teacher, my parent, my friend, my constant companion. And God, I love the old man. He gave me everything. But he also taught me that anything beyond the mountain is bad, that it's only going to bring pain."

And he was right.

I learned that lesson at four years old and am still paying the price for it.

"He told me to shut it all out. That even when I had to go into town for something, that I shouldn't stop and linger, that I shouldn't talk to anyone beyond what was *necessary*, that I shouldn't make connections, that I shouldn't..."

Her brows rise, so dark over her light eyes. "Live?"

The question makes my back throb and my shoulders tense. "I guess you could see it that way."

She releases a sigh. "Look, I didn't grow up here. I didn't spend my whole life on this mountain. But what I can tell you is that all those things Pops warned you about are true. When you open yourself up, you do give someone else the opportunity to hurt you—intentionally or not. But it also gives you the opportunity to *feel* something you never will experience any other way. Caring isn't *failing*."

How I wish that were true...

"It is, Camille. Because I care about you and Davey and this baby who isn't even born yet, more than I should, more than I have a *right* to."

My eyes drift down to her stomach, and she reaches out

and grabs my hand, placing it there with her own pressed over it.

The baby kicks against my palm, and I jerk my head up, meeting her gaze again.

"The baby reacts when you talk." A tiny smile forms on her lips. "She knows you..."

Fucking hell.

I curl my palm tighter against her, fighting the need to pull her fully against me and crush my mouth to hers. "I'm worried about you and the baby and what's coming."

"Winter? The delivery? Or the fact that people are trying to take the mountain from you?"

Shit.

She definitely overheard our conversation that night.

"How much did you hear?"

Her lips twist. "Enough. And I'm sorry for eavesdropping—"

"No, you aren't."

A little sigh slips from her. "Okay, I'm not. But if that important conversation you need to have with Pops had been about me, I didn't want you to be taking on something that you couldn't or that you shouldn't..."

"Isn't that for me to decide, not you?"

She shakes her head. "Not when you just admitted that you'll never concede weakness or admit defeat. Can you really handle getting both homesteads prepped? Can you really ensure you and Pops are ready when you're spending so much time up here with us?"

I slide my free hand to her cheek, brushing the stray strand of hair away. "I'm exactly where I want to be, Camille."

The words are true.

Truer than even I knew they were the second they left my lips.

In only a few short months, I've grown attached to that little boy and something far worse to this woman in front of me who's been through so much, who's taken on too much, who doesn't need the added complication of my unwanted affection for her.

But she doesn't back away as I lean in closer.

Her shoulders press against the wall in the tight space, and I cage her in with my hands on either side of her head.

"Dalton, what are you doing?"

Something so damn stupid.

"I told you, apologizing."

Her hands slide up over my chest, and the warmth of her palms pressed over my heart permeates deep into my skin. "This doesn't seem like apologizing. In fact, you just reiterated exactly what you said at the dinner table about me."

I looked down at her, so small, yet so strong, so damn resilient. "You're right, I did. But there's something else I need to say, and I can't have you running away while I try to do it."

———

CAMILLE

My entire body trembles and heats under Dalton's intense green gaze. He searches my face for something—maybe the objection I *should* be making—then steps in even closer, until the heat of his body radiates into mine. His rock-hard stomach brushes against my belly in a way that sends a little flutter through my stomach, or maybe it's the baby moving again.

I don't even know anymore.

Things have taken such a quick turn that it feels like the whole world is spinning wildly around me while I try to find some stable footing.

Only a few minutes ago, I was so angry at him. Pissed that he pointed out something I've always known about myself and that Dave loved to point out during our seven years together.

That sometimes, I'm too damn stubborn.

That more often than not, when I should be accepting help, I push it away, trying to do things on my own.

Like this morning when Dalton offered to take me to my appointment.

A huge part of me wanted him there.

Going through this pregnancy and all it entails alone after having Dave beside me every step of the way with Davey has been one of the hardest parts of losing him.

But I couldn't bring myself to allow Dalton to do it.

Not when I know how much he needs to get done around both homesteads and that I'm the cause of all this extra burden on his time and energy.

He's become my friend, my only true one in years.

Maybe it was through default because we're the only people up here, or maybe it was through fate that he came to my rescue, but I never, in a million years, thought it would go beyond that.

Yet, the way he's looking at me now is anything but "friendly."

The intensity and heat in his gaze send a shudder of awareness through me.

"What do you need to say, Dalton?"

He brushes his calloused fingertips across my cheek, and I have to fight the urge to lean into the reverent, intimate touch. "That I'm not going anywhere. That no matter what happens on this mountain, I will take care of you and your children."

"That isn't your responsibility. It's mine."

"There's that stubborn streak." He grins, and the way the gold in his eyes seems to twinkle makes my stomach do a stupid flip-flop thing I haven't felt since I was a damn teenager. "I know it's none of my business, but I need you to tell me"—he glances down between us—"what is your plan once this baby comes?"

God, I wish I had one.

Since the moment Dave died, I've been trying to figure that out, just like I was trying to determine how I could stay on the mountain when things were crumbling before my eyes.

Dalton and Pops have made *that* possible, but it doesn't solve the long-term problem. I will still be alone on the homestead with an almost-five-year-old and a newborn, with winter coming, one that will be long, harsh, and that will take every ounce of my effort just to keep my head above water even with Dalton and Pops helping.

But one thing has never wavered.

My determination to find a way.

Squaring my shoulders, pressing them back against the wall so I'm at my full height, I stare Dalton down. "I'm going to do whatever it takes."

"Me, too..."

His gaze dips to my lips, and my entire body freezes as he stares at them.

Even I don't know what I want him to do.

Walk away...

Kiss me...

Both seem incredibly wrong for completely different reasons.

It is the goddamn pregnancy hormones.

The second and third trimesters were like this for me with Davey, too. Only then, I had an outlet for the tension and pulsating need that seem to have my body in a stranglehold right now.

I close my eyes and suck in a long, slow, steady breath, trying to douse the inferno threatening to ignite in me under his intense gaze.

This isn't really about Dalton.

He's your friend.

That's it.

It's all he'll ever be—a friend and a neighbor who is helping you through a horrible situation.

I try to convince myself of that before I dare open my eyes again.

But as I do, he's right there watching me, searching for something I'm not sure I can give him.

Christ.

I'm thirteen years older than the man, and he's barely lived a life stuck up here on the mountain with Pops.

"I wish you wouldn't look at me like that."

He pulls back slightly. "Why not?"

"Because, like you said, you've never gotten to experience anything beyond James Mountain. Have you ever even had a girlfriend?"

The corner of his lips twitches like he finds the question amusing when it wasn't meant to be. "Why does that matter?"

"It matters a lot."

"No, it doesn't." He casually drags his thumb across my

lower lip, sending a fluttering sensation between my legs. "I told you that first day that I don't expect anything from you in return for my help, and I mean it. But I want you to know that if you ever need more from me, all you have to do is tell me so I can give it to you."

Oh, God.

His words wash over me, reigniting that flame I've been trying to extinguish the entire time he's had me cornered in this hallway.

I grit my teeth, fighting my body's natural reaction to having such a handsome man press his hard body against mine when it's been so long since I've been touched in that way, when the hormones raging through my body want so badly to do something utterly stupid.

"I don't need anything else from you, Dalton."

It's a lie.

One I hope he buys.

His hand pauses with the palm resting against my cheek. "Are you sure about that?"

I nod.

"Okay." He leans in slightly and brushes his lips to my forehead in the most gentle, chaste, sincere gesture I've ever experienced in my life. He lets them linger there for a minute, and I close my eyes, breathing in the crisp scent of the soap he used to shower with right before dinner and that smell of freshly cut wood and the forest around us that still clings to him. Then he slowly pulls back. "You let me know if you change your mind."

I swallow thickly through my desert-dry throat as he pushes back and pulls his hands away from the wall and me.

My heart beats wildly against my ribcage as I watch him walk away, taking the answer I still haven't received with him. "Dalton..."

He stops and turns back toward me, his brow furrowing.

"How did you get those scars on your back?"

His jaw hardens, and his shoulders tense.

"That's what I need from you—that information. I need you to answer the question."

Because I won't be able to continue accepting his help when he could be hurting himself.

And I fear that's exactly what's been happening.

He shakes his head. "That isn't anything I want to talk about."

I tilt my head as I examine him and the tension radiating through his body. "Should I ask Pops?"

"It isn't for Pops to tell you that, and he'll say the same thing."

I take a step toward him, then another, until we're standing near the far end of the hallway, with Pops so close behind him in the living room that I can hear the old man turn the page of his book. "Don't you think I need to know? It looks painful, and I've seen you—"

He grits his teeth. "Don't."

"Don't what? Point out your weaknesses the way you just did mine?"

His gaze softens, the anger there only a moment ago vanishing. "If you thought I was pointing out all those things as weaknesses, I think you misunderstood everything I said."

Shit.

Why does he have to go and say something sweet like that?

"Let it go, Camille. It's nothing you need to worry about."

He turns and walks away from me, but his absolute

insistence tells me it's something I *definitely* need to worry about.

Rather than following him, I sag back against the wall and try to regain some control over my body and my head.

My mind races through the potential reasons he would have those kinds of scars—none of them good—and it drifts back to that conversation I overheard months ago but that still stays so fresh in my head.

Dalton dodged my questions about both tonight.

He and Pops are keeping things from me.

Either because they're protecting themselves or they think they're protecting me. But I don't like being in the dark when their secrets could affect my future and that of my children.

I rest my hands over my stomach, and a tiny foot presses against my palm.

There isn't much time before this little girl will make her appearance in the world, and I need to know what kind of world it will be.

Will I have this place?

And if I do, what will it cost Dalton to ensure it?

Chapter Nine

ONE MONTH LATER

CAMILLE

The closer we get to the James property, the harder my heart races, and the more I wish it didn't take so long to make this drive. Blood rushes in my ears, and my vision narrows on the winding, gravel mountain road that will take me there—but not fast enough.

Each minute that passes, the anxiety tightening the vise around my sternum seems to only increase until I have to force myself to take deep breaths before I hyperventilate.

It's almost impossible to keep myself calm with Pops' words ringing through my head ominously.

"You should come down here."

When Dalton didn't show up this afternoon, I wasn't worried—at first.

After all, things have been...tense ever since that night a month ago.

He isn't mad.

Dalton isn't the type who would let his personal feelings get in the way of fulfilling the bargain he made with me, but the atmosphere has definitely shifted the same way the weather has started to.

His heated gaze still lingers when he thinks I'm not watching him, when he thinks I won't notice, but he's giving me space. Spending less time in the cabin when we are there and more out on the land, doing one of the dozens of little repairs and chores that need to happen before winter fully descends.

This afternoon was supposed to be further insulating the barn so the animals will be safe from the sub-zero wind chills that often blow across the mountain.

But he never showed.

I might have let it go as merely him needing a break—from the work or tension between us that feels strung tight enough to snap at this point—if not for Davey mentioning that Dalton *promised* to help him build and paint a sign for Rocky's stall.

Dalton *never* breaks a promise to Davey.

No matter what might be happening—or not happening—between us, if there were something keeping him from coming or making him run late, he or Pops would have radioed to let me know rather than disappoint Davey.

Which is why I finally picked up that radio to call—only to have Pops give me that panic-inducing suggestion to drive across the mountain to them.

Davey remains blissfully unaware that something might be wrong, practically bouncing in his seat, anxious to see Dalton and Pops, only I don't know what we're walking into since the old man didn't want to say anything over the radio.

That uncertainty makes my grip on the steering wheel tighten as I finally turn the truck onto the narrow gravel track that leads back to their cabin.

Nothing looks amiss on the property, from what I can

see. The sun shines through the partial cloud cover, shimmering off the leaves already starting to change color on the trees surrounding the large clearing.

The cabin front door opens as I throw the truck into park, and Pops steps out, his jaw set hard.

None of the usual whimsy fills his eyes when he sees us —only worry.

Shit, something is wrong.

I climb out, a process that has become incredibly, annoyingly difficult the further I progress in this pregnancy, and Pops lumbers down the porch steps and approaches the truck.

Davey manages to free himself from his car seat and get out without my help, and he rushes toward the old man and practically launches himself at him. Pops catches him the best he can and scoops him up, something he couldn't have done when I first met him with as unsteady as he was.

He smiles at Davey, but I catch the wariness in his gaze. "Where's Dalton?"

I'm afraid to ask him what's wrong in front of Davey in case it's something he shouldn't hear. Given how vague Pops was when he told me to come, I don't have a good feeling about any of this.

Is this about that lawyer?

Pops' continued silence on the matter has grown more and more frustrating, and with the lines of communication not exactly wide open between Dalton and me at the moment, it means *anything* could have happened without me knowing a damn thing about it.

With Davey still on his hip, Pops glances back at the cabin. "I think I should take this little guy fishing at the lake this afternoon."

I narrow my eyes on him.

Is he trying to get him out of here?

A foreboding sense of dread settles over me—it's bad enough for him to call me down here and not want Davey to witness it.

Pops releases Davey and points across the yard. "Run over to the barn and find the fishing rods and tackle box in the tack room."

Davey darts away, racing across the property as if it's our own, and honestly, we've spent enough time here now that he knows it as well as he does our place.

As soon as he's out of earshot, I turn back to Pops. "You want to tell me what's wrong?"

"It isn't my place to tell you, darling, but it's about time *he* does." He inclines his head toward the front door. "He needs your help."

Instantly, a vision of the scars crisscrossing his back flashes in front of me, and I suck in a sharp breath, remembering his anger that ignited when I dared to bring it up that night. When he said things that left me unsteady in ways I still haven't wrapped my head around weeks later. "I'll see what I can do."

Pops grabs my arm as I move toward the house, holding me back. "He doesn't want you to see him like this. Doesn't even want me to. If he's harsh with you, don't take it personally."

I narrow my eyes on him, giving him a tight smile. "I didn't when *you* were."

He scoffs. "I was *not*—"

"Whatever you have to tell yourself, old man. Just be careful at the lake."

His hand tightens lightly around my arm in an affectionate squeeze. "I always am."

I slip out of his hold and make my way up the two steps

to their small porch, pushing open the door he left cracked when he came out.

An eerie silence settles over me, so unusual for the home that's typically full of life and laughter when we're here.

Not today.

Unease wraps around my spine and squeezes tightly as I kick off the boots I didn't even bother to tie in my rush out of my place and instinctively move up the steps toward the bedrooms.

Something tells me that's where he'll be.

My bare feet hardly make any noise as I move down the hall. Pops' bedroom stands open and empty, as do Dalton's and the spare room that was his as a child.

I swallow thickly as I approach the half-open door to the bathroom.

A pained grunt carries from inside, freezing me midstep, listening for anything else that might give me some idea what's happening on the other side of the wooden slab.

More silence lingers.

I nudge it open with my hand and find Dalton standing with his thighs pressed against the counter, white-knuckle gripping the surface. His legs shake so badly that it looks like they may give out under him.

"Dalton?"

He tenses and peers over his shoulder. "What the hell are you doing here?"

The sharp edge to his voice has nothing to do with me and everything to do with the obvious pain he's in. If I hadn't dealt with hundreds of patients in the same position, I might let it bother me, but coupled with Pops' earlier warning about the condition I would find him in, I brush it off easily.

147

"Pops asked me to come down."

"Of course, he did." He snorts and shakes his head, squeezing his eyes closed. "I'm fine."

"You don't look *fine*."

"If I needed a fucking doctor, I'd go see him."

I shake off the anger in his words as I approach, examining him for any signs of injury. "Do I need to go back out and ask Pops what happened, or are you going to tell me?"

He gives me an annoyed look, but the edges of his eyes and lips tighten, the pain winning out over his reluctance to come clean with me. "I was working in the barn, moving hay and feed, and my back just...gave out."

Shit.

"Did you fall?"

Dalton presses his lips together and shakes his head. "No. I grabbed a beam to stop myself from face-planting and managed to keep myself upright long enough to get over to the cabin. Pops helped me up the steps."

The waver in his voice tells me exactly how much agony he's in, even if he's doing his damnedest to try to conceal it. "Does this happen a lot?"

He squeezes his eyes closed again, dropping his head low, like he can't even bear to hold it up anymore. "More lately..."

Since he started helping me.

Dalton doesn't need to finish the sentence for me to know that's what he means. He's been overworking himself to make sure that my mistakes are fixed. That old friend guilt grinds down on my heart as much as my worry for the man in front of me does.

I reach across him to open the medicine cabinet above the sink. "Did Doc prescribe you anything? Muscle relaxers, pain meds?"

He reaches out and grasps my wrist, tightening his fingers around it gently. In control even when he's in this state. "I don't take drugs."

The way he says it, I can hear the disdain in his voice.

"They're not *drugs*, Dalton. It's *medication* for a *medical* problem you clearly have."

He releases my arm and shakes his head, trying to hide a wince. "I haven't taken that stuff in a very long time, and I don't intend to, no matter how much Pops or Doc may try to push it on me."

Which means that this battle's been going on for a long time, far longer than he's let me know.

It explains Pops' reaction and warning downstairs, too.

And if Dalton won't take anything to help ease his pain, then I'm going to have to try a different tactic.

I glance over at the large cast-iron tub in the corner, then push away from him and move over to it, cranking on the water as hot as it'll go.

He follows my movements across the bathroom. "What are you doing?"

"Filling the bath for you..."

"Do I look like I take a lot of fucking baths?"

The tension in his voice and the way his legs continue to shake worry me enough that I walk over and wrap my arm around his waist to steady him in case his grip on the counter fails.

"No, and that's part of the problem. If you're not going to take any sort of medication to relieve what's happening to you, then we need to calm those muscles down another way. A long, hot soak in that bathtub is going to help."

He looks ready to argue with me.

I hold up my free hand, silencing him before he can even open his mouth. "Don't even think about it. I might not be a doctor, but I worked in the emergency room for a long time, Dalton. Do you want to feel better or not?"

Our argument, or whatever the hell that was last month that created so much heated tension between us, rushes back, and I can see his eyes darken as he remembers it, too.

He might try to shut me out again, just like he did that night.

But his shoulders slump, as if he's conceding defeat, and he reluctantly nods.

"Good. Let's get you in."

He mutters something under his breath I don't quite catch, then reaches for the hem of his shirt, and I release my hold on him long enough to let him tug it up and off, exposing his muscled chest, abs, and back. "I don't know if I can…"

His gaze drifts down to his boots and jeans like they're Mount Everest and he has absolutely no hope of climbing it.

"I got it."

This certainly isn't the way I imagined stripping Dalton out of his clothes, and I'd be lying if I said I *haven't* done just that. Especially after the way he touched me in that hallway and the words he said that still linger the same way the rough brush of his fingertips does.

I nudge him until he turns and rests his ass against the counter, then I unzip his jeans and slide them down to the top of his boots. His hands slip under my arms, and I look up at him as he helps me lower myself to my knees to untie his boots because there isn't any way I can bend that low.

Even in so much physical and mental distress, Dalton is still looking out for me, ensuring I'm okay when I should be the one taking care of him.

He lifts one foot, then the other, and I tug off the muddy

boots and his socks, tossing them across the bathroom toward the open door.

Leaving him in nothing but his boxers—directly in front of my face.

Hell...

Darting my gaze to the tub, I clear my throat and climb to my feet with his assistance again.

He can get into the tub in *those*, or he can take them off himself.

But I am *not* going there.

I can't.

The heat flooding my body tells me it wouldn't be a good idea for me to even attempt it.

———

DALTON

The almost-scalding water surrounding me up to mid-chest feels so damn good. I release a little strangled groan, even though I try to bite it back. Only a few minutes in here, and already, the trembling of my legs and tightness and spasms in my back have started to melt away slowly.

Camille leans against the counter, hand resting on her protruding belly, and even though my eyes are closed, I can feel hers on me like they have been since the second she walked into this bathroom.

Analyzing every little move or sound I make.

Raking over me as I lie in the water in nothing but my boxers.

Fucking hell, Pops.

He didn't need to call her down here.

I would've been fine on my own, eventually.

Like I always am.

This might be the worst it's ever been, but it didn't require getting Camille all riled up or making her drive over here with Davey when she surely has other things to be doing at her place today.

"Feeling better?"

Dammit.

Apparently, she didn't miss that little groan I just released—not that she would have. Camille doesn't miss *anything*. And since that night I told her exactly how I felt about her, every moment we've been in the same room has been sheer torture, wondering what's going on in her head.

I crack one eye open and peek at her, afraid to see that pitying look there from the sole person I *never* want to see me so broken and helpless. "A little."

She fights a smirk but fails miserably.

"You don't have to look so smug."

Her eyes widen slightly in feigned ignorance before she fully grins at me. "I'm not trying to be smug. I'm genuinely happy it's helping and you're feeling better."

"Not *that* much better."

She chuckles softly at my clarification, then moves closer to the tub, making me tense all over again.

After crossing that line and baring my soul, I knew things would be different, but I've managed to avoid situations like *this* for the past month.

The two of us *truly* alone...

With either Pops or Davey always around, it's been easy to keep things light, to appear unaffected by her presence, when all I've wanted was to pin her to a wall again and kiss her senseless this time.

But I would never do that.

Not unless she *asks*.

And that's nothing more than wishful thinking from a man who is too sore and exhausted to really process what she must be thinking as she looks down at me now.

I lift my hand out of the water and run it across my face. "I'm sorry about when you got here. I shouldn't have snapped at you like that."

"No." She cautiously kneels next to the tub and sits back on her feet, resting one hand across her stomach and rubbing it idly. "You shouldn't have." She sets her left hand on the edge of the tub and drums her fingers on the porcelain. "But I understand why you did."

"Do you?"

She bobs her head slowly, the dark strands pulled back in a messy bun fighting the hold with the movement. "The way you live out here, the way your grandfather is, I imagine showing any amount of pain gets a certain reaction."

I snort and drop my head back to stare at the ceiling beams again. "You have no idea. He's very overprotective."

"Shouldn't he be?"

I glance at her and her raised brow.

She holds my gaze, waiting for me to say something. "Tell me what happened, Dalton."

It isn't a request.

Not this time, like it has been the others she asked about the scars.

Camille expects me to do it, and honestly, I don't know why I bit her head off when she asked about it that night she first saw them.

Maybe because I've never talked to anyone about it.

There was never anyone to ask before, so talking about it felt wrong.

But now that she's seen the scars and seen me like this,

there really isn't any hiding it from her anymore. Plus, I don't know that I *want* to keep it locked up where it has been for so long.

"The car accident that killed my parents..."

Camille tenses, her eyes softening with that same look I saw there the first time she spotted the scars.

"The car was partially crushed, and I was pinned. Six broken vertebrae. I lost feeling in my legs off and on for a while."

Her fingers tighten around the edge of the tub, and the hand rubbing her stomach stills. "Jesus..."

"I was in the hospital for months, had three surgeries, so on top of losing my mom and dad, I was dealing with that... at Davey's age."

She's quiet for a moment, studying me with compassion in her blue gaze I've never seen from anyone else who wasn't paid to care about me, like the doctors and nurses who put me back together—except Pops. "I am so sorry, Dalton."

I blow out a long breath. "It was a long time ago. Almost twenty years now."

"What about since then? Any revision surgeries or complications?"

I know her question comes from her medical training and her concern for me, but I bristle at it. She must sense it because she presses her lips together and glances at the water rather than at me.

"Two other surgeries over the years. I was so young and still growing. They had to go in and adjust some things. The last was six years ago."

Her fingers trail over the cast iron. "An injury like that, no matter how well the surgeons piece you back together, living like this, what you do up here, it's probably the worst possible thing for your body."

I snort a mirthless laugh. "You think I don't know that? That Pops doesn't?"

It's been a constant source of tension and disagreement between us for years.

Pops worried I'm pushing too hard.

Me worried I'm not pushing hard *enough* to get everything done as he ages and isn't able to help with as much as he used to around the property.

I may be broken, but I'm still only twenty-three, and he's seventy-five.

It can't rest on his shoulders to keep this place running, even if it hurts to have it on mine.

"Then why did you stay? Knowing the toll it would take? You're only twenty-three, Dalton. What's going to happen when you're forty or sixty or Pops' age?"

I squeeze my eyes closed as an agony that has nothing to do with my back threatens to swallow me whole.

I'm not ready to think about that yet...

"This is the only life I ever knew, the only life my mom ever knew, and my dad grew up in James Creek, so it wasn't much different for him, either."

"I always meant to ask, why is your last name James? Were your mother and father married?"

A grin pulls at my lips, and I let my eyes drift open. "When my dad wanted to marry my mom, he asked Pops. And Pops told him the *only* way that was happening was if she kept her maiden name. He said, 'A James has always lived on this mountain, and it will continue that way.' So, she stayed a James and ensured I was one to keep Pops happy."

Camille's light laughter splits some of the tension in the

air brought on by such a heavy conversation. "That sounds like Pops..."

I shrug, the water shifting around me. "He's always lived here. There was never any question in my mind that I'd come back after my surgeries. He won't ever live off the mountain."

"Why does he hate that world so much?"

"He didn't always." I watch Camille casually rubbing her belly, wondering if the baby is kicking and reacting to my voice the same way she did that night. "But *that* world is what took his daughter from him. What did *this* to me. The only reason we weren't on the mountain that day was because I begged my parents to take me to the circus."

The familiar guilt ices my veins even though the water remains warm.

"So, what? He blames you for asking to go see something every child wants to?"

I release another sardonic laugh. "According to Pops, a circus is a travesty that just tortures animals who should live in the wild like this mountain provides. He lectured them on agreeing to take me, but we went anyway..."

She pulls her bottom lip between her teeth, chewing at it idly.

"Once I came home from the hospital, there was no way he was letting me off this mountain again except to go to James Creek, and even *that* bothers him. He knew we would figure out a way to make it work, regardless of what my physical limitations might be as I grew older. And we have...mostly."

Camille releases her lip, now pink and plump and so fucking tempting, and she resumes rubbing her stomach, looking down at it rather than at me. "How often does this happen?"

She asked me the question before, and I tried to be vague and brush it off because I know what will come of it if I tell her the truth. This beautiful, resilient woman will blame herself for something that has absolutely nothing to do with her or what I'm doing for her and Davey.

But I've given up trying to conceal things from Camille.

It's too damn hard when all I want is to be a fucking open book for her, to allow her to see how genuine I am in what I told her that night.

"A lot. More than it used to. But I was already having trouble before I started helping you, so please don't get it in your head that this is your fault somehow."

She presses her lips together. "I wasn't going to."

I chuckle. "Bullshit. We may not have known each other for very long, Camille, but do you really think I don't know what goes on in that beautiful head of yours?" I raise a brow at her. "I do. And you said it yourself that the reason you were eavesdropping on Pops and me that day was because you wanted to make sure it wasn't about you, that you weren't causing any trouble for us."

"I am..." She sucks in a little sob, tears forming in her eyes. "I *am* causing trouble for you."

Against my better judgment, I reach out and rest my wet hand on top of hers on the edge of the tub. "No, you're not. Having you and Davey around has been wonderful for me and for Pops. I haven't seen him this energetic, excited, dare I say *happy*, in years."

"That's probably just the B12."

She forces a smile that isn't very convincing, and I squeeze her hand as she drops her gaze to her stomach.

"It's not, and that wouldn't explain why I've felt that way, too."

Shit.

I definitely shouldn't have said that. Not after what my confession the other night did to the easy, comfortable companionship we had created. But she doesn't pull away her hand, and her eyes finally lift to meet mine.

"Why won't you take the medicine? I understand the fear of becoming addicted to narcotics. Believe me, I saw enough addicts in my time in the ER to know what that looks like and how awful it is. But muscle relaxers and taking an occasional pain pill when it's really bad aren't going to hurt you. They're designed to help you avoid *this*."

"I can manage the pain, Camille." I squeeze her hand again. "I always do."

She gives me an incredulous look. "You shouldn't have to."

I don't disagree with her, but it's beside the point.

In a perfect world, the surgeries would not only have repaired the damage to my back but also done it in a way that left me completely pain free.

But that isn't reality.

This is.

And I am not about to shove those pills down my throat —again.

"I was young when it happened, when I spent all that time in the hospital. But I remember how what they gave me made me feel like I was constantly stuck in some sort of nightmare I couldn't get out of and couldn't control. I always felt out of touch with reality and not in a good way." I shake my head. "I don't ever want to feel that as an adult. Not when Pops depends on me. Not when the homestead does. Not when you do—and I don't say that to try to make you feel guilty. I say it because it's something I have to do, even if you fought me tooth and nail on it, which I feel like you might now."

"That's why you were hiding it from me." She glances up, a single tear sliding down her cheek. "Because you knew I would try to stop you from continuing to help us."

I nod. "That and I hate anybody seeing me like this."

She offers me a sympathetic look. "I can understand that."

"Can you?"

A little humorless laugh falls from her lips. "Why do you think I didn't want your help when you showed up?"

I laugh, the sound booming in the small room. "Oh, I know why you didn't want it. Stubborn woman."

Her mouth pulls into a half grin. "Dave always said I was stubborn. I guess it wasn't just with him."

"No, it wasn't."

She releases a long, drawn-out sigh, glancing out the window in the corner. "So, what now?"

It seems like such a simple question, but the answer I want to give her is far from it.

Because I don't know *what* she's asking.

About us?

I wish that were true, that this has somehow broken through all the reasons we shouldn't act on *whatever* this is and allow her to try to find some sort of happiness again.

But I won't presume to put her in that position by pushing it again.

"I rest the remainder of the day, and I get back at it tomorrow."

She scowls, shifting slightly, like remaining in that position for so long is taking a toll on her—which it probably is, considering her current condition. "You can't keep doing this to yourself, Dalton. It's only going to get worse."

It isn't anything I don't already know or that Pops hasn't brought up at least a dozen times since he finally realized the extent of what I was doing up at the Bower property. But there's nothing else *to* do.

"I don't have a choice, Camille."

Her jaw tenses at my soft words. "Maybe it's time for me just admit defeat and go."

My hand tightens around hers as a vise clamps down on my chest and squishes my heart, threatening to eviscerate it. "Don't ever do that."

"Do what?"

"Talk about leaving like that."

"Dalton..."

She doesn't say anything else, but the way my name floats from her perfect lips makes my cock twitch against my wet shorts that are concealing nothing under the clear water she can definitely see into.

I never knew the danger that exists on the mountain could come in the form of this woman.

But she has become my greatest weakness.

Chapter Ten

DALTON

By the time the water cools enough that Camille reaches over to add more from the hot tap for the third time, I grab her arm to stop her and shake my head. "I'm good."

Some of the pain and tension may linger, but it's light-years better than the constant spasms and agonizing sharp, stabbing torture I was experiencing before Camille arrived and *forced* me into this tub.

She offers me a concerned look, her dark brows furrowing. "You're sure?"

"Positive."

Her gaze drifts to my hand wrapped around her arm, and I let it linger there a little too long. The feel of her smooth, soft skin under my rough fingertips might be the most decadent thing I've ever experienced.

But it isn't right for me to be so selfish when it comes to this woman.

Shit.

I release her quickly, and she reaches down to pull the drain plug.

Water starts rushing away from around me, and I watch the woman I've sat here with for the past hour in a comfortable silence—yet somehow, still one filled with a thousand unsaid things.

Very *serious* things that aren't going to remain unsaid forever.

She saw the way my body reacted to her, the way *I* reacted when she mentioned leaving, but she doesn't know the half of it.

How the panic welled instantly at the thought of her and Davey not being here.

How I wanted to scream that she better not *ever* leave and had to rein myself in from doing just that.

I have no right to say it.

No right to *ask* it.

Camille Bower isn't *mine,* no matter how much I may want her to be.

She retreats to grab a towel for me, and I take the opportunity to push off the sides of the cast iron tub to get to my feet without her being able to see my grimace at the twinge of electric pain that radiates across my back and down my right thigh.

My legs shake, but it isn't the violent, barely holding-me-up type of quaking that it was an hour ago when I thought I might collapse before I ever even made it up here.

She twists and hands the towel to me, keeping her gaze on my face rather than on my nearly naked body and soaked boxer briefs that cling to *everything* they cover.

At least my cock is cooperating now.

Though I don't know how.

I've had enough dreams about this woman that I've

162

woken with it hard and in my hand to last a lifetime, and in the tub, she kept looking at me in that *way* that she always did in those fantasies.

This is reality.

And reality is always stark and cold.

Not warm and inviting, the way Camille's arms would be.

I dry off my torso and wait for her to turn around again before I slide the soaked underwear off, letting them remain in the tub. Because there's no way in *hell* I'm bending over to grab them.

It can wait 'til tomorrow...

Wrapping the towel around my waist, I hold my breath for a moment, trying to ready myself for the inevitable jolt that will come with climbing over the edge.

Just do it.

I grit my teeth and swing one leg over, then the other, to stand on the bathmat she kneeled on. Keeping watch over me for so long. Ensuring I would take her advice, even when I never wanted her to see me like this.

Her stubbornness helped me today—something I'm sure she won't ever acknowledge since she can't seem to see that it isn't a fault. Not by a longshot.

She finally turns to face me and leans against the counter, examining me with a keen, practiced eye that I'm sure sees everything I want to hide. "How are you feeling?"

I offer her a half smile that I hope does a good job of hiding my continued discomfort. "Better."

"Pain level?"

"Six."

Her eyes widen slightly. "Still?"

"But considering I was definitely at a ten *plus*, I'd have

to say your little home remedy worked." I move toward her cautiously. "This is *bearable*."

Each step might send a little spark of agony up through my spine, but it's not like I haven't lived in constant pain for twenty years, anyway.

This is more like my normal end-of-the-day level.

One I'm used to and can *manage*.

Her mouth twists, her lips pressed together in a way that screams she isn't happy about the current situation. "What do you normally do when you're like this?"

I lift one shoulder and let it fall as nonchalantly as I can. "Climb into bed. Getting horizontal and keeping the pressure off helps."

"Then that's what you should do."

I nod. "That's the plan."

She watches me carefully for signs that I might be downplaying how bad it is, but I've been honest with her since I finally gave up trying to hide it. "I have a suggestion."

My eyes drift over the sink. "I hope it's not related to the bottles of pills that are in that cabinet."

Camille shakes her head, shifting on her bare feet awkwardly. "No. Another pretty basic home remedy."

"Okay..."

Why is she being so weird about this?

"If you'll let me—"—she glances down at her hands, resting on her belly, and then back up at me—"if you'll let me massage you, I could get more tension out of the muscle."

Fuck.

My throat closes with sudden dryness, and I try to swallow through it, willing my cock to stay down at the thought of her hands on me. "I don't know if that's such a good idea..."

The corner of her lips twitches slightly. "I didn't think you spending all this time and energy helping me on the homestead was a good idea, either. You ignored me, and look where it got you."

Fuck is she quick and smart.

"Touché."

She pushes from the counter. "This is my opportunity to make up for it, for all the pain you must have been going through for the last several months while you were helping us."

"Camille..."

She's so close to me that I can smell that faint orange blossom scent that haunts my dreams.

Her shampoo?

Her lotion?

Or maybe it's just *her*.

I lean even closer, knowing full well I shouldn't, given the tension permeating the room and the fact that my cock was hard for her less than half an hour ago. "You don't owe me anything."

When she looks up, I can see the determination in her gaze and know I've lost. "I do, though—whether you want it or not. And I'm far from a massage therapist, but Dave used to have some issues in his back and shoulder, so I know how much I can help, if you'll let me."

Shit.

Denying her the opportunity to do something like this for me is just as selfish as allowing it.

She doesn't just *want* to help. She *needs* to.

I draw in a long, slow breath and release it, gathering the strength I know I'm going to need to handle what's about to happen. "Okay."

One thing I learned quickly about the woman standing

beside me is that she doesn't back down easily, and she also clings to her guilt like an old friend. Unfortunately, I'm more than familiar with that sentiment.

If helping me with *this* will help ease some of *that* for her, I can't say no.

I slowly walk to my room, keeping my right hand against the wall to steady myself rather than risk collapsing onto the floorboards. Things may be better, but I don't trust my legs not to give out on me again at any moment the way they did out in the barn earlier.

Camille stays at my side and slightly behind me, like she's waiting to catch me if I should lose my balance—or worse.

But she doesn't touch me.

She lets me do it on my own.

And Christ, do I appreciate that about her.

By the time I finally lie down on the bed, I release a relieved groan at the almost instant release of pressure.

Thank fucking God...

Camille steps in and pushes the door closed behind her as she eyes me spread out on top of the quilt. "Are you okay to lie on your stomach?"

I nod.

Maybe that will make this easier.

Not having to look at her.

Not having to see her perfect, soft, pink lips or the way her blue eyes roam over me like they do now, taking in every inch of my exposed skin like she's taking stock.

I know I'm not imagining the pull between us that's developed over the last several months. I'm not just seeing what I want to or reading into the situation because she's vulnerable.

Camille isn't in any place to want anything from me

166

other than my help on her homestead—and I may have offered her more, but I won't bring it up again.

Never.

Not even when she finally lays her hands on me.

Pushing up on my elbow, I roll over onto my stomach, turning my head to one side so I can watch her out of the corner of my eye.

She moves toward the bed slowly, cautiously, like I'm a wounded animal who might strike, but I am far from it. If anything, she's like a fucking lion tamer who has somehow managed to wrangle me into submission just by being kind, by doing something no one else ever really has, forcing me to take care of myself.

Her knee hits the mattress, and she shifts closer to me.

The towel still lies wrapped around my waist, covering me from lower back to mid-thigh.

She clears her throat. "I'm going to have to move this down a little."

I nod my approval, afraid of trying to voice my consent when it feels like I'm hanging on the razor-thin edge of something I *can't* fall off.

Her soft fingers brush against my skin as she slides them beneath the terry cloth. My whole body twitches, then tenses at the electrical current that buzzes through every nerve ending with her simple caress.

Not pain.

Far fucking from it.

She tugs on the towel hard enough to release the loose tie at the front and nudges it down until I can feel the cool air of the room brush against the top of my ass.

Her eyes linger on my lower back, on the scars criss-crossing it, and she worries her bottom lip between her teeth and looks like she's fighting something she wants to say.

Part of me wants to know what it is, but more of me just needs her hands on me again.

My cock stirs, pinned between my pelvis and the mattress beneath me, just anticipating that soft caress again.

"You're going to have to tell me if it's too much, if it hurts in certain places, what feels good and what—"

"Camille..."

She glances at me, and I push up on my elbow so I can turn my head fully back to her.

"I will be fine."

I hold her gaze for as long as she allows it, trying to ensure she sees how much I mean it.

How *not* worried I am that she could inadvertently hurt me.

She finally gives a little bob of her head and reaches forward, pressing her palms flat against my back, drifting over it in a way that makes me release a sharp hiss before I drop my forehead into my pillow.

Camille thinks this will help, but it's going to be absolute fucking torture at the same time.

———

CAMILLE

Dalton trembles under my touch, and I push my thumbs into the tense muscles along the base of his spinal column, feeling along the rigid bone and metal hardware there.

God, these surgeries must have been agonizing...

He issues a low groan with the increased pressure, a sound that sends a rush of heat between my legs embarrassingly fast.

Hell.

When I walked into that bathroom and saw him like that, I certainly never expected I'd end up like this, with him mostly naked under my hands. Or that my body would react so damn inappropriately to it.

The man is in *pain*, he's *suffering*, and I'm starting to feel like a bitch in heat.

I squeeze my thighs together and shift on my knees, trying to work out the ache forming there without being obvious.

It's the hormones.

It has to be.

You were the same way when you were pregnant with Davey...

I keep telling myself that.

The same way I did a thousand times while I sat beside Dalton in that bathtub after I glanced into the water and saw how hard his cock was straining against the wet fabric of his boxer briefs.

After I heard the break in his voice, when he begged me *never* to consider leaving again.

It was all too much.

Too overwhelming when I'm already a hormonal and emotional mess.

And now I have my hands on him.

His hot, smooth skin and raised scars.

The hard, rippling muscles.

Stop thinking about it and just help *him.*

I shake my head to try to clear the images running through it, then reach up and press my hand against the middle of his shoulder blades, urging him down fully. "You need to relax."

If he stays so tense, this isn't going to benefit him at all. And that's the entire reason I'm putting myself through what is turning out to be both a test of my own strength and proof of how little control I have over my own body when I'm in this condition.

The dull throb between my legs continues as Dalton releases a deep sigh and collapses onto his chest, letting his arms fall out to his sides. He turns his head to the right, and his eyes drift closed.

Thick, dark lashes flutter against his cheeks, and I shift to the sides of his spine, digging into the tight muscles across his lower back that cut out across his ass.

Dalton winces and clenches his eyes and fists.

"Is it too much?"

He shakes his head, and his hands relax on the bed. "No"—he swallows audibly—"it feels so good. You have magic hands..."

I laugh lightly at his comment, and it feels so fake, so wooden, considering the tension building in me and in the room around us. "You're not the first person who has said that."

That thought helps cool my heated body slightly, but I don't let myself go down the road that will lead to memories of the man I thought I'd spend the rest of my life with.

Just keep working on him.

I'm careful not to press too hard in the places where I can feel the hardware, where his body was literally pieced back together after it was shattered.

An image of him as a child flashes through my head. A mop of sandy-blond hair. Green eyes rimmed with red from the constant tears of loss, pain, and fear.

It quickly morphs into Davey in the same situation.

Tears blur my vision, and I blink them away, trying desperately not to let my concern and my feelings that have grown for this man overwhelm my common sense. But he shifts under me, moving his hips in a way that makes my core clench around something that isn't there.

"Are you all right?"

He glances back at me again, his eyes hooded. "Just trying to get in a more comfortable position."

I do the same, transferring my weight and inching my legs together to better gain control of what feels like an utterly uncontrollable ache between my thighs.

Dalton resettles, and I breathe through my reaction to him the best I can. Working his taut muscles until I start to feel them give way and relax under my fingers. Digging into places that feel exceptionally tight, where his body has compensated for the injury and the ways he abuses it on a daily basis in order to complete the tasks necessary to keep this place—and ours—running.

The occasional groan and gasp that slip from his lips as he practically melts under my touch only coil me tighter, make the aching need unbearable, until I feel like I'm going to snap if I don't get relief.

My body is shaking by the time I've worked on him for almost half an hour, and I finally have to pull my hands away, resting them on my own quivering thighs before I act and do something I know I shouldn't.

He pushes up on his elbows and looks back at me. "Thank you, Camille."

Our gazes lock, and the heat I see in his matches that searing through me, threatening to consume me alive.

All logic tells me that this is my cue to leave.

To slide back off the bed and to walk away from him.

To let him relax and sleep.

Allow his body to calm down from the trauma it experienced today.

But I can't bring myself to move, not when my hands still tingle with the feel of his hard, hot body under them.

His green eyes darken in a way that makes my heart flutter, and my clit does the same.

Hell...

I shift restlessly, pressing my thighs together against the growing need for release. "Don't look at me like that, Dalton."

It isn't the first time I've issued him the warning, and the last time I did, he didn't heed it. That only led to a more complicated situation. To both of us walking on eggshells around each other, afraid to do or say anything that might be taken the wrong—or right—way.

"Why not?"

His voice comes out in a deep rasp I've never heard before.

Full of so much *need* that clearly matches my own.

I shake my head, swallowing through the emotion clogging my throat. "Because I can't."

"Why can't you, Camille?"

It's such a stupid question when he knows the answer, when it's glaringly obvious. But when I open my mouth to answer, the words won't come out.

All those reasons seem less important when my body is thrumming and desperate for this man's touch.

"Camille..."

The way he says my name draws my focus back to him, and the pain there has been replaced with a searing lust that makes all the walls I've built up to keep my attraction to him at bay shatter far too easily.

"Roll over."

Dalton's eyes flare, his body tensing, but he slowly

rotates onto his back, exposing himself to me fully. His hard cock lies thick and heavy across his stomach.

Fuck...

He is clearly just as affected as I am.

My clit throbs again, and I bite back a groan at the thought of what it would feel like to have him inside me.

Goddamn these fucking hormones.

It's the last thing I should be thinking about.

He's my friend—my savior, really—but he can't be anything more. Still, the thought of climbing on top of him and letting him slip inside is far too appealing to simply erase from my thoughts.

His hand slides over mine where it rests on my thigh, and I jerk my gaze up over his perfectly formed abs and honed chest, built by years of hard, manual labor. That work may have destroyed what was already broken, but it has sculpted Dalton into an exquisite, perfect example of the male form.

My eyes finally reach his, and we stare at each other, tethered by shared need, while both of us are restrained by our own reasons not to act on what we clearly both want in this moment.

His Adam's apple bobs as he swallows thickly, watching me. "Maybe you should go."

The words seem almost excruciating for him to speak, but the flash of distress that rushes through me with his suggestion says far more about what my choice is going to be than what my head wants to say.

This doesn't have to mean anything.

It can just be relieving this tension that exists between us and that these damn hormones are building inside me...

That's what I tell myself as I slide my hand out from under his and grip his hard length.

He hisses, his eyes drifting closed as I stroke him in one long, slow movement that takes my palm up across the head of his cock where a bead of pre-cum glistens.

"Fucking hell, Camille."

The throaty groan only throws more gas onto the inferno already blazing inside me, and I shift impatiently on my knees, trying to find a position that helps alleviate the ache between my legs.

His eyes fly open and drift down to his hand resting on my thigh.

So close to where I want it.

Where I need it.

I tighten my grip on him.

His jaw clenches, a muscle there ticcing violently as his hand drifts low to the seam of the maternity stretch pants I never had time to change out of before I rushed over here today. "I don't know what I'm doing, Camille."

The painful-sounding admission should be a stark reminder of why we should stop.

He's so much younger than me.

Completely inexperienced.

And in absolutely no position to be making these types of decisions.

Yet, I can't bring myself to pull away.

I stroke him again and again, dragging my palm across the slick head of his cock as I turn slightly to give him better access.

He murmurs something under his breath I can't quite catch, too focused on the heat building between my legs before he's even touched me there.

I shift my knees wider, and his hand glides up between them until he's cupping me. That flicker of contact is enough to make me buck against his hold, and he groans, then pushes his fingers up along the harsh seam of the material, rubbing it into my already-soaked underwear.

My eyes drift closed on a silent gasp, my hand tightening around his cock. His hips arch up into my fist, and he glides his fingers across me in a slow rhythm that creates the most beautiful friction but doesn't quite give me what I need.

Practically panting now, my hips grinding against him in a frantic search, I release his cock. His eyes fly open with concern, and I reach down to the waistband of my pants and shove them down my hips far enough to give him better access.

I grasp his wrist and guide his hand right over me, where only a thin piece of already-soaked silky fabric separates us.

He groans again and starts gliding his fingers back and forth, but still not hitting the right spot to send me spinning.

Taking him in one palm, I place my other hand over his and start guiding his movements, teaching him what I want, what I need to find the release that's been taunting me for what feels like forever.

I help press his fingers up against my clit and rub in harsh, quick circles, and he moans as my tempo stroking his cock increases. His hips roll up to meet my hand until he's basically fucking it as I ride his.

It doesn't take long for that low heat centered deep in my core to spread, and my mouth falls open on a gasp as those first little sparks start to fire off.

"Camille..." My name comes breathy, strangled, and I force my eyes open to meet his as my orgasm hovers on the periphery of reach. The green blazes with the type of need I don't think I've ever seen before. "I'm going to—"

He swallows the final word, his body tightening and going completely rigid as he starts to come.

Hot spurts shoot from the head of his cock over my hand and across his stomach, every muscle in his beautiful form going completely rigid as my own release finally blasts through me.

My body jerks and twitches as he continues to stroke the wet fabric and glide across my clit in the motion I taught him until I can't take it anymore, until I'm too sensitive to bear even a feather-light touch.

I whimper and tug his hand away with mine, then drop forward, pressing both my palms against his bare skin—one covered in his release, the other over his hand that just got me off for the first time in five months.

Tears well and start to trickle down my cheeks.

But it isn't regret.

It isn't pain.

It's just pure, unadulterated relief.

Chapter Eleven

DALTON

The door slamming downstairs jars me out of my dazed eye lock with Camille, and I push up onto my elbow, my head still spinning from what we did as much as from the mind-bending orgasm and the fact that she came on my hand.

She snags the towel and scrambles back off the bed, wiping the evidence of what just happened on it before she tosses it onto my still-prone body.

Her hands shake as she nervously shoves them through her already tied-back hair, then she slips out the door, closing it behind her without a glance back at me.

Shit.

Pops and Davey—they're back.

And at the literal *most* inopportune time possible.

I let out a shuttered breath, trying to slow my racing heart as I wipe the cooling cum from my stomach.

She ran...

Before I even had a chance to talk to her, to discuss what the hell just went down.

I'm not sure what to make of that, but I force myself to try to climb off the bed, anticipating the agony that will rack my body so soon after being incapacitated like I was earlier today.

Only a dull ache radiates across my back as I climb to my feet, and I manage to tug on a clean pair of jeans far easier than I ever have when my body has given out.

Camille is a miracle worker.

Not only did she manage to diagnose and treat Pops, but she's already helped me in more ways than I can even put into words. Most of which have nothing to do with the way she just touched me—though I certainly can't say I could ever regret it.

Fuck.

Did that really just happen?

I scrub my hands over my face and give myself a moment to try to process how quickly things changed with Camille. It's been four months since I first stared down the barrel of her shotgun, but the shift seems to have happened in almost the blink of an eye.

Of course, it wasn't really that fast.

We've grown closer and closer over the time we've spent together, but I never allowed myself the luxury of hoping or believing it might become more.

Not after she lost Dave.

Not when she's carrying his child.

Today changes things...

There isn't any way I can let her walk away and pretend *that* didn't just happen. I won't allow her to shut down or drown in whatever she's feeling right now. We definitely need to talk about it. But not when Pops and Davey are around.

I snag a T-shirt and open the bedroom door.

Davey's excited voice carries up the stairs, and I slowly make my way down to find all three of them in the living room.

Camille squats in front of her son as he excitedly tells her about the successful fishing trip in jumbled sentences so fast that I barely catch more than a few words.

A single small trout on a string hangs from his little fist, and he lifts it proudly, proving their "success" and explaining his bubbling excitement.

Pops glances up at my descent, brows raised. "You're up…"

I understand his confusion. The other *very* few times I've allowed him to see me like I was earlier, I didn't move for the rest of the day and barely did anything the next few except what was absolutely necessary around the home-stead that he couldn't accomplish.

"Yeah…"

I don't intend to offer any other information about *how* this miracle happened.

The bath.

The massage.

The *very* personal release of all that tension…

His eyes dart between Camille and me, and she quickly looks away, refocusing on Davey with a smile to avoid the knowing scrutiny of the old man who reads things all too well.

I'm sure he has a million questions about what happened between the time he left me practically collapsing upstairs and now, and given the pink rising in Camille's cheeks, he probably already has a guess.

But what Pops *does* have is some common sense and tact.

He knows better than to confront me about it in front of Camille and Davey.

"I'm glad to see you up and around." His eyes scan over me. "I expected you'd be down for a while."

"I'm okay."

Instead of the relief I expect to see crossing his face, his jaw tightens, and he inclines his head toward the kitchen with the clear intent of getting me away from prying ears.

I follow him in there, tugging on the shirt as I go. "What's going on?"

He glances over my shoulder to ensure Camille and Davey are occupied before he leans closer. "We weren't alone at the lake."

All that tension that just got released in the most delicious way immediately returns to rest between my shoulders. "What do you mean?"

It's squarely on our property.

Private property that's well-marked as such.

No one should have been anywhere near the lake, and everyone in James Creek knows that. They also understand that all they need to do is *ask* and we would give them permission to fish or swim there any time they wanted, which immediately tells me more than Pops has so far.

"Strangers?"

He nods. "Definitely not locals. They were already there when we arrived and seemed surprised to see us."

They probably thought no one would be out there this late in the day, which is a pretty good assumption, since the fish are usually biting early in the morning or at dusk, not at the height of the afternoon.

"What were they doing?"

"Looked like they were taking some sort of samples from the water."

"Shit." I shove a hand through my hair, clutching the ends of the strands as I start to pace. "Do you think they're connected to that Gallo guy?"

Pops leans back against the counter and crosses his arms over his chest, chewing on the inside of his cheek. "Probably."

That's it?

Someone threatens the mountain.

Invades the land.

And he acts like he isn't worried in the least.

"You still haven't told me this brilliant plan to ensure they don't come after the mountain. It's been months since Gallo cornered me. If you're working on something, I should know, Pops."

He scowls at me and drums his fingers on the counter behind him. "We surprised them, and they headed back off into the woods. There was no way I was going to catch them on foot. Even you probably couldn't have."

And he dodged my question again.

After our conversation that day on the porch, I thought Pops would open up more about what he's been up to and why he seems so confident that we don't *need* to worry about any threats.

Yet, the old man has remained suspiciously silent on that super-important topic. He has avoided my questions over and over. And while I'd love to rail at him right now about that, there are more urgent issues to address.

He scrubs a palm across his stubbled cheek. "There's no way they hiked up here from town."

I nod my agreement. "It's too far. I'm going to go out and see what I can find. Maybe they left something behind."

He reaches out and grabs my arm before I can move away. "Dalton, you can't."

"Why the hell not?"

Pops shoves off the counter, invading my personal space and lowering his voice. "Because when I left here, you could barely *walk,* and you were in fucking *agony.* Not to mention, we don't know who they are, what they want, or why they might be up here."

"You want them roaming around the land? What's stopping them from coming over here and showing up unannounced with less-than-pure intentions? I'm *okay,* and I'm *going.*"

"Wait until tomorrow."

I grit my jaw.

"They're long gone by now, Dalton. Anything that's there tonight will be there tomorrow."

He has a point.

It isn't supposed to rain tonight, so any prints or other evidence of their presence should remain intact until I can get there at sunrise.

"Fine, but I'm going to radio the sheriff."

Pops bobs his head in agreement. "We need to, but I don't want to scare Camille."

I glance back at her as she takes the strung fish from Davey and holds it up, admiring it. "Agreed. Let's head to the office as calmly as possible."

We step back into the living room.

I do my best to look casual, relaxed, and if I don't, hopefully, Camille thinks it's because of what just happened upstairs and *not* something else.

She lifts the fish. "I'm not sure this is enough for dinner, but..."

Pops chuckles and ruffles Davey's hair. "Maybe an appetizer. Dalton and I need to take care of something in the office quickly. Do you know how to clean it?"

Camille scoffs, rolling her eyes at him. "Dave was quite an accomplished fisherman. I'm an *expert*."

For the first time since I met her, Camille said Dave's name and discussed him without the immediate pinch of pain crossing her face.

Progress.

Even if after what happened upstairs might set *us* spiraling backward—or God knows where else—if it in any way has made her grief easier to handle, then I am not one to question it.

Her gaze meets mine for a split second as I walk past them and follow Pops into his office, but I can't get a read on her. I shut the door behind me before I'm tempted to stay and try to get her to talk.

Pops eyes me as he settles into his chair behind the desk. "Something I should know?"

"About what?"

He nods toward the closed door. "You and Camille."

I run my hand through my hair and sigh. "Nothing to tell."

"Uh-huh."

He doesn't sound at all convinced but reaches out and snags the radio, calling the sheriff on the dedicated channel without giving me the third degree.

Though I know it's coming—eventually.

I listen intently as he gives a more detailed rundown of what he saw, growing more and more uneasy with the whole situation the more he talks.

Sheriff Wilson releases a long sigh after taking a second to consider the information. "I haven't noticed anybody unusual near town today, but I'll tell you what. I'll go out now and do a quick patrol to see if anything stands out or anyone who shouldn't be around pops up."

"I'd appreciate that." Pops leans forward, resting his elbows on the desk. "Let us know what you find...if you find anything."

"I will."

I don't dare try to sit in the chair with the way my body still feels, so I stand behind it and grasp the back, watching Pops set the receiver down. "I'll go out tomorrow and see what I can track down. Hopefully, the sheriff comes up with something, but in the meantime, we stay vigilant."

He nods. "What you said earlier...I don't want you to worry. I'm not sure if what happened today has anything to do with Gallo, but that situation isn't anything you need to spend any of your energy on."

"There you go, shutting me down again without ever actually telling me anything." I tighten my grip on the leather under my palms. "You can't keep me in the dark forever, Pops."

"I'm not trying to." He motions absently around him. "You have enough to worry about between running this place, getting Camille's in shape, and keeping me alive."

"You could make *that* part easier, you know." I point an accusatory finger at him. "Stop giving her shit when she gives you your shots. Stop complaining about the balance exercises and the brain-game shit she has you doing to try to get your body back to where it should be."

He crosses his arms over his chest and leans back in his chair with a *humph*. "I'm fine. Doing much better."

"Only because she keeps making you do it. Because she *pushes* you."

A single white brow rises over his glasses. "Is that what she does to you, too?"

Shit.

I drop my head, trying hard to wipe out the images of what she just did to me in that bedroom. How she *pushed* right over that imaginary line we had drawn between us. "She does, Pops, but not the way you're thinking..."

"I'm pretty sure it's *exactly* the way I'm thinking it is, Dalton."

Damn him.

Slowly lifting my head, I meet his green gaze. "And if it is?"

I raise a brow at him, and the corners of his lips twitch into a little half grin.

"I'd be happy for you and for her, but there are a lot of complications there."

"No shit."

She's not in any position to offer me something that belongs to another man, nor am I in any to offer her something when I don't have any idea how to *give* it to her, even if she said yes.

We should have just left things as they were—as friends.

Stuck to the bargain we made to help each other and nothing more.

But instead, I've gone and fucked everything up by falling head over sanity for Camille Bower.

———

CAMILLE

Tension at the dinner table made me shift restlessly in my seat and push the food around on my plate rather than actu-

185

ally eat much of it. Every second, I could feel Dalton's eyes on me, watching my every move, the heat of his gaze igniting parts of me I'm too embarrassed to think about even now that I've escaped the James homestead and any possibility of him cornering me to discuss what happened.

Did I really do that?

The flutter between my thighs and my still-damp panties confirms I did. Yet I still can't wrap my head around the fact that I actually shut down all those reasons we shouldn't have to act on my attraction to him.

It was reckless.

Thoughtless.

Selfish.

It's only going to end one way—with one or both of us getting hurt.

Even Davey's continued excited chattering about fishing with Pops as I drive us home hasn't been enough to quell the worry that I might've ruined everything. That I might end up pushing away the only person in my life I've actually been able to count on since Dave died.

The only person *in* my life, really.

"And then we saw the two men—"

I glance up at him in the rearview mirror. "I'm sorry, kiddo, I didn't hear you. What were you talking about?"

He releases a little exacerbated sigh that can only come from a four-year-old who thinks *everything* is excruciatingly important. "Fishing!"

"You just said something about two men..."

He nods, grinning. "They were at the lake."

My hands tighten on the wheel, and I try not to let panic seep into my next words as I peek at him again. "Did Pops recognize them?"

Davey shakes his head. "Don't think so..."

I return my focus to the road, relieved to see how close we are to home. "Did he talk to them?"

"No, they left when we got there."

Shit.

That certainly isn't a good sign.

Why would anyone up at the lake leave *when Pops arrives?*

Unless they shouldn't have been there...

All that worry about what's been going on behind the scenes with the lawyer who confronted Dalton in James Creek rushes back.

Are they connected?

Does Dalton know?

The way Pops pulled him into the kitchen when they got back and then disappeared into the office shortly thereafter suddenly makes a lot more sense.

Of course, he knows.

That's why they were acting so strangely at dinner.

Quiet.

Reserved.

Sending each other quick looks when Dalton wasn't busy trying to assess me with his heated gaze.

They're worried.

And now panic starts to creep in, despite my best efforts to keep it at bay.

It's been months since I overheard that conversation between them, since I learned that someone might try to interfere with their land, with their ownership of the mountain. As far as I know, nothing has happened, but that doesn't mean it won't. It doesn't mean it *can't*.

This could be that *something*.

By the time I pull onto the property and park in front of the cabin, my anxiety has ramped up so much that my hands shake as I try to open my truck door. I manage to get Davey out of his car seat in the back and turn toward the front door when the sound of tires crunching on gravel hits my ears, coming from the winding road that leads to our homestead.

Shit.

I quickly scoop him up, balancing him on my hip as much as I can, ready to run with him into the house to where I have the shotgun stashed if I need to.

Whoever those men were might still be around, might be after whatever they came here for, and God only knows what that could be. Or whether they would come *here* looking for it.

I back toward the house, keeping my focus on the dark gap between the trees where any vehicles coming will appear.

Bright headlights momentarily blind me as they make the final turn, and I raise one hand to dampen them as I almost reach the porch. A truck stops a few feet behind mine and shuts off, but the lights stay on, impairing my ability to see the driver.

Every muscle in my body tenses, ready to take the few steps up to the porch and dash into the house to snag the shotgun...

The truck door opens and closes, and someone steps into the light. With it backlighting whoever it is, it would be impossible for anyone to identify the driver.

If I didn't know that body so well...

A relieved breath rushes from my chest as Dalton rounds the front of the truck fully and moves toward us.

"Jesus, Dalton, you scared the shit out of me."

He approaches with a furrowed brow. "I didn't know you left."

"I didn't know I had to *tell* you I was leaving…"

When he and Pops went out to the barn to check on Apollo and some of the other animals, leaving me with Davey to finish cleaning up after dinner, it gave me the perfect exit without having awkwardness between me and the man now staring me down with a strange mix of anger and concern brewing in his gaze.

I tighten my hold on Davey, who waves excitedly at his friend. "What's wrong, Dalton?"

He clenches his jaw and glances away.

"And don't tell me nothing."

Dalton approaches, his gaze softening, and he takes Davey's hand in his and grins. "Everything's fine, bud."

He wasn't the one who asked the question, but the fact that Dalton is being so careful about what he says in front of him only concerns me more.

"Is it?" I raise a brow at him, trying to keep my voice level. "Because he told me about the men at the lake…"

Dalton winces, confirming exactly what I feared.

They don't know who it was.

And they're worried about it, too.

He steps closer and rubs his hand up the side of my exposed arm. A breeze flows over us, but the goosebumps that pebble on my skin could be from either touch. "Look, we don't know if there's any reason to be worried yet…"

"Bullshit. If there wasn't any reason to be worried, you wouldn't have that look on your face or have chased me up here."

He leans in, brushing his lips against my ear in an intimate move he never would have attempted yesterday. "Yes, I *would* have. I wasn't going to let you run away from what happened today as if it didn't. I would have come after you, *regardless* of the reason."

Shit.

Pulling back slightly, he locks his gaze with mine. "But that conversation can wait. I need to check the house and make sure no one's been in there or on the property."

Oh, God...

"You think...they came *here?*"

All that calm I experienced only a moment ago upon seeing Dalton arrive vanishes in an instant.

"I don't know. That's the problem." He scans around us, as if he can somehow see through the darkness and dense trees. "We don't know who they were or why they were up here. Even the sheriff doesn't have any idea."

I clutch Davey tighter, thankful he doesn't seem to understand the tense situation surrounding him.

"Where's your shotgun?"

Swallowing back dinner as it threatens to rise up my throat, I incline my head toward the house. "On top of the bookcase to the right of the door. Shells are behind the first row of books."

His hand glides across my arm again. "Follow me up to the porch. I'm going to go in and clear the house. Stay in the doorjamb until I tell you it's safe to come in. If you hear anything suspicious—"

I suck in a sharp breath before he even says the words. "I get back in the truck and go to your place."

He nods, then lifts his hand to cup my cheek. "It'll be okay."

Will it?

I want to believe him when he says that, want to believe the words are true, but it's hard to when I can see that hint of panic in his gaze, too. The concern there matches my own. The very real possibility that somebody could have come onto the property while we were gone and done something...or worse, be lurking to do something *more*.

All I can do is put my faith in Dalton as I follow him up the steps and onto the porch. He turns the handle of the door we never lock—which I will start doing after this—and slowly eases it open to utter darkness.

We both stand still and listen, but all I can hear is the sound of my own heartbeat and blood rushing in my ears.

Dalton turns back to me and motions for us to stay there, and I nod as he reaches up onto the top of the bookcase, grabs the gun, and then slides the books over to get to the shells.

He loads it quickly, then steps deeper into the house.

Davey clings to me, giggling, and I press my finger over my mouth to tell him to be quiet, pretending it's a game. He presses his lips closed again and slaps his hand over his mouth, and I force a smile he's too young to know is fake.

Dalton disappears into the blackness, and I hold my breath.

The cabin isn't big.

It shouldn't take him long to check everywhere, but each second that ticks by when he's gone feels like an hour.

The darkness that usually doesn't bother me up here somehow feels threatening tonight.

Each sound makes me flinch, tightening my hold on Davey.

A light finally flips on in the living room, and Dalton stands there with the gun at his side, no longer at the ready. "The house is clear. Go into the back with him. I have to check the rest of the property for any signs that someone was here. Lock the door behind me and don't open it unless you're sure it's me coming back."

"Dalton..."

He approaches and takes my cheek in his palm again, running his calloused thumb across it in a way that sends a little shiver of pure warmth through me. "I promise I'll be okay."

Only hours ago, he was barely able to stand, in so much pain that *I* almost felt it. And now, who knows what he might face out there, what might wait for him?

Tears burn my eyes, and he presses a kiss to my temple before he steps around us through the open door and out into the inky blackness of night. He motions for us to go, and I close the door behind him, throw the lock, and rush back to the bedroom with Davey.

Please, God, let him be okay...

I haven't prayed in so long. I haven't even *thought* to.

After Dave died, I wasn't even sure there *was* a God anymore, yet here I am, begging Him to protect the man who spent the last few months protecting us and is still out there doing it.

No matter what it might cost him.

Chapter Twelve

DALTON

Every snap of a twig, each rustle of a leaf in the chilly night-time breeze, draws my attention, tensing every muscle in my body as I make my way around the property, searching for any signs that someone was here who shouldn't have been.

Which is *anyone*.

This mountain has always been a haven—somewhere free of threats beyond what's always lived in these trees. The people of James Creek respect it and our place, and we've never had to even *consider* a breach of that trust before.

The fact that it's brought that kind of fear to Camille only strengthens my grip on the weapon.

I pause next to the paddock and pop into the barn for a minute to check on the animals, but everything is quiet and appears untouched—whoever was at the lake doesn't seem to have come to the property.

Or if they did, they are good at covering their tracks.

At least in the dark.

Tomorrow may show something different in the light of a new day, but at least for tonight, I know Camille is safe with me here.

The satisfaction that washes through me with that knowledge rivals that of earlier today brought on by Camille's touch. I want to do the same for her; that's why I made her that promise—that everything will be okay.

It may have been stupid to say those words when I don't even fully understand the situation myself, but seeing that terror return to her eyes that I thought I had vanquished was enough for me to tell her *anything* to ensure it went away.

Even if it wasn't true...

Something in my gut tells me today's intrusion on the mountain wasn't an innocent tourist sightseeing at our pristine lake. Camille clearly knows that, too, or she wouldn't have been so shaken when I arrived.

The relief that flooded her gaze when she realized it was *me* who pulled in behind her was enough to give me a flicker of hope that what happened today between us won't ruin everything.

It's that warmth that mixes with the pure heat of my anger toward the assholes who brought that fear back to her.

By the time I reach the cabin and knock at the front door, I'm struggling to rein in my rage over the entire situation, and I don't even know how long I've been gone securing the property.

An hour?

Two?

It feels like forever, though I know it hasn't been that long given the fact that my back hasn't returned to screeching in protest.

I just don't like to be away from her.

Any distance between us feels too great.

That's a dangerous feeling to have when she isn't ready for it.

I should have given her space to process what happened between us today, but as soon as Pops said they had left, nothing was going to keep me from coming after them.

Because I needed to see her.

To know they were safe.

To know I didn't fuck up everything between us by allowing her to touch me. Allowing myself to touch *her* like that.

My body thrums with the memory as I climb the porch steps, my hands itching to take her into my arms and hold her again. To do all the things I *didn't*, that I *couldn't* before.

If she'll let me...

Camille's face appears in the window beside the door where she once stood to eavesdrop on Pops and me about likely the very situation I'm dealing with tonight. When she sees me, her shoulders sag, and she unlocks the door and yanks it open.

She throws herself at me, wrapping her arms around my neck, her belly pressing into mine tightly, like she can't get close enough. "Oh, God, I was so worried."

I cling to her with my free arm, the shotgun still clasped at my side in my other hand, and bury my face in the thick, dark amber hair she's let down from the messy bun she typically keeps it in. "I'm okay. Nothing seems amiss on the property. I don't think anyone came up here, but I'll check again in the morning before I head to the lake."

She tugs back, her brows raised, searching my face like she doesn't quite understand. "In the morning?"

"You really think I'm going to let you stay up here alone tonight?"

"But your grandfather..."

Shifting my hand from around her, I brush the hair back from her face. "Pops is the one who taught me how to fire a gun, and he has better aim than anyone I know. He also has a *shoot-first, ask-questions-later* mentality. He'll be fine. You and Davey won't be. I don't want to scare him by trying to take him back to my place, and I wouldn't sleep, knowing you were up here alone without any sort of protection."

She scowls at me, the twist of her lips insanely beautiful, despite her best efforts to toss me the strongest reproachful look in her arsenal. "I protected myself pretty well against you."

The memory of the way she leveled this very gun on me the first time I came up here makes me grin at her. "That you did, but I don't want you to *have* to do that again, ever. I'm staying here tonight."

Her body tenses, and she backs away from me, retreating into the living room fully as her gaze darts toward the two bedrooms.

I lean the gun carefully against the wall beside the door as I close and lock it, securing us inside. When I turn back to her, Camille has that plump bottom lip pulled between her teeth again.

But I don't think this concern has anything to do with the potential there may be someone out in the miles of wilderness surrounding us.

This has to do with something much closer.

Me.

"I'll sleep on the couch so I can be near the door."

She releases her lip with a little sharp breath, her shoulders relaxing.

A pang hits my chest that feels an awful lot like disappointment, even though I never intended to put her in a situation where she would ever be uncomfortable.

That was never what *this* was about.

I just wanted to help Davey and this incredibly brave and stunningly beautiful woman in any way I could.

Pinpointing when things changed would be impossible because it wasn't one single moment in time. It was the passage of it. Every hour, each day we spent together working and getting to know one another, I feel a little more in love with the woman I thought I could never have.

How could I when her heart belongs to someone else?

Her focus has to be on herself, her baby, and her son.

And protecting all three of them is my only concern. The old man can fend for himself tonight...

"Where's Davey?"

"I got him to fall asleep." She rubs at her side, like the baby is kicking or it's bothering her. "I think Pops wore him out."

"Well, the walk to the lake isn't an easy one."

"No, it isn't." She shakes her head. "Dave brought me down there a few times."

The ghost of a smile that crosses her face, thinking about the memory, renews that spark of hope that she will make it through all of this.

Her grief over losing Dave will last a lifetime.

It may never fade.

But lately, it seems as though she's been taking my advice to look for the moments in each day that are pure joy.

That's certainly what I experienced earlier today.

After one of the most agonizing moments I can remember, this woman somehow morphed it into one of the most beautiful.

Almost as if she can read my thoughts or somehow *see* what I'm thinking about and the way my skin heats remembering her hands on me, she blushes and retreats a few steps, then glances back at the couch. "You can't sleep out here."

"Why not?"

Her throat works on a slow swallow. "Your back…"

I scowl at her, opening my mouth to explain that I will be doing just that, despite any objections she may make.

"Don't give me that look, Dalton. I saw you earlier today, remember? You can't argue that sleeping on a couch isn't going to mess up your back even more."

Probably.

The fact is, I never know *how* I'm going to feel when I wake in the morning, regardless of where I end up crashing, so this argument is irrelevant.

"I've slept in far worse places than on a couch, Camille. I've spent many nights in the barn because one of the animals went into labor and I didn't want to leave it or out on the property to watch over some of the livestock when there was a bear in the area. I'm no stranger to sleeping places other than a bed."

One of her dark brows rises slowly. "And was your back as bad those times?"

She's got me there, and the look she gives me tells me she knows it, too.

I told her far too much today.

Revealed all those little secret cracks in my armor I've done such a good job of hiding for so long.

"That's irrelevant."

"It's far from irrelevant to me, Dalton."

The unwavering way she cares about me and worries, even if she has no reason to, is what ultimately draws me across the room to her, even when I should be giving her space.

I take her face between my palms. "You have no idea how much I appreciate your concern and the help you gave me earlier. I wouldn't be up and walking around like this right now if it weren't for what you did. But if I am in your bed, I am not going to be concentrating on protecting you from anything that might be happening outside. All I'm going to be thinking about is how it feels to have you beside me."

She shudders against me, her eyes drifting closed as a little sigh slips from her lips so close to mine.

And God, I want to kiss her.

I want to know what she tastes like and feel the press of her lips to mine.

I want to swallow those little sighs she makes into my mouth and breathe her into my lungs and hold her there forever.

I want Camille like I've never wanted anything in my life before.

And I don't want to fuck it up with her.

I don't want to do anything that'll send her running the way she did from my room earlier. If she shuts down and shuts me out, I won't ever get us back to where we were when she wrapped her hand over mine and directed it between her legs.

I'll never get to experience the pure bliss of seeing her come or the pride of knowing I did that for her.

It may have only happened once, but I'm already addicted to it.

But if I kiss her now, if I give in to this pull that draws me to her so powerfully, I *will* send her fleeing from me.

She's not ready.

She may never be.

Don't blow it, Dalton.

I've probably already said too much, revealed far more about how I feel and what I want from her than I ever should have. But I want even more than what I admitted.

I want it *all*.

This woman.

This life with her and her children.

A family and a future on the mountain.

My cock aches between us, desperate to do whatever it takes to make that happen, but I pull away before she can feel the hard length pressed against her. "I'm sleeping on the couch, Camille. That's final."

Her eyes flutter open to meet mine, and she stares up at me from under thick, dark lashes.

The look in her warm blue eyes says she wants to argue her point further, but after everything that's happened today, I watch the fight drain out of them and her.

She leans into my palm on her cheek for a split second before she slips from my hold and slowly turns and walks away down the short hallway toward her room across from Davey's.

I follow after her.

Not because I have any intention of going in, but I need one last look at her before she goes to bed.

To know she's really okay.

Her door is already closed by the time I reach it.

Which is probably for the best.

Despite my pure intentions, only God knows what I might have done if it had been open.

Maybe something stupid—again.

But Davey's door is cracked so Camille can hear him if he gets up during the night, and I stick my head in to check on him.

He lies sprawled on his back, arms wide, with his favorite teddy bear resting across one. The soft glow of the nightlight plugged into the wall to his left illuminates his soft features, making him look even more angelic in his sleep than he already does.

My still-booted feet draw me across the worn floorboards and over to him, and I lower myself to the side of the bed and brush the thick, dark hair back from his forehead.

"You take such good care of your mom..." He's always so aware of her, helping in any way he can, trying to be a mini version of the woman he's watched around the homestead since his dad died. "I wish I could do that, too."

It feels like I'm failing, though.

If I were really taking care of her, none of this would have happened.

There wouldn't be this looming threat.

She'd be safe and secure without me having to sleep armed on her couch.

I release a heavy sigh, and Davey stirs slightly. He shifts more onto his side, turning toward me, as if my voice is drawing him closer. I pull my hand away, not wanting to wake him when I also want to lift him into my arms and hold him tightly.

It's strange to care so much about someone else, to be willing to do *anything* to protect them.

I never thought about being a father, about what it might be like to feel this way about a child.

He isn't even mine.

Yet, the thought that something could have happened to

him today while he was at the lake with Pops, or up here when they came home without me, is enough to make acid crawl up the back of my throat.

Somehow, since he first stared up at me all those months ago, I've fallen in love not only with Camille but with her son, too. Come to think of him as mine to protect and to take care of.

I climb off the bed and turn toward the door to leave, but Camille stands there, watching me, her temple dropped against the jamb.

How much did she hear?

Enough to send her running?

The question worries me enough to slow my steps as I approach her. When I finally get to her, she leans into me, resting her cheek on my shoulder and feathering her lips over my neck. "Thank you for loving him."

She pushes away and walks back to her room, closing the door behind her before I have any chance to react.

I never said that out loud.

Never dared utter those words.

Yet she *knew*.

And it makes me wonder what else she knows without me ever admitting it.

———

CAMILLE

My own strangled scream rips me from the nightmare, and I bolt upright in bed. Ragged breaths rasp through my chest, and my heart slams so violently it feels like it might crack my ribs. The tank top I sleep in clings to my sweat-dampened skin that somehow still has goosebumps raised across it.

The bedroom door flies open, and Dalton stands in the frame, illuminated by the faint moonlight filtering in from the single window on the exterior wall.

His eyes widen, scanning over me carefully. "What's wrong?"

I shudder and drop my face into my hands, trying to catch my breath and wishing I could melt away and disappear rather than have to admit the embarrassment of waking him like this. "Just a dream..."

He releases an audible relieved sigh; then the bed dips beside me. His arm wraps around my shoulder and tugs me against him, and I let my head fall to his shoulder, absorbing all the warmth and strength he's brought instantly when I needed it.

Another shudder rolls through me, and he tightens his hold, reminding me of what I saw and heard earlier. "Did I wake Davey?"

"No." He feathers his lips against my temple. "I just checked on him before I opened your door, and he's still asleep."

Thank God.

I don't need him being any more panicked than I already made him today. Pretending it was all a game worked to a degree, but he's a smart kid and can sense when things are off. He must have asked where Dalton went and when he would be back a dozen times before I finally got him to settle enough to fall asleep.

He loves the man holding me as much as Dalton does him.

And that only complicates this so much more.

Dalton rubs his hand gently up and down my back, and each time he reaches my bare shoulder blades, a little shiver runs through me. Every simple touch only makes me want to find a way to crawl closer, to allow him to take on the weight of all the ways I failed that I can't escape—even when I sleep.

His warm breath flutters my loose hair, and he pulls a strand from where it's matted against my cheek and tucks it behind my ear. "What was your dream about?"

Bits and pieces of it flash through my head.

Vivid.

Bright.

Crystal clear.

As if it really happened and wasn't just some creation of my psyche.

I shudder and snuggle closer to him, welcoming the comfort of his solid arms and body supporting me. His hand settles over mine on top of my stomach and moves with me as I rub at the spot the baby loves to use to get my attention.

The longer he's here, the more he talks, the more likely she is to respond.

It's been like that since very early in this pregnancy.

This little girl loves the sound of Dalton's voice as much as I do, and if he weren't here right now, I might still be down the black hole that nightmare had me trapped in.

I hadn't even realized how long it's been since I've had the dreams about that day until this very moment.

They've slowly vanished over the last couple of months, as things started to fall into place, as I finally started to have hope that everything might actually work out for Davey and me and this baby. When I started to see beyond my own pain to the possibility of a life after it.

But the dream came back with a vengeance tonight.

And it was *different* this time.

In the throes of the nightmare itself, I didn't realize it, but now that my brain is coming out of that fog, those details start to emerge more clearly.

I inhale deeply, taking Dalton's woodsy, masculine scent into my lungs as I cling to him. "It was the day Dave died..."

The day everything changed.

Dalton's body stiffens, his hand stilling for a second against my skin before he resumes the soothing movement. "Do you dream about it a lot?"

I haven't talked about what happened with him at all.

Not with *anyone* after that day.

Talking about it makes it feel too raw.

Too real.

But I can't avoid it forever.

Not now that Dalton and I have grown so close and the line between friendship and more seems to have blurred into nothing today.

"I used to. Haven't in a while." I pull my head back and look up at him. "But it was different this time."

"Different how?"

Though the images flicker in my head, I can't make sense of what they mean, of *why* the dream changed.

The explanation burns in my throat, but I force it out, needing to talk about what it could mean. "This time, when I got there, when I found him, he wasn't alone." Another little shiver hits me. "There was someone else in the barn who ran off as I came in..."

Dalton's brows draw low as he narrows his eyes on me. "What do you mean?"

"That day...he was *alone* in the barn stall with one of the horses—Wilder. And that's the way the dream has always come before, *exactly* as it happened. But tonight, it was like, I don't know..." I shake my head, trying to make any sense of it. "Like maybe someone else was there and hit him? Like maybe it wasn't the horse. But...it's just a dream, right?"

I know what happened the day I lost him.

It would be impossible to forget any of those minute details that are so seared into my brain.

I remember exactly what time he walked out of the house to head to the barn. I recall the moment I realized he was late coming back in for lunch. And I could never wipe away the image of what I found when I went looking for him...

So, the dream is just *that*.

A dream.

It has to be.

Dalton swallows thickly, and his eyes dart to the window before they come back to me. He doesn't say anything, but his silence speaks volumes.

"You don't think—"

He shakes his head. "I don't. I mean, is it possible that whoever Pops saw at the lake has been up here before, snooping around?" He shrugs. "Of course. People have been after the land and what's on it for a lot longer than I've even known about it. But would they go so far as to actually attack Dave to try to get you off the property, to try to send a message to *us*?" His eyes meet mine. "That would be crazy, right?"

I nod slowly. "It would be."

"And you said it was the horse..."

"I assumed it was. What else could have caused a head injury like that? There weren't signs of anyone else or any*thing* else around." I squeeze my eyes closed, trying not to picture Dave, but I can't keep it out. "Wilder has always been just that—*wild*. It's one of the reasons I never tried to ride him, and Davey knew to keep his distance in the pasture and barn. Only Dave could ever handle his attitude. And it looked like Dave got *kicked*." That bloody image makes me wince. "But I suppose anything blunt striking him could have caused that if he were hit hard enough."

During my years in the ER, I saw *plenty* of blunt force trauma head injuries, but it *never* crossed my mind that it could have been anything else until now.

Wilder is precisely the type of horse who *would* throw an unexpected fit and injure someone.

That's why I sold him immediately after Dave died.

Dalton tugs me up against him fully, my belly pressing against the side of his solid body, his arm rigid around my back. "I think everything that happened today is just messing with your head, making it spiral to create this crazy alternate situation. It's your subconscious. Nothing more."

"Do we really know that?"

How long has Gallo's client been after the land?

And who is to say what lengths someone might go to in order to get it?

He presses his lips together. "I guess not, but it doesn't make sense that anyone would come after Dave." He cradles my face in his hands and brushes the hair back from my cheeks. "They would have come after Pops or *me* if they really wanted to scare us. And worrying about something that popped up in a dream isn't going to change what *did* happen."

I release a heavy breath.

My heart finally starts to slow.

"You're right."

Just having him here, holding me, sitting in the peaceful darkness, knowing he will stop anything that ever threatens us, is enough to start calming me from that sheer terror that gripped me only minutes ago.

He presses his forehead against mine, and I let my eyes drift closed, absorbing all the things this man is offering.

His strength.

His determination.

How insanely protective he is.

All of it washes over me, coating me in a warmth that heats my soul, lifting it from the very dark place I was in when I woke. "Thank you."

He lifts his head. "For what?"

"For being here."

"Fuck." He shakes his head. "Don't thank me, Camille. Please. It isn't altruistic. I'm here because..." His lips press together, like he's fighting the words. "Fuck it. I'm here because I *want* you, Camille. I have for a fucking long time, far longer than I should have. Far longer than it was appropriate, given everything you've been through. And after what happened today..."

My body heats at the mere reference to what I allowed to occur in that bedroom.

"I want it *all*, Camille. I want you. I want you and me. I want you, me, and Davey together like *this*. And I know it's stupid for me to even suggest it. It isn't fair for me to say this to you, but..."

He doesn't finish.

He doesn't actually say the words.

The unasked question just hangs in the air between us.

Do you feel the same way?

It shouldn't be an easy answer.

Not when things are *beyond* complicated.

My heart is a mess. My head is, too. My young son, who just lost his father, sleeps right across the hall, and this little girl growing inside me will be coming into the world soon without one.

But I don't have to think about how to respond because only one word sits on my tongue. Only one answer feels *right*.

"Yes."

It comes out on a whispered breath, so quiet that he wouldn't even be able to hear it if we weren't pressed so closely together, but it sounds like an explosion going off in my own head. The weight such a simple word carries is like an atom bomb detonating and blowing away everything that stood between us.

I lean forward and drift my lips over his.

Doing the thing he's so afraid to—*pushing*.

For so long, I've been holding back, preventing myself from *feeling* the things I do for this man.

And he's always been there.

Never expecting anything from me.

Never demanding it.

He's held back, too.

Giving me space and time.

Never pushing for what he wants.

But the time to hold back is gone.

The kiss is soft and sweet, tentative, because I don't know how he will react to any of this, but he responds to it quickly, groaning and trying to tug me closer, which is impossible with my stomach between us.

His hands shift back to tangle in my hair, and he angles my head, kissing me deeper, devouring me in an eager rush that matches the intensity of the need consuming me.

Being right here, right now, with Dalton James, feels like the only thing that has been right in almost six months.

I'm not about to lose the moment, not going to let it slip

away because of fear or anxiety or the guilt that threatens to rear its ugly head if I allowed it even an inch of space in my mind.

Those are tomorrow's problems.

Tonight, I'm going to savor every single kiss. Every touch. Everything Dalton can give me.

Chapter Thirteen

DALTON

Camille fists my shirt tightly, struggling to drag me closer to her, despite the physical impediment her body creates between us. She kisses me with a wanton recklessness and frantic need I've only ever dreamed of. An urgency underlies it, the same as what surges through my own veins, heating my blood until it feels like I'm going to boil over.

Our first kiss is *everything* I thought it would be and somehow more than I ever could have fantasized about at the same time.

Because I've never done anything like this.

Never met anyone like *her*.

Never felt my heart beat in time with someone else's or experienced this rush of almost panic-laced desire that I do when I'm with her.

She mewls softly against my lips, shifting herself onto my lap fully. Her ass grinds against my hard cock, and I groan, my fingers digging into her hips to steady her before she inadvertently ends this far too early.

None of the trepidation or hesitation that lingered in her gaze earlier today seems to be here with us tonight, but it could just be the fear talking, the lingering effects of the nightmare that woke her so violently, making her do something she'll regret in the morning.

I can't let that happen.

No matter how badly I want this and her, I can't let her do it if she's not in her right mind, if she's still reeling from that trauma and only using me as a distraction from it.

Burrowing my hands in her thick hair, I tug her head back, and her eyes fly open, meeting mine in question. "Camille, are you sure you want—"

She leans forward and captures the rest of my words with another brutal kiss. Her tongue glides along the seam of my mouth, and I open for her, allowing my control to slip even further the harder she pushes for this.

Fuck...

So much for trying to be the gentleman.

Whatever happens tonight, we'll deal with it in the morning.

Because she doesn't want to stop.

The way she moves in my lap, clings to my shirt, and releases those needy little whimpers against my lips, God knows I don't want to stop, either.

She is *everything.*

And I want to give it to her, even when I have no fucking clue how to do it.

My cock aches, and she tries to shift her position, but her belly prevents her from moving or changing the angles. A little frustrated moan falls from her mouth to mine, and I angle her head to better collect those little noises.

I want them all.

I *need* them as much as I do her.

But I don't know what to do, how to make this work for her, how not to hurt her or the baby and still give her what she seeks.

The helplessness mixes with her frustration, turning our movements and kisses even more frenzied until she tears her mouth from mine. Wild, lust-hazed eyes meet mine, and she nudges my shoulders.

I follow her command, falling back on the bed and the tangled sheets still askew from her dream.

Camille slides her leg across me, fully straddling my hips and settling her heat only covered by thin, silky panties directly over my hard cock. A searing blaze spreads out from where our bodies touch, seeping into the marrow of my bones and igniting a firestorm in my heart.

In the moonlight filtering in from the window, her dark hair falling around her face as she stares down at me, Camille is the most stunning creature I've ever seen.

I take her face in my palm, brushing my thumb across her pinkened cheek. "You're so fucking beautiful."

Her entire body shudders against me, making her grind against my hard length in a way that has me near the brink of my restraint. My fingers itch to touch every part of her. To feel her smooth, soft skin against mine. To explore the woman who has so easily stolen my heart.

She shifts back slightly and glides her hand along the hem of my shirt, urging me to shift up enough to let her pull it off. Her appreciative gaze roams over my chest and stomach almost greedily in a way she didn't allow herself to earlier. Every muscle tightens in response to her assessment, my body primed and ready for whatever Camille decides she wants.

I'm more than happy to give her all of me.

As far as I'm concerned, the woman already owns me.

Her eyes drift to my cock straining against the confines of my jeans, and her lips slide open on a little mewl that makes me twitch in anticipation.

She grasps the hem of her tank top, gliding it up over the smooth expanse of her stomach and freeing her breasts before she drops it off the side of the bed.

Hell...

All the air rushes from my lungs, my hands fisting in the rumpled sheets beneath me.

Good God.

I have *always* thought Camille was beautiful. Her beauty stunned me speechless almost from the beginning. But seeing her like this—her perfect, full breasts, just begging for me to touch them, to taste them, her swollen belly, her glowing skin in the moonlight...I don't stand a chance of maintaining control.

Fuck.

Like the young, inexperienced virgin I am, I almost come on the spot just looking at her.

Only by a razor-thin thread of sheer willpower do I manage to wrangle my body back under control. But when her soft, warm fingers slide to undo the buttons on my jeans, I catch her hand, stalling her progress.

I have to give her one more chance to stop before she does something she might regret later. Something I never would've rushed her into. Something I never intended to happen at all.

Her eyes lift to meet mine, and she closes her other hand over mine and squeezes.

This is what she wants.

Maybe it's more than want. Maybe she needs it. Needs me. Needs the connection and the safety and the release she'll find from all the uncertainty and demons chasing her.

I could never deny her that.

Literally, *anything* this woman asks of me is hers.

She moves off my thighs so I can shove down my pants and boxers and kick them off, freeing my cock and giving her free rein over my body without the fear that held her back in my room.

Was that really only a handful of hours ago?

It seems like a lifetime since she last touched me. Since I felt her wetness on my fingers and saw her come undone as she rode my hand.

Thinking about it makes my cock ache, and I lower myself down fully as Camille tugs off her underwear and completely exposes herself to me in the silvery moonlight.

Good God...

An appreciative groan falls from my lips as she starts to swing her leg over me again, and I grasp her hips, helping to guide her when she stills, hovering over my waist.

Her brow furrows, her gaze clearing for a moment, long enough to see the concern darkening the blue when all I want to see there is the same unbridled lust overwhelming me. "Your back..."

I push up with one hand and tunnel my other in her hair to drag her down as close as she can get, pushing myself up until our mouths can meet in a searing kiss intent on silencing her trepidation.

If I let her spiral down that rabbit hole, she'll never come back up.

We'll never get back to *this* place without me assuring her that she won't hurt me.

By the time I pull away, we're both panting, and my cock throbs hard enough to warn me I'm close to reaching that limit of restraint. "The last fucking thing I'm thinking about at this moment is my *back*. I'm fine...now tell me what you need."

She lowers her forehead against mine and releases a rush of warm breath that tickles my lips before she grasps my cock and aligns it, dragging the head through her slick core.

Fucking hell.

Heat slowly engulfs my entire world.

My hips twitch.

And she sinks down on me, her mouth falling open on a silent gasp as I drop my head to the mattress and release a groan that sounds far more animal than it does human.

"Sweet mother of God..." I grip her fleshy hips as she finally settles on me fully, cementing my cock deep inside her with our pelvises perfectly pressed together. Not a fucking hairsbreadth of space separating us. "Camille...I—"

Can't even talk.

I struggle to even form a coherent thought through the cloud of sheer bliss her hot, wet pussy has created around me.

She clenches around me and releases a little mewling sound that has my eyes drifting open again.

God, I hope I didn't hurt her.

This is all so new.

So blissful and confusing.

My body urges me to move, to end this erotic torture by finding my release, but I tamp down that urge and cling to her, fighting the spinning in my head to ask her if she's all right.

Before I can get a word to form at the back of my throat, her eyes flutter open to meet mine. "I'm okay." She nods, almost as if she's reading my mind and trying to convince me. "It's just, God..." A shiver rolls through her, and she squeezes my cock again. "You feel so damn good."

Thank. Fucking. God.

Instinct takes over, and I press my heels into the mattress, lifting my hips and somehow managing to get even farther into her, until the warm, slick comfort of her core completely cocoons me.

She moans, then braces her hands against my shoulders and starts to move. Her thighs clamp around mine, and she lifts herself agonizingly slowly, exposing my cock glistening in her arousal, then sinks back down, tightening around me with each inch she takes.

How do people do this?

Maintain control.

Keep a clear head when this is the hottest fucking thing I've ever seen in my entire life.

I grit my teeth, fighting against that tingle at the base of my spine and the tightening of my balls that warns I'm close to coming already.

No!

Not like this.

Not so fast.

Fuck...

She needs this.

She needs me.

She needs strong Dalton.

The one who helped her.

The one who told her he would give her anything she wanted or needed.

Not the young, inexperienced Dalton, who can sometimes make impulsive decisions without fully thinking them through and lets his emotions take control.

If I let that happen now, I'll only disappoint her, leave her wanting and desperate without any way to fix it.

And I *refuse* to be that to her.

I slow my breathing, dig my fingers into her hips, and help her move and sustain the rhythm she seems to need.

She angles herself forward, grinding down against my pelvis when she reaches the hilt. Her breaths fall from her parted lips in harsh rushes of warm air, her fingers curling into my skin as she pushes down so hard on my shoulders that it feels like there might be bruises there tomorrow.

I'd fucking welcome it.

This woman could mark me anyway she wants to, and I'd let her and then find a way to make it permanent.

Because what tonight has made abundantly clear, besides the fact that I'm putty in Camille's hands, is that I am utterly, hopelessly, completely in love with her. There is nothing she could do that could drive me away or make me question this all-consuming emotion as I watch her ride me.

She rolls her hips almost violently, her belly brushing my abs with every forward swirl and downward grind, and I bite down so hard to keep myself from immediately emptying inside her that my teeth hurt.

Every muscle stiffens and begins to shake, like I'm on the verge of shattering, no matter how badly I try to cling to power over my reaction to her. The longer I watch her, the darker the flush that spreads across her breasts, up her neck, and across her cheeks, the harder it becomes to control what my body wants in favor of what *she* needs.

Because fuck, she's beautiful riding me like this.

Taking what she wants.

What only *I* can give her in this moment.

I feather my fingers across her warm cheek, and her eyes flicker open to meet mine, half hooded under thick, dark lashes. Clouded by the same lust and need I'm feeling.

She keeps gliding up and down my length and grinding against me, and I can see her frustration and feel it in every jerky movement.

"Tell me what to do, Camille..."

If she doesn't help me, I can't help her.

That utter sense of inadequacy I've tried not to let overwhelm me at times when it comes to her threatens to rear its ugly head. Especially when she clenches her jaw and shakes her head, squeezing her eyes closed again, like she's fighting it and me.

Maybe she is.

Her body or her mind are unwilling to let go of something still clinging to her and holding her back.

I drag her down to me again, pushing up on one elbow and meeting her halfway so I can ghost my lips over hers and beg. "Please, Camille." I kiss her hard and deep, slamming my mouth to hers greedily, and she moans as she keeps moving, keeps grinding, keeps seeking it, even as her body trembles as if she's battling some unseen force working against her. "Tell me what you need and stop fighting it. Let me give you it. Let me give you everything."

She whimpers against my lips and drags her head back, grinding against me more aggressively, her short nails biting deeper into my skin. "I need—"

Her breath catches.

But somehow, I *know*.

Just like I knew the very first moment I saw her that she was going to change my life.

―――――

CAMILLE

My body trembles.

Each fiber of my being wound so tightly that it feels like I might shatter with every roll of my hips and decadent sink down around Dalton's immaculate cock.

The pleasure that courses through my veins and over my heated skin threatens to consume me and bring me to the ecstasy I'm so frantically chasing.

But.

I.

Just.

Can't.

Get.

There.

I can't grasp that bright light that's hovering just out of reach. That relief, that release I need so much taunts me. Toys with me by sending flickers of blinding heat out from where our bodies connect. But never giving me more.

My frustration grows with each jerky movement of my hips as much as the promised ecstasy does.

And Dalton *wants* to help so damn badly.

His dogged determination to learn what it takes, to get me off before he finds his own bliss couldn't be sweeter.

But it isn't *sweet* I need right now.

I need—

Dalton squeezes my hips, digging his fingers into the flesh there almost painfully, then braces his feet on the bed and thrusts up into me as I come down.

"Fuck!"

The word tumbles from my lips on a rush of air as pleasure spirals wildly.

Yes.

THAT!

"Shift back."

I open my eyes to meet his. "Wh-what?"

He tries to angle my hips back, and it finally clicks what he's asking but not why. I *need* that friction, that angle...

But the insistence in his gaze makes me pull my hands from where they're braced against his shoulders and lean back, allowing cool air to slip under my belly and across the place where we're joined.

Dalton slides his hand down across my stomach, pausing with his palm pressed fully against it. His eyes drop there as he caresses me reverently, skimming the rough callouses across my smooth skin in a way that causes tears to pool in my eyes.

But I refuse to let them fall.

I refuse to let them ruin this moment.

The fact that he looks at me with so much yearning, so much appreciation, so much love, and seems to love *both* my children the same way makes it almost impossible to breathe.

His hand slips lower, and his thumb finds the apex of my thighs, brushing across my clit.

I twitch against him, losing my rhythm, but he holds me steady with one hand at my hip and continues to thrust up into me.

Hitting exactly the right spot.

Over and over again.

I gasp as he increases the pressure and speed of the swirl against the most sensitive place of my body. My pussy ripples and clenches around him, clinging to the feeling of having him buried so deeply.

Right fucking there...

"Fuck, Camille. I'm—"

He's close, and so am I now.

Dalton gave me exactly what I wanted, exactly what I needed, without even having to voice it. Just like when he arrived and saved me from crumbling alone into the dark abyss I had found myself in on the homestead, he's bringing me to the light now.

It finally bursts through me.

An epic explosion of pleasure that makes me buck on top of him, clasping his cock as I try to keep moving through the seemingly endless, frantic spasms.

A low, deep groan rumbles through his body under me, and he continues to stroke me through my orgasm with his cock and his fingers. He plunges deep one more time and releases a strangled moan and goes completely rigid, drawn as tight as a bowstring as he comes deep inside me.

My orgasm finally fades, and I sag forward, trying to catch myself with an elbow on his chest. He pulls his hand away from between my legs and wraps it around my back, rolling us onto our sides, facing each other.

We both try to find our breaths.

My belly presses into his as it heaves with his effort to slow his heart, the same way I am.

Calloused fingertips trail across my temple and drift down over my lips. "Are you all right?"

That was incredible.

It felt like I momentarily lost six months of pain. All that anguish and torture disappeared in only a few minutes in Dalton's arms. But the words to express that to him won't leave my lips.

Instead, everything I pushed down before I kissed him threatens to bubble back up.

Guilt washes over me just as quickly as my orgasm did, and my body tenses instead of relaxing into his arms. I try to shift away from him even though he's still partially inside me, but he holds me to him with his hand at my lower back.

"Open your eyes, Camille. Look at me."

I struggle to do as he asks, afraid to see disappointment or worse in his gaze, but it's too hard to deny him.

My lids flutter open, and the compassion in the emerald green staring back at me instantly helps melt away some of the icy chill threatening to overtake me.

His fingertips move to my chin, holding me there, preventing me from looking away. "Tell me you're okay."

I nod. "I am."

He shakes his head and brings it closer to mine to lower his lips to my forehead. "I can see that you're not."

"I'm just..."

Confused.

Lost.

I don't know how to describe it without hurting him, without destroying the few moments of peace we have managed to find in each other's arms, without ruining everything—our friendship, the future I have on the mountain with Davey and this baby, a potential for one with Dalton.

God, is that what I've done?

Did I ruin everything?

The tears start to burn in my eyes, and he pulls his head back from mine and brushes them away the moment they trickle down my cheek. "Why are you crying?"

"I just feel like maybe..."

I close my eyes again, unable to look at him when my

mind is such a dark spiral of uncertainty. He's so strong. So confident in what he wants.

Why can't I be that?

"Maybe what, Camille?"

God, this shouldn't be so hard.

I force my eyes open to meet his again, and understanding lies in their depths without me even saying anything.

He gives me a soft smile, one that's as kind and genuine as he has always been, then leans forward and presses his lips against mine so gently it almost makes the tears come harder. "It's okay for you to love him and want this at the same time, Camille. The two things are not mutually exclusive."

My heart seizes with his words.

How did he know?

Because he's Dalton.

Because he always seems to just understand what I need to hear.

He seems to just understand *me*.

It's one of the reasons we've ended up like this, because things are just *easy* with him. They have been since the minute he walked onto the property and I aimed that gun at him.

It shouldn't have been, not with the way I attempted to ice him out, how I tried to decline his assistance, my vain struggle to keep him at arm's length. Yet, slowly but surely, he managed to work his way under my skin and into my heart.

With how he loves Pops.

With how much he loves this mountain and the people on it and in the town below.

With how he loves Davey and *me*.

He dips his head to catch my gaze again. "Okay?"

One sandy-blond brow rises, and I nod, then bury my face against his chest. He tunnels his hand in my hair and holds me there, rubbing his other palm up and down my bare spine in a soothing motion that sends goosebumps skittering across my skin and makes me shiver in the best way possible.

His touch disappears for just long enough for him to reach down and grab the nearest edge of the sheet and tug it up over us. Then he presses a kiss to the top of my head and resumes the trickling fingers. "Are you cold?"

I shake my head. "No." The heat of his body could keep me warm forever. And I want that more than anything right now. I lift my head to search his face for any sort of reservation I've been fearing. "Dalton?"

"What?"

It seems so stupid.

Especially after the warning he gave me earlier about what would happen if he ended up in this bed with me.

Because he was right.

But the thought of having to fall asleep again without this is enough to make me ask.

"Please don't go back and sleep on the couch."

The corners of his mouth curl up slowly, amusement lighting his eyes. His hold on me tightens, and he adjusts his hips slightly, easing even further into me, as much as the position and the baby between us will allow. "Okay. I won't..."

I can't fight the grin pulling at my lips, and I score my nails lightly across his hard pecs, around the sides of his hips, and to where the scars mar his otherwise flawless skin. "I wouldn't want your back to hurt."

He chuckles low.

The vibration from his chest rolls through me, and his cock gets even harder inside me. I groan at the sensation, my body tingling with the memory of the first release, and clench around him.

He makes that deep rumbling sound again and crushes his lips to mine. "I told you before, and I'll tell you again, Camille, whatever you need, anytime, anywhere, always, I'll give it to you."

Chapter Fourteen

DALTON

Normally, on a beautiful fall day like this, when the leaves are just starting to change and the cool breeze washes over me, being able to ride Apollo would wipe away worries.

Anything bothering me would disappear the harder I pushed him.

The faster we run, the further I would move from any problems.

But not today.

I'm riding *toward* the very thing that has caused the tension. Searching for an explanation when what I might find could make things worse.

This isn't a joyride to take in the pristine wilderness and allow Apollo to unleash his restlessness and power.

I'm out here because somebody *violated* the mountain in a way that could threaten my life—and those of the only people I care about.

Being in these woods means I'm not there with *her*, with *them*, and leaving Camille and Davey with Pops this morning took every ounce of strength I had.

I can't even count the number of times I looked back at them on the cabin porch before I led Apollo into the trees toward the lake to try to track the men who were here yesterday. Or the number of times I've considered turning around and going back, regardless of whether I've completed the task I've set out to accomplish.

Deep down, I know Pops will protect them.

That everything will be *fine* while I'm gone, but leaving was made a thousand times harder because of the looks Camille gave me all morning before we left her place to come here.

Watching me out of the corner of her eye.

Staring when I was talking with Davey and she thought I wouldn't notice.

Chewing on her bottom lip as she moved around the kitchen, making breakfast like she's still unsure about what happened last night and considering what it means.

I can't say I blame her.

Not really.

I could never regret it.

Not in a million years.

Not in this fucking lifetime or any other that might come.

But *she* has every reason to—first and foremost because she still loves Dave with all her heart and probably always will.

Every word of what I said to her last night was true, though.

I could never be jealous of him. Being with Dave is part of what made Camille into the woman I've fallen in love with. His love for her helped make her strong and resilient and all the things I find so fascinating about her. And he's Davey's and that little girl's father. He's the reason they're all *here.* The reason I might have a chance for something I never imagined could ever be possible.

If there were a way, I would thank him for this tremendous gift and beg him to find me worthy of it.

Things may feel very uncertain right now—both when it comes to the mountain and what's happening between Camille and me—but just like with the pain that's become my old friend, it's temporary.

My feelings for her aren't.

If she still needs time, I'm not going anywhere.

I'll be right here when she's ready for what I can give her. I just wish I didn't have to ride off so early this morning when talking to her about it might have helped ease some of her insecurities and worries.

She'll be there when you get home.

That's the only thing that keeps pushing me forward through the thick forest to the lake.

Seeing its smooth, glassy surface, undisturbed and completely peaceful the way God intended it, all I want is to turn around and head back to her.

So I can assure her it will all be okay.

So I can hold her in my arms again.

So I can wipe away that uncertainty furrowing her brow.

So I can tell Camille that she and Davey and her unborn daughter are safe with me and always will be—no matter what happens between us.

But I can't make *that* promise until I do what I came here to accomplish.

I push Apollo into a gallop and let him race along the

shore until he reaches the spot Pop said he saw the two men —on the far western side of the glacial lake near where two large boulders jut out into the water from the natural beach entrance.

What the hell were they doing here?

If they were taking water samples or doing a survey of the clearing the lake sits in, then my first inclination to believe it was that asshole lawyer and his "interested party" is probably true.

There wouldn't be any other reason to be messing around up here and to run. They were either looking to make plans for the land that doesn't belong to them or for a way to force us to sell.

Either possibility makes me twist the reins hard enough for the leather to bite into my palms.

I welcome the pain, though.

It reminds me of my purpose and to move quickly to get back to the woman who can erase that pain.

What should be throbbing through my back after almost collapsing yesterday barely registers anymore. All because of Camille's touch and what she has done for my body and my soul. Offering me the kind of acceptance and affection I never thought I'd find from another person.

"Whoa, boy."

I slow Apollo and finally pull him to a stop, then slide off and make my way down the pebbled beach, letting him graze in the long grass in the clearing that won't be accessible in only a few short weeks once the snow comes.

The entire ride here, I imagined finding some glaring evidence of the intrusion. But there isn't any sign of anyone having been here. Only the pristine shoreline and crystal-clear water. The birds flying overhead in the breeze. The smell of the fire from the cabin drifting in the same wind.

Nothing out of place.

Not even a single footprint or track in the mud at the edge of the bank.

Dammit.

I scan the trees in the direction Pop said they fled, but instead of climbing back onto Apollo, I grab his reins and lead him that way, surveying for any signs of human activity or anything they might've dropped.

Even the smallest clue or tiniest confirmation could give us some ammunition against whoever might be coming after us.

Though Pops still insists he has this "under control," that doesn't dissuade me from feeling like we need the biggest arsenal possible if they *do* come—physically or otherwise.

I reach the tree line where the trunks are packed so densely that there's no way Apollo will be able to get through. "Wait here, buddy." He whinnies his annoyance, and I rub his neck as I tie him to one of the branches so he doesn't wander off too far. "I'll be back."

The quicker I make my sweep, the quicker I can get back to the cabin.

I have no intention of lingering any longer than necessary to ensure the men are long gone and gather whatever I can that might identify who was involved.

The woods thicken even more as I head down the most obvious route. Though there isn't a true trail, only places where there's enough room between the towering trunks for people to slip between, broken twigs lead the way.

Proving the old man right.

They definitely came this way.

But where the hell did they go?

231

We're so far up the mountain that they couldn't have come all the way on foot.

It takes hours to reach James Creek in a truck—or car, if you dare attempt that gravel and incline in one—from our place, double that by horse, which they couldn't have led through this part of the forest, anyway.

Which means they had to have another mode of transportation.

I push my way through the trees, stepping over fallen logs, broken branches that they hastily snapped on their way out, and pick my way down the slope, away from the lake and both our and Camille's property.

Another hour passes of following their obvious route before the trees start to thin, and I reach the small clearing that always has the most magnificent wildflowers every spring and summer.

It was one of Mom's favorite places.

Somewhere she would come with *her* mother before she passed and left Mom alone with Pops, who never had time to trek down here with her, too busy running everything else to actually enjoy the mountain he owns.

Memories of running through the field with her, bright buds in hand to bring back to Pops and Dad, flow through my head, simultaneously making my heart warm and my eyes burn.

I only have to take a few steps into the familiar open space to know how the two men got up here—deep tire marks mar the otherwise pristine clearing, moving from one side across it and toward the end that would be closest to the road coming up the mountain.

The fuckers came up on ATVs, then they hiked up to the lake and back.

Which means I'm likely not going to find anything

useful, nothing that could help tell us who they are or why they were here. Certainly not a way to track them beyond here.

Once they hit the road, they no doubt loaded up into a trailer and used a big truck to disappear themselves and their equipment out of the area quickly.

Motherfuckers.

Not only have they invaded our land, but they've shaken Camille's sense of safety when she's already faced enough for ten lifetimes.

That nightmare that hit her last night wasn't random.

She had it because of what happened at the lake.

I dismissed the contents of it easily last night—both because I didn't believe it was actually possible anyone could have hurt Dave and because if I even remotely entertained it *was* possible, it would've sent Camille into a further downward spiral.

But now, standing here, it seems a lot less crazy a proposition.

They could have gotten to her property the same way they made it to the lake, all without anyone ever knowing if they were careful about where they left the ATVs to ensure no one heard the engines.

Is it really possible?

Even if they did an autopsy, the type of blunt force trauma inflicted by someone else using a weapon could easily be mistaken for a horse kick...and that's assuming they even bothered with the examination when everyone assumed the most obvious cause of his death.

A shiver rolls through me that has nothing to do with the chilly breeze lifting the branches and rustling the leaves all around me.

Something flutters in my peripheral vision—a flash of

white that definitely isn't natural up here. At least, not until the snow starts.

Squatting, I snag the tiny piece of paper before it gets carried away with another gust. I narrow my gaze, trying to read the letters on the scrap that appears to have been torn off of a larger document.

The familiar handwriting taunts me.

Rage floods my veins as I shove to my feet and stomp back through the woods, likely scaring off any and all wildlife by not bothering to try to hide my presence like I normally would.

I can't.

Not when I have the proof in my fucking hand that I was *right* to be so worried. Not when I'm starting to believe that maybe Camille's nightmare wasn't just that.

Maybe she did see something else that day, *someone* else, or maybe it *is* just her subconscious.

The mere possibility that it could be the former is enough to make me rush faster than I should through the dense underbrush.

By the time I make it back to the property, after pushing Apollo as fast and as hard as I dared in the open areas that allowed for it, I'm vibrating with pure wrath.

My entire body feels like a rattlesnake, coiled and ready to strike.

I unsaddle Apollo and get him back into his stall with a treat, then stalk up to the house, pound up the steps and across the porch, and yank open the door.

Pops jumps slightly where he sits in the chair just inside, and his gaze locks on me. "Did you find something?"

I give him a sharp nod and step forward, slipping the piece of paper into his hand as I kick the door shut behind me with a boom that reverberates through the cabin.

He glances down at it, lifting his glasses to his forehead and pulling the paper closer. His eyes widen. "Shit."

Camille steps out of the kitchen with a flour-splattered apron around her, her hair twisted up in a messy bun, several strands falling across her cheeks. The amber undertones glint in the light as she steps forward.

God, she's beautiful.

My throat dries just looking at her, but it can't quell the fury roaring through me right now.

Nor my fear for *her*.

For what this potentially means for all of us.

Her brow furrows as she takes in my agitated state, and she glances behind her, then disappears into the kitchen. She reappears a second later, sans apron, brushing her hands on her leggings and leaving little streaks of white across them as she makes her way over to us. "What is it? Did you find something?"

Pops and I exchange a look.

She presses her lips together and steps forward, hissing under her breath to keep Davey, who must be in the kitchen, from hearing her. "Do *not* keep things from me."

"I'm not." I run a hand through my too-long hair. "It's just—"

Pops holds it out for her to examine, and I know the second she understands what it means because her eyes widen and her back stiffens.

Camille hands it back to Pops and glances over at me, a thousand questions swimming in her blue eyes.

"You and I need to talk."

She nods, appearing just as shaken as I was when I found it.

I reach out and take her hand, tugging her toward the door.

This is not a conversation I'm going to have anywhere Davey might be in earshot.

———

CAMILLE

Dalton leads me away from the cabin with a firm grip on my hand and sure strides that carry the same tension his rigid body does.

Everything about the man screams, "leave me alone," yet he pulls me with him, seemingly intent on getting me somewhere private. And quickly.

The afternoon sun hangs low on the horizon, a chilly breeze wrapping around us as we cross the yard in front of the house and cut toward the outbuildings.

"Where are we going?"

He squeezes my fingers with his and slows his steps so I'm not struggling to keep up with his pace, considering I mostly waddle these days. "The barn."

I can understand why he might not want to have certain conversations in the cabin with Davey sure to be all over him the moment he realized he had returned, but the way he vibrates with anger makes me wonder if there's more than just the piece of paper.

Something he didn't even tell Pops.

Did he find something else?

Something he left out here somewhere that he wants to show me but keep concealed from his grandfather?

There's a second option.

Dalton could want to talk about something completely separate from what that tiny slip of paper could mean.

He may want to delve into what happened last night.

And that's a topic I'm not completely sure I'm *ready* to leap into yet.

He keeps walking, tugging on my hand gently to follow, and leads me into the now-familiar barn. Past the animal stalls, allowing me to run my free hand over Apollo's snout briefly. All the way to the tack room at the back where they store various tools and the infamous fishing rods whose use led to the unsettling discovery of strangers on the mountain in the first place.

It's an odd place to want to talk, but Dalton urges me in with a gentle hand on my lower back, letting his touch linger for a few extra moments, the heat of his palm seeping through my Henley and warming me from the chill the short walk brought on.

Once we're inside, he nudges the door closed and immediately starts to pace the small space.

He rubs at the back of his neck, craning his head from side to side as he burns a path on the already-worn floorboards with the incessant back and forth.

Each time he passes me, I hold my breath, waiting for him to say something. Anticipating an explanation for why he needed me to come out here with him instead of talking with Pops privately in his office once we got Davey sufficiently distracted by something.

Unless this isn't about the paper at all.

Maybe it's about us.

But he doesn't say anything.

He just lets the tension build with each pass. His heavy boots thump on the wood in a steady tempo that starts to drive me mad. The longer it goes on, the antsier I become, unable to stand still myself, shifting on my feet both because of the nervous energy he's putting off and the discomfort I'm feeling this late in my pregnancy.

After what feels like an eternity but is likely only a handful of minutes, I finally can't take it anymore. "Does that slip of paper mean what I think it does?"

It would certainly explain why he's so worked up, why it appears like he's about ready to either implode or explode.

In all these months we've spent at least a portion of almost every day together, I've never seen him like this.

So agitated.

So off balance.

So close to losing control.

He's always so calm, facing each problem logically until he finds the most reasonable solution and implements it effectively. It's how he has managed to make so much progress at my place while splitting his time.

But this isn't the same man who left the cabin this morning, not the one who held me all night and well beyond when he should have risen from bed this morning.

And his distress is starting to make what I thought was a *normal* amount of worry on my part about the discovery on the paper seem woefully inadequate.

Dalton rubs at his temple, and I lean back against the old wooden table that runs along one wall, resting my right hand on my belly, where the baby seems intent on moving around and making her presence known during what appears to be a conversation that's going to be very intense.

He pauses mid-step, glancing down at my palm pressed over her tiny foot. "Are you okay?"

I nod and smile, trying to encourage him to relax by faking that I am. "She's just kicking."

His lips twitch slightly, but instead of reaching out to

feel it himself like I had hoped, he resumes pacing, alternately digging his fingers into the base of his skull and forehead like he's trying to work through and process something he can't quite wrap his head around.

"Will you please tell me what's going on?" I release an exasperated sigh. "I mean, I think I understand, but—"

He pauses his movement. "You *do* understand."

That handwriting was so distinct.

So recognizable.

He knows even *I* would be able to place it right away.

"Okay, but is it possible it was left up there at some other time?"

Dalton shakes his head, lacing his hands at the back of his neck. "I don't think so. There wouldn't be any reason for him to have been down there. It's just an empty clearing. And a tiny piece of paper like that wouldn't have stayed *right there* for long."

He knows this mountain better than anyone except Pops. So, if he says there isn't any other reason for *that* particular slip of paper to have ended up in the clearing except for if it was brought by the two men who were at the lake, then I believe him.

"Shit, no wonder you're so rattled."

"Shouldn't I be?" He releases his grip on his neck and lets his arms fall to his sides. "You know what this means. You're not safe here. You and Davey need to go."

My back stiffens, and his plea from only yesterday— *God, was it really only twenty-four hours ago that I sat next to that tub?*—rushes back so clearly it's as if he just said it. That insistence that I never consider leaving the mountain. If this is what he's been contemplating, it would explain the nervous energy. "Go where?"

He stops pacing and approaches me, stopping close enough that I can see the tension in his jaw, his muscles twitching under his T-shirt. "Somewhere safe until all this blows over, until I can get it resolved, until I can bring you and Davey back here, where you're supposed to be."

Where we're supposed to be...

Such a simple statement that is anything but.

"Where's that?"

Last night was incredible—in spite of all the reasons it shouldn't have been—and when I woke this morning, it finally felt like things were settling. There was this sense of belonging, stronger than I've experienced since Dave died.

But we never got a chance to discuss what any of it meant or where my children and I belong in all this.

Dalton reaches out and slides his hands along my waist, pressing against me right over where my little girl was just kicking. "Wherever I am."

My heart skips a beat, and I draw in a long, slow breath. The finality and surety with which he made that statement isn't the kind you hear the day after you sleep with someone for the first time. "You know, you kind of went from one to one hundred pretty quickly."

He presses a kiss to my forehead. "Does that scare you?"

I open my mouth to answer "yes," because *anyone* would be overwhelmed and terrified by a man saying something like that so damn fast.

But the word won't come out.

Because it isn't true.

We may have only met a handful of months ago, but it feels like I've known Dalton and Pops my entire life. Like they've always been a part of my every day. All the things we do together—working, eating, playing, laughing—are just so natural.

240

It feels like a *family*.

I shake my head. "No."

He grins, some of the tension melting away from his handsome face. "Does it scare you that it *doesn't* scare you?"

A little laugh slips out from my lips, and I nod. "Yes. Is it that obvious?"

Here I thought I did a pretty damn good job of keeping my reaction contained.

He brushes a stray strand of hair behind my ear. "It is to me because I watch you all the time. The way you move. The way you handle Davey and Pops. All the little expressions you make when you're concentrating on something or upset...or angry. I have your beautiful face memorized—the thousands of looks you give me. I can read them all."

His confidence permeates his grin, and seeing the playfulness return when only moments ago he was so agitated makes me relax against the table.

I rest my hands on his chest, fingering one of the buttons as I hold his evergreen gaze. "And what am I saying now?"

A smirk pulls at his lips. "That you want me to kiss you."

Damn.

He is smug.

But he's also right.

"You can read me well."

Because I *do* want him to.

All day, my body has thrummed with the memory of the way he touched me last night, the way he held me, how perfectly we fit together and how goddamn incredible it was to be loved by him that way.

It shouldn't have been that easy, shouldn't have been that good, considering the emotional toll it had on me.

But he ensured it would be.

He took care of me just like he promised, and now, it's my turn to take care of him when he's the one rattled.

I slide my hand to the back of his neck and tangle my fingers in the thick hair there, drawing him closer to me until my lips can brush over his. "I'm sorry if I've been giving you mixed signals. This is just a lot. *You're* a lot."

He kisses the corner of my mouth, then across my cheek all the way to my ear. "I am, and I'm sorry if I've done anything to make you feel like I'm pushing you into something you're not ready for."

My hand tightens in his shirt, the other tugging the sandy-blond silky strands in it until he returns his gaze to mine. "No." I shake my head. "I mean, there are definitely parts of me that aren't prepared, that are trying to convince me to hold back, but I don't want to listen to those parts. Not when it feels so good not to."

"Jesus, Camille."

This kiss is long, slow, and deep.

A thorough exploration.

His tongue gliding along mine as if he's trying to memorize every bit of my mouth.

Strong fingers tighten on my hips as he tries to push closer, but my belly won't let him. I release a little frustrated groan, and he chuckles, kissing me again lightly and drawing back his head.

My pussy clenches at the need in his gaze and the heat that matches the fire burning through me now.

It was so much easier to blame it on the hormones in the beginning—and they may have played a role in finally sending me over this edge—but it's never been just that.

It's been Dalton.

What he does to me, what he does *for* me. How caring and kind, thoughtful and protective he is. How much I can feel the sincerity of every fucking word he has ever said to me.

He's never lied, never withheld information that he didn't think was to protect Davey or me. And that's what he's trying to do now by asking me to leave.

"You really want me to go?"

He shakes his head and kisses his way to my ear, where he sucks gently on the lobe, making my body twitch and my thighs clench against the throb between them. "No."

"Then I'll stay. I don't want you and Pops up here alone, either."

"Take Pops with you." Warm breath flutters over my skin, raising goosebumps. "It'll be safer for him away from the mountain."

I shake my head and tilt my neck, giving him better access as he explores it and the area behind my ear in a way that sends little jolts of pleasure through me.

His hand glides over my stomach, and he caresses me gently. The baby kicks against his hand, and I feel his lips curl into a smile against my cheek. "I know you want to stay, and God, I want you to be here every minute, but until this is resolved, I need you to go. I need to be able to concentrate and know you're safe. I don't want you to tell me where. I don't want to have that information. But when you come home, it'll be forever."

He draws his head back, and I release a pitiful sigh at how ridiculously fast I seem to have fallen for this man.

"This is what you need?"

Dalton nods, even though the pain in his gaze tells me it's the furthest from what he wants. "I promise it won't be for long. I have no intention of dragging this out..."

"Good, because even the thought of leaving the mountain, of leaving you..." I squeeze my eyes closed and shake my head. "I can't."

His hand slides lower and slips between my legs, rubbing the same way I taught him yesterday. "Then let me give you something else to think about."

Chapter Fifteen

DALTON

Camille glances around the tack room, her warm blue eyes swimming with interest and surprise. "Out *here*?"

I grin before I drop a quick kiss to her lips. "Would you prefer we go back up to the cabin and try to find some place where you'd have to be quiet?"

A pink flush rushes up her neck and over her cheeks, and she shakes her head, pulling her bottom lip between her teeth.

For such a confident, outspoken woman to be rendered speechless is a true accomplishment, and the fact that I am capable of it just by *suggesting* we have a repeat of last night makes pride swell in my chest.

"That's what I thought."

I reach for the waistband of her stretchy pants and gently slide them down over her stomach and to her ankles. Sliding my hands to her ass, I lift her onto the edge of the table and make quick work of her boots which hit the floor with two distinct *thunks* wherever I toss them.

In order to proceed with my plans, I need her spread wide open, and I tug off her pants and set them beside her, then press my palms against her inner thighs, urging them apart as she shudders under my touch.

My cock aches, pressed against the fly of my jeans so hard that it feels like I may end up with an imprint of the teeth on it by the time I finally free it from its confines.

I'm desperate for her in a way I never knew I *could* be for another person. Even last night, it was more controlled, a far more measured satisfaction of need.

This is something else entirely.

This is *desperation*.

Camille's eyes flare wide as I keep nudging her legs wider and wider until she's spread open completely before me. "What are you going to do?"

I let my focus drift to the apex of her thighs, and out here in the broad daylight streaming in from the small window, I can see her in all her glory. "Besides staring at the most exquisite part of the most gorgeous woman I've ever seen?"

Her hand drops to my shoulder and squeezes, and I slowly sink to my knees before I lift my gaze to meet hers.

Those pretty lips of hers part on a little, "Oh..." as she realizes my intent.

I don't bother fighting my grin as I slide my hands around the back of her thighs and adjust her to the edge of the table, giving me the perfect angle and height to finally taste her *everywhere*.

"Fuck, you're beautiful, Camille."

Her hands grip the old wood as she watches me

intently, her chest heaving rapidly even though I haven't touched her yet. At least not in the way I want to.

But just like yesterday, I am a complete rookie in the getting-my-woman-off-with-my-mouth department, and the last thing I want to do is fail at this.

"You're going to have to help me out here, Camille, because I'm fucking clueless about how to do this right."

She releases a little laugh, the table creaking as she adjusts her position to get more comfortable with her elbows behind her, supporting her weight. "You're not clueless; you're just—"

"I'm fucking clueless." I laugh as I dip my head closer, letting my warm breath flutter across her skin. "It's okay to say it. But I promise I'm a very fast learner..."

A humored huff floats down to me. "You certainly proved that last night."

I lift my head to raise a brow at her. "Did I now?"

Her cheeks flush even redder as I return my focus to her pussy, now glistening so beautifully with her arousal.

Jesus...

My mouth waters for what I've been fantasizing about tasting, and I lean in and glide my tongue across her.

The flavor of her need coats my mouth, and I groan as my cock throbs in appreciation of it. She gasps and grips the wood tight enough to make it creak again.

"Dalton..."

"Like that?"

I pull my head back and tip it to the side to see her face around her belly in this position. She nods vigorously, and the trembling of her thighs against my ears makes me grin again as I dip my head and do it again and again.

Exploring her.

Savoring her.

Memorizing how everything I do makes her react.

Like flicking the tip of my tongue across her clit...

Her hips buck off the table, and I reach up with my left hand and press it across her to help keep her down.

"So, basically, I should just do with my tongue what I did with my fingers and my cock?"

She mewls in that needy way that makes pre-cum eke out and wet the front of my jeans. "God, yes..."

If I thought everything else we've done was a test of my control, I greatly underestimated what it would be like to feast on Camille Bower.

I chuckle against her damp flesh, and she twitches slightly, her thighs tightening on the sides of my head.

She likes that.

Which means *I* like it.

A-fucking-lot.

I do it again, allowing the vibration to roll through her, and the force with which she pushes against my hold with her bowing hips makes me confident that I know exactly what she needs—even if I've never done this before.

What kind of a man would I be if I couldn't figure out how to get my woman off this way?

Not the kind I would want to be.

I slip a finger inside her, and she groans, her head dropping back against the wall behind the table hard enough to knock something off the shelf above her, sending it clattering to the floor beside me.

Her pussy squeezes around me, and my cock throbs at the memory of her doing that last night around *it*. My balls seize up, threatening to make me come in my pants like the inexperienced kid I am if I'm not more careful about where I let my thoughts go while I should be focused on *her*.

She tunnels a hand in my hair, tugging on the strands slightly as her hips begin to roll against my mouth.

I work her over, thrusting my finger inside her while I lash at her flesh and suck her clit between my lips.

Her movements eventually find a rhythm I match, letting her take the lead.

Showing me how she likes it by her body's responses.

The quivers.

The whimpers.

The way her pussy clenches around me, seeking...

Her head shakes from side to side, almost frantically.

She needs more.

I slip another finger inside her, spreading her wider, and she groans—an agonizingly sexual sound I feel all the way through every nerve in my body.

I've never tasted anything so sweet, so satisfying, as her, or experienced anything as gratifying as the knowledge that I'm about to make her come.

That I'm doing this to her.

That I'm giving it to her.

Her body starts to tremble violently, and the old, uneven table rattles on its legs. "Curl your fingers..."

I do as she instructs, curving them deep inside of her and dragging my fingertips along the walls of her pussy as I withdraw. A strangled moan fills the room, and I suck her clit between my lips hard while flicking my tongue across it.

Camille stills and cries out as her orgasm slams into her.

Her hips grind against my face, pussy clasping around my fingers, and the wash of her sweet release flows down my throat.

God, I could drown in this woman and go happily.

But right now, I only want one thing, and that's to be

inside her, to feel this all over again, this time around my cock.

When she finally sags back, her body lax and sated, I pull my head and hand away and climb to my feet.

She lies panting on the table, hooded gaze following my every move as I slide my hands around her back to tug her up to me, so I can press my lips against hers.

Her arms loop around my neck, and she entangles her fingers in my hair, clutching me to her the best she can, allowing me to devour her mouth the same I just did her pussy.

I finally slow the kiss, drawing away long enough to search her face for any signs of distress or—hopefully—bliss. "How did I do?"

Camille grins lazily. "Fucking magnificent."

The compliment shouldn't make me preen like a fucking peacock, but it does.

Warmth floods my chest, and I shift away from her. At this angle, with as big as her belly's gotten, there's no way this will work and allow her to be comfortable on that table.

Stepping back, I gently ease her off the edge until her feet hit the floor. She wobbles slightly, her hands grasping my upper arms to keep herself upright on shaky legs.

I brush my lips over her ear, enjoying the little shiver of anticipation that rolls through her. "Turn around."

Her eyes flare, and that blush creeps up her neck and over her cheeks again as her mouth falls open. But she doesn't hesitate. She releases her grip on me and gives me her back, pressing her hands flat against the table, then leaning forward onto her elbows.

I move in behind her and press against her bare skin, hot even through the confines of my jeans that feel about five sizes too small at the moment.

There is nothing about this woman that isn't stunning, but bent over like this, with her lush ass and glistening pussy in the air in offering to me, I don't think I've ever seen anything more beautiful.

If I could take a picture to capture this moment forever, I would carry it with me everywhere, but a mental snapshot will have to do for now.

Though I can guarantee it's been seared into my memory like an erotic tattoo I will never want to remove.

I lean over her, kissing along the back of her neck to her ear where I nip at the lobe and make her shiver. "You tell me if this is too much, too hard, if I'm hurting you or the baby."

She shakes her head. "You won't."

Sliding my hand around her neck, I force her head back until our eyes meet. "You'll tell me."

It isn't up for debate.

I appreciate her faith in me, but I don't have the experience to know if what my body will want me to do is what I *should* be in this position or her condition.

She nods, and I reach between us and unzip my pants, freeing my aching cock from the constrictive prison. I shove the fabric down only to mid-thigh, unwilling to wait even the few extra seconds it would take to get them all the way off before I align with her slick heat.

I push in on a long, slow glide, giving her time to accept me, to adjust.

Fuck, this angle, this position...

My balls seize up again, and I grit my teeth and still myself because if I move even another fraction of an inch, I'm going to come instantly.

Camille squeezes around me, only half inside her, and

glances over her shoulder at me in question. Her body trembles under my hands at her hips. "Dalton?"

"I...need...a second."

She clamps down harder, a whimper falling from her lips and striking me square in that spot in my chest that belongs only to her. "I need you. Now."

Her words snap the last thread of my restraint, and my control slips as I push into her all the way, until her ass presses against my pelvis and my cock is buried to the hilt.

"Fucking hell, Camille."

I drop my hands down on top of hers on the table, entwining our fingers, and burying my face against her neck. Her orange blossom scent invades my choppy breaths as I draw my hips back and slowly plunge into her again.

She releases a strangled cry, and I immediately freeze my movements.

"No!" A keening whimper comes from her parted lips. "Keep going."

Camille is strong.

Determined.

She can take so much more than I ever give her credit for.

Thank God, because I feel like my control is about to slip even more.

———

CAMILLE

Each thrust of Dalton's hips propels him deeper, rocking me against the rickety table. He seems more confident than I am that it will continue to hold our weight.

His fingers twined with mine tighten on top of it, and he

brushes his lips along the column of my exposed neck until he makes it to my ear, leaving goosebumps pebbling across my skin. "You're. So. Fucking. Beautiful, Camille."

He punctuates each word with a drive of his hips, and they race through me like a wildfire, threatening to sear me from the inside out with the intensity.

I squeeze around his cock in response, my body struggling to process the blustering flames liquifying me at my core where our bodies connect. He groans his approval, his chest rumbling against my back, and he pushes into me even harder.

Stretching me to the brink of what I can take.

Filling me completely and still finding a way to seek more.

But he would never hurt me or the baby.

I know that even if he doesn't.

Given his question earlier, his *demand* that I let him know if it's too much, I don't think he does believe he'll know when that line not to cross appears. Yet last night proved that he not only recognizes it but will never make that jump across it.

I trust him completely with everything.

Our safety.

Our lives.

And even what's left of my heart.

What he said to me last night rings in my ears as loudly as the slap of our bodies coming together in the intense rhythm he's set.

You can love him and want this at the same time...

It was like he was speaking directly to my soul when he said those words. As if he could see everything I had been struggling with for months when it came to my growing feelings for him and the fact that my heart still yearned for Dave.

God knows I want them both.

I can never stop loving Dave.

He was my *everything*.

The first man I ever truly loved. Who offered me a different life and gave me all I ever dreamed of. He was the perfect partner and father. And he never took any of it for granted. He loved unconditionally and completely.

But Dalton has taken my shattered, splintered, practically disintegrated heart, and somehow managed to find a tiny piece that still beat.

A single shard that was worth trying to save.

He latched onto it, and he stoked it like one does the tiniest hint of a spark until it finally bursts into a flame.

Dalton brought me back to life, made me believe I could be happy again by pointing out those individual moments each day where I could find joy.

There have been so many with Davey, Pops, and him.

None of them compared to this. To being with him, to feeling alive again with every drag of his hips and the way the head of his cock catches inside me in just the right spot to steal my breath.

I move back against him, trying to meet his driving rhythm, and he pulls one hand from mine and slides it around my belly, protectively.

It draws a low whimper from me—the act so sweet, so careful and protective.

Then his hand slips lower still until he finds my aching clit.

My body twitches at the lightest brush of his calloused fingertips, and he draws back and snaps his hips in a way that forces a throaty moan from deep inside me.

"Does that feel good? Like that?"

He does it again, and I practically choke on my breath but manage to nod.

Dalton may not have a lot of experience where women are concerned, but what he lacks there, he makes up for with absolute, unbridled passion and attention to detail.

His commitment to ensuring this is good for me, to giving me the release I know he's also chasing before he finds his own is so damn sweet.

It only makes me want him more.

And the longer he strokes and glides his fingers over my clit, the harder he thrusts into me, the more I want this to continue.

I want it for more than just last night and today.

I know he does, too.

Even if he's afraid to say it, even if he's scared that I'll run away if he does.

We want the same thing.

All this time, I've been relying on him. I had to give myself over and trust him to take care of us and fix what had become broken. And he has, time and time again.

He's been there for me, for Davey, the same way he is for Pops.

And now he's taking care of me again, making absolutely sure I get exactly what I need so expertly that my body is primed and ready for it when he pinches my clit slightly.

I explode, that scalding heat of release rippling across my skin and out through every nerve in my body.

Dalton keeps working me over. Pumping his hips. His hand tightening on top of mine on the table as his ministrations with the other drag my release on and on.

By the time it finally ebbs and my body is nothing but a twitchy, Jell-O-y mass, I can tell he is close.

His movements become erratic.

Frantic.

Desperate.

He lifts his hand from between my legs and uses it to tilt my head back until he can take my mouth with a soul-wrenching kiss.

Were you really going to fight this?

Were you really going to deny what this man has made you feel?

In only a handful of months, he has brought me back from the brink of disaster, when I thought I couldn't go on without Dave. And now, I can't imagine my life without *him*, without *this*. Without waking up with him beside me like I did this morning. Without him kissing me like his very life depends on securing the oxygen from my lungs.

I can't imagine living without Davey's laughter as they play in the rain, or when Dalton takes him on a ride on Apollo, or chases chickens around the yard with him.

Dave may have been the love of my life, but Dalton has slowly become the center of it without me even realizing it was happening.

He is the cornerstone, what has kept me strong and allowed Davey and me time to heal, time to process.

And no matter what comes, I know he'll keep me safe in his arms like this. He won't let go.

Never.

He finally plunges deep, his gasp falling from his lips into mine as he comes, and I squeeze around him, dragging out his orgasm the same way he did mine until he finally groans.

His arms slip around my belly, and he tugs me against him upright.

His lips trail down my neck to my collarbone. "God, Camille, that was incredible. *You're* incredible."

I laugh lightly at the compliment as I reach back and wrap my arms around his neck, threading my fingers through his thick, sometimes unruly hair that no doubt looks a hot mess after what we just did.

"You know I'll always protect you, right?"

His question makes me stiffen slightly, and I glance at him over my shoulder. "Of course. Why are you asking me that?"

"Because I changed my mind." He squeezes me gently, possessively. "I don't want you to go. I thought it would be easier to know you were safe somewhere away from here. But honestly, the thought of letting you and Davey and Pops out of my sight when everything is so unclear actually means it would be the only thing I *was* thinking about."

"So, you want us to stay?"

He nods, and my heart lifts. "I know this mountain better than I know myself. Every leaf, every tree, every stream, every inch of it is part of me, and knowing it that well is going to be what allows me to protect it and you better here."

The sincerity of his words makes my chest ache.

I can see the benefits of both options.

If we go, we would be safe, at least temporarily, from whatever's happening up here. But there is no guarantee there would be anything to come back to if we did leave. If we stay, Dalton has backup for whatever might be coming, and we'll be on home turf.

"What do I have to do to get you to say yes?"

I press my lips to his cheek. "Nothing. You just did it.

You promised you would take care of us and protect us, and I believe you."

"That's all I need to do?"

He sounds surprised, and I turn the best I can to see his face fully.

His eyes search mine, like he's half-expecting me to change my mind. "You should want to go, Camille. You should want to take yourself and Davey somewhere that none of this can reach you."

I shake my head, hating the darkness overtaking his gaze. "No. I want to be where I feel the safest. And that is with *you*."

He shivers against me, clutching me to him tighter, his hands settling over the expanse of my stomach. The way his eyes drift down to that spot, the sheer wonder and love in them, is enough to help assuage any fears I have that staying might be the wrong choice.

This is James Mountain.

This is his home.

This is *my* home.

And I won't let anyone scare me away from it—even temporarily.

This little girl will be coming into the world soon, and I want it to be this one. With Dalton at my side, Pops watching our backs, and Davey running around the homestead free from the complications of life below the mountain.

If that means facing down the reality of what that slip of paper has brought to our doorstep, then so be it.

I've faced worse situations and won't back down from this one.

Chapter Sixteen

DALTON

The tiny scrap of paper easily fits in the palm of my hand, and the few hand-scrawled letters written on it might seem completely innocuous to anyone who doesn't know what they mean.

A shitstorm is coming—all because of this minuscule piece of stationery.

Despite its diminutive size, it feels like a massive, heavy weight in my hand, a burden I now have to carry to protect this mountain and the people on it.

I stare at it in the firelight where I sit in Pops' old leather chair, as if examining it longer might somehow change what's on it or what it means for all of us.

With Pops, Camille, and Davey long since headed to bed, all I'm left with are my thoughts—and they aren't good ones.

Any efforts to try to keep the welling panic at bay have failed.

I can't help but feel like something is coming—something we won't be able to win against.

Even what happened with Camille in the barn this afternoon hasn't been enough to quell the tide of rising anxiety over what we could be facing.

She did her best to help ease my fears. Her strength should have bolstered mine, but all it did was make me realize that, if push comes to shove, she will be the first one to step into the line of danger to protect *us*.

And the thought of that happening has only made things *worse* in my head as darkness has descended both inside and out.

I take a sip of my beer and set the glass on the small table beside the chair, then return to analyzing the piece of paper that has changed everything.

How can Pops even sleep right now?

I'm too amped up, too worried about what might come through that door to ever be able to close my eyes, let alone let myself drift off. Not even having Camille in my bed will be enough to allow that tonight.

The stairs creak behind me, and I turn my head back, expecting to find Pops coming down for something or even Camille checking on why I haven't come to bed. But a different set of sleepy blue eyes stares back at me from the base of the staircase.

Teddy bear clutched in one hand, his blanket in the other, Davey blinks slowly, like he's trying to decide if he wants to be awake or go back to dreamland.

"What are you doing down here, buddy? You should be asleep."

He shrugs slightly, hugging his stuffy closer. "Can't sleep."

No shit, kid.

I feel you on that.

Probably because he feels the energy and tension that has permeated the air all day, even though we've all tried to keep things light with him and have avoided discussing anything that might upset the almost-five-year-old.

I motion for him to come over and set the scrap of paper on the table beside my glass. "Come here."

He pads across the wood floors on bare feet, then climbs up into my lap and settles there, snuggling close and pressing his cheek directly over my heart.

I wrap my arms around him, his tiny weight so much more welcome than the one I just had in my palm. "Did you have a bad dream?"

He shakes his head. "No. Where's Mama?"

"Mama's sleeping." I run my hand up and down his back softly, trying to get him to calm enough to go back to bed. "She is very tired. We should let her sleep."

He nods, shifting to get a better grip on his blanket.

I can't imagine how exhausted she must be.

Not only from the physical toll her pregnancy is taking on her but also the emotional one of everything that's been going on, of all the changes that have been happening and the revelations that are starting to paint a very dark picture.

All I can do is hope she's as prepared to face it as she seems and that this little boy doesn't suffer from the fallout.

I squeeze Davey tightly and press a kiss to the top of his head. "Are you scared about something?"

He shakes his head, snuggling even closer, like this is the only place in the world he wants to be in this moment.

And despite all the uncertainty swirling around us and permeating the air, it does feel pretty damn good to have him in my arms.

Right.

I don't want him to ever have to worry about anything. Just like Pops did for me as a child, I want Davey to always feel secure and loved, even when things get hard.

Like now.

"You know I'll always protect you and your mom, right?"

He nods and pulls his head back, looking up at me with sleepy eyes and little furrowed brows. "Are you my new daddy?"

Fuck...

I swallow through the emotion lodged in my throat.

How the hell do I answer that?

It isn't a simple one.

What I might want, how I might *feel*, doesn't mean it's necessarily what Camille or Davey needs. And we haven't discussed any of this.

Not really.

Not beyond the promises we made to each other in the barn earlier today.

But I know what I want my future to hold with her and this little boy—and that baby who will enter the world so soon.

"I would never try to take the place of your daddy." My voice breaks on the final word, picturing the man who *should* be here with them and everything he's missing. "He loved you and your mom very much, but I do, too. And I'll always be there for you guys, no matter what."

I hope that's a good enough answer.

One that doesn't further confuse the little boy who has had so many life changes in the last six months.

He offers me a soft smile and nods, then returns to resting his cheek against my chest.

The fact that he's so trusting, that he feels comfortable

enough with me to do this makes old memories and long-suppressed feelings bubble to the surface.

It's hard to think that twenty years have passed since I lost them. Sometimes it feels like yesterday, and often, it feels more like a distant dream I have trouble clinging to.

I wrap my arms fully around him and lower my cheek to his thick mop of dark hair. "You know, I used to sit like this with my dad in front of the fire."

"Where is he?"

Long gone...

Some days, it's hard for me to even remember his face, and I have to seek out the old photo albums we keep on a shelf in Pops' office to remind myself what he and Mom looked like. So I can convince myself I haven't fully forgotten them.

"He died when I was about the same age you are."

Davey pulls back and looks up at me again.

"Pops raised me. He's my grandfather, but he's also like my father in a way because he taught me everything I know."

"Like you're teaching me?"

Oh, God.

That heavy emotion I can't quite place thickens my throat again.

Honored that I've been put in this position with him?

Terrified I don't deserve it and am going to fuck it up?

Guilty that it should be Dave?

"I'll teach you everything I know, buddy. You're such a big help and a good learner."

"Are we going to stay here on the mountain"—he looks around the room he and Camille have spent so much time in—"at your house?"

Hell, I haven't had a chance to give that any thought yet, either.

I brought them down here where we'd all be together, where they'd be safer with Pops and me around until things get sorted out. But I've just spent months fixing up the property that's *always* been his home and has been Camille's for even longer so that they could stay.

This might be my home, but that's *theirs*.

Where Camille built a life for him with Dave and created all those memories I don't want Davey to forget.

I don't know if I could ever take him away from that.

Squeezing him gently, I shake my head. "I don't know, bud. We'll figure that out."

He seems to accept my vague answer easily and lowers his head again as his lids start to droop.

A little sigh of contentment falls from his parted lips, and he snuggles deep, bringing his blanket up to almost cover his face.

The fire distorts before my eyes as tears fill them.

How the hell do I fix any of this?

I've always been good with my hands. More than capable of repairing just about anything on the property that might need it. But this goes so far beyond my capabilities.

Maybe Pops was right in keeping me in the dark about what was happening with Gallo and the other threats that have been made to the mountain over the years.

For a long time, it kept me blissfully unaware that there *was* anything to worry about beyond the chores on the homestead.

Or maybe not.

If he had told me, I could have been better prepared for this or anything else that might get thrown at us.

It's naïve to think this mountain will remain untouched forever. After two hundred and fifty years, something was bound to try to taint the sanctity of our safe haven.

But even Pops couldn't have known it would come to *this*.

I glance over at the paper again, and that same anger that burned through me after I found it reignites. Only the soft weight of Davy against my chest keeps it from exploding.

Just like his mother did earlier, having him in my arms soothes the fiery fury and allows me to drop my head back against the leather chair and let my eyes close.

Tomorrow will be filled with problems and questions and things I don't even want to have to face, but for tonight, I'm going to try to let it go long enough to relish this moment.

Knowing Davey feels safe enough with me to fall asleep like this. That Camille trusts me enough to allow herself to open up to me the way she has in the last few days.

Rather than wondering what's coming when the sun rises, I'm going to be thankful for what I have today and pray to God that it won't be taken away.

———

CAMILLE

Bright morning sunlight pours through the window of Dalton's bedroom, and I blink awake slowly, trying to let my eyes adjust to it. I shift and struggle to find a more comfortable position, which is almost impossible at this point during my pregnancy.

It was the same way with Davey.

By this far along, my body was ready to be done with all this, and it's the same this morning. Yet, given how light it already is, I somehow managed to sleep in far later than I normally do.

I push myself up on one elbow and glance to the side of the bed where Dalton should have slept last night, but his pillow looks unused, the sheets cold.

Not that they'd still be warm if the sun's this far up.

He's usually out on the property long before dawn, taking care of his livestock and anything else that needs to happen before he goes to work on our place.

Chances are good that he's out in the barn with Apollo.

A smile pulls up my lips as I think about yesterday and that small room I will never be able to set foot into again without my body and cheeks heating.

Every look he gave me after. Each fleeting touch or brush of his hand sparked that light deep inside me that I thought would never glow again.

It warms me even now, and I dread having to move.

But the world beyond this bed won't wait.

I toss back the covers and carefully climb from the mattress, snagging a hair tie from the nightstand. My fingers catch in tangles as I pull my hair up into a bun and pad toward the door.

Tugging it open, I still and listen, but the house is silent even at this late hour.

I nudge open the cracked door to Dalton's old room where we put Davey to sleep last night, but the bed is empty, the sheets pushed aside haphazardly. For the briefest second, a knot of worry forms in my stomach, but the door to Pops' room also stands open, so even if Dalton is out on the property, Davey isn't alone.

One of them may even have taken Davey back to our

place to check on the livestock—Rocky especially, since the best part of my little man's day is getting to see his best friend.

Making my way down the stairs, a slight chill rolls over me as the cooler air raises goosebumps on my skin.

The flames typically roaring in the fireplace have dwindled down to only embers, explaining why the usual warmth of the room has dissipated. Given the way the temperatures have been dropping, it feels like an early snow may be coming sooner than we anticipated.

I shiver as the living room fully comes into view, and my heart stops.

Dalton sits in Pops' leather chair, head tilted back to the side, sound asleep with Davey in his arms, curled tightly against him.

I don't bother trying to fight the tears that well at the image.

They're so peaceful.

Content.

Comfortable.

And it looks so *right*.

I press my hand over my mouth to keep myself from releasing a sob that might wake them. Old wood creaks to my left, and I rip my gaze from them to find Pops coming out of his office.

He presses a finger over his lips to tell me to be quiet and moves over to the bottom of the staircase near me. "I didn't want to wake them."

I clear my throat and swipe at my eyes. "No. Don't. They both need as much sleep as they can get right now."

Pops offers me a sympathetic look and places his weathered hand over mine on my stomach. "So do you. How are you feeling?"

"Tired, but..." I give him a slight shrug.

He nods his understanding without me having to offer any further explanation.

Even if I didn't feel as big as Winny before she gave birth to Rocky, the events of the past few days would exhaust anyone—as is clearly evidenced by the fact that Dalton didn't even make it up to bed last night.

I start to move off the steps, but the sound of a heavy-duty engine and tires crunching over gravel whips my head toward the front of the cabin.

Pops scowls. "Who the hell could that be?"

Dalton twitches in the chair, starting to wake. He slowly lifts his head and turns it to peer back at us with half-lidded, still sleepy eyes.

Lumbering toward the door, Pops glances his way. "Someone's here."

The shift in Dalton's gaze is instant.

His eyes clear of the last remnants of sleep as he climbs to his feet with Davey clutched to his chest protectively. He turns toward me and moves quickly to the staircase. "I'm going to put him back in his room." His focus darts to his grandfather, whose hand rests on the knob. "Pops, wait for me before you go out."

Pops gives a sharp nod, and Dalton rushes up the stairs, taking them two at a time easily, even with Davey in his hold.

I grip the banister so tightly my knuckles whiten. "Who is it?"

Shifting to the side of the door, Pops glances out the window, and his shoulders immediately tense. "The sheriff..."

Dalton returns before I can ask him anything, moving down the steps as quickly as he ascended them. He pauses on the bottom one next to me and kisses my cheek, pressing a warm, reassuring hand to my lower back. "It'll be okay."

Without him even saying it, I can already tell he's going to order me to stay in the house.

I wrap my hand around his wrist. "I'm going out there with you."

His nostrils flare, his normally soft green eyes hardening like emeralds. "Like hell you are..."

"Dalton, I need to know what's going on."

He presses his hand on my back tighter. "You need to stay in *here*."

I slide my hand from his wrist to twine my fingers with his, squeezing. "We're a team, right?"

His shoulders sag slightly, as if my question physically hurt him. "Of course we are."

"Then let me back you up."

He releases a sigh, then gives me a sharp nod and gently tugs me down the final step toward the front door. Pops grasps the knob and turns it. Chilly air blows in as he pulls it open, and we step out onto the porch and into the bright morning sunlight that so vastly contradicts the dark foreboding settling over me.

Sheriff Wilson is already halfway up the steps. He recoils slightly, almost like he didn't expect us. "Oh, you *are* here. I figured you were in the barn or out on the property and was going to come look for you after I knocked."

Pops forces a smile, but I can see how tight it is, how filled with unease and mistrust. "If you're here, it must be bad news. You could have just radioed."

The sheriff pulls off his cowboy hat and rubs at the thinning, gray-streaked hair near his temple. "You're right. It isn't good."

Dalton tightens his hand around mine. "You found something?"

He nods, leaning an arm on the banister behind him. "Did some digging after you radioed about the people being at the lake. Had to call all the way to Saranac Lake to find a company that rented two ATVs."

Pops raises a white brow. "And…"

I hold my breath, waiting to see who is behind this, and Dalton's entire body goes completely rigid.

This is the moment we've been waiting for. After literal *months* of trying to get answers—from Pops and elsewhere—we might actually finally find out who we are fighting.

"Well"—Wilson rubs a hand across his jaw—"it's a name you'll be familiar with."

Dalton's hand tightens around mine, and he subtly tugs me closer. "That scumbag lawyer Gallo?"

He nods. "Yes, but I made some phone calls to some friends in the city, people who might know him or at least *of* him, and now, I've got more information on that fucker."

I glance at Pops, waiting for him to ask the ultimate question, but he just casually leans against the porch railing, like all of this is boring to him. "Who does he work for?"

Sheriff Wilson's jaw hardens, his already dark eyes turning steely. "You aren't going to like the answer."

Dalton scowls. "We need it, anyway."

"It isn't just some big-shot investors like you thought. It's *one*. And he's not just *connected*. He's one of the pariahs at the top of the food chain where the New York mob is concerned."

"Shit." Dalton wraps an arm around my waist protectively and glances away, his jaw tightening.

"These are dangerous people, far more than you thought. These aren't the type of men who take no for an answer. If they want this land"—he follows Dalton's gaze out toward the barn and beyond—"they're going to take it any way they have to."

The ominous warning makes the strange dream come barreling back, and my legs start to give out slightly, but Dalton's strong arm keeps me steady.

He feathers his lips across my temple and holds them there for a moment, until I can regain my strength by taking his.

Pops pushes off the banister. "I have no doubt they're dangerous people. The kind who use everything at their disposal, every means."

The sheriff nods, putting his hat back in place. "Exactly."

Only months ago, Pops was unsteady on his feet, confused, unable to hold a basic conversation without having to search his foggy mind for memories that should have been at the forefront of his mind.

But the man who puffs out his chest and steps closer to Sheriff Wilson isn't that version of him.

Strong, broad shoulders form an immovable force between the person who is supposed to protect James Creek and the mountain and us. "And what did they promise *you* to secure your help?"

Sheriff Wilson stiffens, his eyes darting between all three of us. "What do you mean?"

Dalton releases me, then slips his hand into his back pocket and steps forward, holding out the scrap of paper he found yesterday. "Want to explain how this ended up in the clearing halfway down the mountain that whoever was up here at the lake was using as a base of operations?"

Wilson glances down at it, squinting like he's having trouble reading it. "I can't tell what it is."

"Bullshit." Dalton says the word calmly—*too* calmly. The rage building inside him mirrors how he acted yesterday when he realized what that piece of paper meant. "That is *your* handwriting. You've always done that strange swirl at the end of your *A*s and crossed your sevens. I knew you had written it the moment I laid eyes on it."

I did, too.

All the paperwork Sheriff Wilson had to fill out when Dave died still sits in a drawer back at the cabin, but I've looked it over so many times that I would have recognized the distinct features of his writing anywhere.

Pops glowers at him, crossing his arms over his wide chest. "What was it? Directions up here? Times that we were least likely to be at the lake? A map to get them through the woods without being detected?"

Dalton steps around his grandfather and into Sheriff Wilson's space, stopping only inches from his chest. "What the fuck did they promise you for your help?"

Whatever it was must have been big for this man to betray the people who rely on him so much. Who *trusted* him to always look out for the interests of the residents of this mountain and the town below it.

Pops shifts to the left, putting himself behind the traitor so he can't retreat.

Sheriff Wilson's eyes soften, and his shoulders slump in defeat. "I didn't want to do it."

Fuck.

That's all the confirmation we need.

He glances between Dalton and Pops. "But the kind of money they're offering, that they'd be bringing in here—"

Dalton grabs the front of his uniform, fisting the crisp deep-blue fabric. "You fucking sell out! You've lived in James Creek your whole life. Your whole family has, and you're willing to let this mountain, this land, be destroyed to put dollar signs in your bank account?" He seethes, his face so close to the bastard that he can probably smell his fury. "Fuck you!"

Pops nods. "My sentiments exactly."

Wilson tries to stagger back a step, but Dalton's hold and Pops block him. "You don't know who you're dealing with. They were going to come no matter what—"

Dalton regains the space between them, using his size to intimidate the smaller man. "So, you just thought you would take advantage of it?"

"Better me than somebody who doesn't care and isn't trying to protect you." He glances toward me. "All of you."

"Did they..."—my stomach drops, my legs starting to shake again as I wrap my arms around myself—"did they have anything to do with Dave's death?"

The sheriff recoils slightly, his eyes widening. "I don't..."—he shakes his head—"I don't think so, but shit, I guess I don't know."

Dalton peers over his shoulder at me, then releases his grip on the sheriff and comes to my side to wrap his arms around me again and hold me steady. "If I find out they did and that you knew about it or had any role in it, you're going to answer to me. As it stands, you're already at the top of my shit list."

The menacing tone he uses should frighten me.

Especially when it's so out of character for him.

But the situation definitely warrants it.

"I'm sorry, guys." Wilson blubbers. "Really, truly I am. But you can't fight this. It's going to happen one way or another. They're too powerful. They know too many people in far higher places than James Mountain. They're going to get this land and use it for whatever the hell it is they want it for." He sweeps out his hand absently. "I suggest you start making plans for when they do."

With that warning, he angles himself to slip between Pops and the railing and hustles back to his department truck.

We all watch him drive away, but no one says anything.

We're all too stunned.

This is all about *money*.

Greed.

They weren't even blackmailing him in a way that would have posed a threat we might have been able to understand.

He just wanted the cold, hard cash they offered.

And his assurance that they didn't have anything to do with Dave's death wasn't really one at all.

Chapter Seventeen

ONE MONTH LATER

CAMILLE

Abiting wind blows the season's first snow across the yard, battering the house and rattling the window above the sink, but I seem to be the only one who notices.

Davey's too focused on the plate of cupcakes in front of him, and Dalton is busy digging through the drawers, looking for the candles I swear I put in one of them recently.

The way my pregnancy brain has basically turned my memory to mush hasn't made the last month easy. I'm constantly forgetting things and finding myself standing in a room without any idea why I went there in the first place.

I'm dreading what these final two weeks before my due date will bring—both for my body and for all the people in this room.

Even the joy of Davey's birthday celebration seems subdued by the fact that we've spent the last several weeks on edge. Between the changing weather, last-minute prep on both homesteads, and the growing uncertainty brought on by Sheriff Wilson's warning, none of us have really relaxed.

But I intend to change that today.

I have to.

Davey shouldn't suffer because someone else wants to hurt what we have here on the mountain.

Pops leans over to grab one of the frosted treats from in front of Davey, and Dalton smacks his hand away as he returns to the table with the missing candles in hand. "Knock it off."

The old man scowls but leans back in his chair, crossing his arms defiantly.

Dalton smirks and inclines his head toward me. "She wants to sing."

At least Pops has the decency to look properly reprimanded as Dalton tears into the package and starts placing the candles on the cupcakes.

Another gust of wind blows snow across the window, and I shiver even though the roaring fire in the living room has the cabin bright and warm.

Pops slides his hand over mine on the table and squeezes it, raising a brow as if to ask if I'm all right without actually saying it and alerting Dalton that I might not be.

God knows if he thought I was spiraling, he would rush in to rescue me from it—even to his own detriment.

He's already working himself to exhaustion every day.

Shoring up the security around both properties as much as he can. Stocking supplies before the weather that would keep us trapped on the mountain hits. Moving Rocky down here to their place because Davey insisted we couldn't leave him there, even though Dalton goes twice a day to feed all the animals and handle anything else. Pushing himself beyond what he's physically capable of.

And he's paying the price for it.

His back has acted up more and more, to the point that most nights, he's spending an hour in the tub trying to release enough of the tension from his muscles to be able to actually sleep.

Which is a rare luxury for both of us these days.

I can't get comfortable, and he can't turn off his brain or stop worrying about the fact that it's basically impossible to secure the mountain completely.

No fences line the properties.

Nothing to physically deter anyone from coming straight onto them the way those two men did to the lake.

Even if there were, given who we're dealing with, a stupid fence wouldn't be enough to stop what might be coming for us.

The vague assurances that Pops keeps offering that "things are in motion" and will "work themselves out" haven't done anything to convince Dalton *or* me that we shouldn't be terrified.

But not today.

Dalton slides his arm around my neck from behind and leans down. "Where are you right now? Because it isn't here."

Shit.

I glance up at him and smile. "Sorry."

"You don't have anything to apologize for." He peeks over at Davey, who is counting the candles to ensure the right number made it on top of his cupcake. "He hasn't noticed. I just want to make sure you're okay."

A near-constant ache in my lower back and hips.

Swollen feet and ankles.

Heartburn that won't go away no matter what I eat or don't.

So many reasons to say I'm not all right.

But looking around this table, none of them really matter.

I slide my hands around my belly and press against the spot my little girl usually kicks me, but for the moment, she's quiet. And she'll be here soon. Things will feel... complete. "I'm good."

And I actually mean it.

Dalton grins and kisses my temple, then retakes his seat as Davey bounces excitedly in his chair, clapping his hands. "Cupcakes!"

Pops snags the lighter off the table and ignites the candles. "Don't touch these. Hot!"

Davey nods his understanding, the flames flickering across his wide blue eyes.

He probably doesn't even remember his last birthday, when his father stood behind him and helped him blow them out...

Before the tears come, I clear my throat and clap my hands. "Time to sing!"

Pops launches into the most God-awful, off-key rendition of "Happy Birthday" I've ever heard, and Dalton and I join in, fighting laughter until Davey finally blows out the candles.

Dalton pulls them from the cupcake so Davey can dig into it, and we all sit back and watch him become an absolute disaster. Chocolate frosting covers his face and hands, but he doesn't seem to care as he shovels more pieces of the crumbling confection into his mouth.

I reach out for my own, but a sharp tug at my side makes me wince. Pressing my palm over it and massaging at the muscle, I shift in the chair to try to find a position that isn't so uncomfortable on the hard wood.

Of course, Dalton didn't miss the movement, his intense gaze zeroing in on my hand. "Are you okay?"

Getting this little celebration together means I've spent more time on my feet today than I have in a few weeks, and I am certainly paying the price for it now.

I nod and give him what I hope is a reassuring smile. "I'll lie down when we're done. Maybe on the couch by the fire for a while…"

His hand glides across the back of my neck, and rough fingertips dig into the tense muscles at the base of my skull.

Groaning, I lean into his welcome touch. "You have no idea how good that feels."

Dalton chuckles low, leaning in even closer, until I catch a hint of that woodsy, fresh scent that always clings to him. "Oh, I do. And I promise I'll take care of you later."

The promise in his words makes me shiver again. "Take care of me, how?"

He moves even *closer* and kisses my cheek so that I'll be the only one who can hear whatever he's about to say. "However you want me to. You know that."

Heat spreads across my cheeks and between my legs, the pain in my side long forgotten.

Pops slams his palm against the table hard enough to make both of us jerk away from each other. "Will you two lovebirds knock it off? I'm trying to eat here." He takes a massive bite of his cupcake, and Dalton glares at him, even though the old man couldn't care less. "These are really good, sweetheart. I could eat ten of them."

I snort and nod. "I bet you could."

And he will, if I don't stop him.

The man may be "as healthy as a horse," as he likes to

say, but at his age, he doesn't need to be devouring almost a dozen cupcakes.

Davey finishes his and rushes off into the living room, probably to play with the few new toys he already opened before we got to the singing and cake portion of the day.

Something tells me the bright-yellow dump trunk that makes real sounds will be both his new favorite and the most annoying, especially when the baby comes and I need the house quiet at times.

But I knew as soon as Dalton showed it to me that it was the perfect gift.

Because he knows Davey so well.

And me.

"Go lie down. Pops and I will clean up in here."

Pops' brows rise. "We will?"

Dalton glares across the table. "We *will*."

That seems to settle any further debate, and Dalton rises to his feet to help me to mine with a supportive arm. His hand lingers on me, and he searches my face. "You're sure you're okay?"

I'm already getting sick of hearing him ask. I still have two more weeks to go before this baby arrives, but I can't be annoyed by it. Not when he's genuinely concerned and willing to do anything I need to ease my discomfort.

I kiss his cheek. "Positive. Just need to rest."

And watching Davey enjoy his birthday surprises will help, too.

I waddle into the living room, expecting to find him right in front of the fireplace, using the dump truck to move around the little balls of wrapping paper he created earlier.

But the room is empty.

Where did he go?

I glance up the stairs and pause to listen for him

running around in his room or even using the bathroom, but the only sounds in the house are Dalton and Pops debating something and water filling the sink for the dishes.

With worry starting to take root in my chest, I return to the kitchen. "Davey didn't come back in here, did he?"

It wouldn't have been impossible for him to have snuck around the couch, going one way, while I came into the room from the other, and hidden from me.

My gaze drifts to the back door that leads to the porch where Pops likes to sit with his coffee, and I move toward it and peek outside. Snow already blankets everything, including Pops' favorite Adirondack chair, and the wind kicks up a cloud of it as I turn back toward the sink.

"No..." Dalton comes to my side. "What's wrong?"

"He's not in the living room, and I didn't hear him upstairs."

Dalton immediately rushes from the room, bolting for the stairs. "I'll check the bedrooms and bathroom."

Pops dries his hands on a kitchen towel, and I follow him back into the living room, where most of Davey's gifts still sit strewn in front of the hearth.

Most but not all.

"His new truck is gone, too."

Pops' gaze drops to follow mine, and Dalton's heavy footsteps coming down the stairs only increase the panic starting to fill me.

Dalton reaches me and grasps my elbow, the concern furrowing his brow. "He isn't up there..."

"Oh, God..."

Pops makes it to the front door before I can even pull out of Dalton's hold, and we quickly follow him.

An icy blast sends snow across the floor, and Dalton

tugs on his boots and places mine on the floor for me to do the same.

The obvious question finally makes its way up my throat as Dalton rises to his full height. "Do you think he went out *there?*"

In this storm?

Not only is it freezing, but we're expecting to get several inches before midnight, maybe more than that before daybreak tomorrow.

There isn't any reason for him to step foot outside this cabin—especially in weather like this. It may only be the first week of October, but it already feels like the dead of winter.

But the frigid chill isn't what catches my attention.

It's the smell permeating the air.

Smoke.

And it isn't from the hearty fire roaring only a few feet away from us.

Pops scans out the front door as he pulls on his own boots, and his eyes widen. "*Shit.*"

Dalton shoves past him in nothing more than jeans and a Henley, his vigilant gaze cutting over the porch and then to where Pops looks. I follow him out, not caring that I'm only wearing thin leggings and a sweater.

Smoke billows from the barn, thick flames licking across the roofline. "Oh, God..."

I tear my eyes from the inferno and search the accumulating snow for any sign that Davey was out here, but it's coming down so fast that it's nearly impossible to see anything through the near whiteout.

"Davey!"

The howling wind quickly swallows my cry, and Pops

and Dalton rush down off the porch, calling out for him the same way.

There are so many hiding spots on the property, so many places he could go, but my gut tells me something I wish it didn't—that he went to go see Rocky.

And Rocky is in that barn.

———

DALTON

My feet slam into the snow as I race across the clearing from the cabin toward the barn, now partially engulfed in a spreading inferno.

The exterior gate to the paddock that always stays closed now stands open, banging against its hitch in the wind that seems to be fanning the flames on the building just behind it.

Oh, God...

There's only *one* reason for it to be like this—because Davey came through it.

I hope I'm wrong as I shove it all the way open and rush to the barn, but chilly awareness ripples through me as I see tiny boot tracks in the snow closer to the structure, where they haven't been covered by the falling, blowing flakes yet.

Thick, dark smoke fills my lungs with each breath I take, and I cough and advance inside, barely able to see anything through the darkness swirling in the air. "Davey!"

I listen for him, but all I can hear is the frantic noises of the animals stuck in their pens as the flames grow closer from the back corner.

How the fuck did that start?

It climbs up the far wall and rushes across the ceiling beams and roof.

There isn't any way to stop it.

This whole place is coming down—sooner rather than later.

Anything and anyone inside it won't stand a chance.

Coughing and covering my mouth and nose with my arm, I make it to Rocky's pen, and my heart stops, along with any of my attempts to breathe.

No.

Davey's brand-new dump truck lies on its side in front of the closed gate.

Only an hour ago, we all sat around him in the living room as he unwrapped it. I saw the joy light up his face. Heard his little squeal of excitement. Felt his arms wrap around my neck and squeeze as he thanked me for the gift.

Now, the only squeals are from the animals desperate to escape the flames.

Camille coughs behind me, skidding to a stop and grabbing my arm to steady herself.

I whirl to face her, gripping her arms and coughing, struggling to draw in any form of useable breath through the thick smoke. "You can't be in here!"

The terror I felt at knowing Davey could be in here triples as I push her toward the open door.

She tries to pull against my hold. "Davey!"

I finally manage to force her out into the blustery wind. It freezes my bare skin instantly, but at least the air is somewhat breathable, the smoke blowing away from us at the moment.

Taking her face between my palms, I lock eyes with her, hoping she can see the promise in mine through her tears. "I'll find him and get him out. I promise."

She sobs, and I can feel the anguish radiate off her.

I lower a hand to her belly. "*You* can't be *here*."

My words finally seem to get through to her, and she nods, taking a few steps back as she stares at the barn going up in flames.

I rush back inside and scan the pens, but there's too much smoke to see more than the frantic movement from the animals trying to free themselves.

"Davey!"

Smoke fills my lungs, and I sputter a cough, dipping my head low to try to keep it closer to the ground where the air seems less tainted.

The fire continues to spread, the roar of the flames consuming the old wood so loud, coupled with the panicked noises from the animals, that there's no way he would hear me even if I could keep screaming.

He has to be in here.

If he were anywhere else, he would have come running to Camille, Pops, or me by now after smelling the smoke and seeing the fire.

Which means, he's either too scared to move or trapped in the barn somewhere.

I start unlatching every pen door to release the animals, letting them race out into the livestock yard so I can check each enclosure to ensure he's not hiding in one of them.

The heat from the growing blaze makes sweat flow down my temples, chest, and back, and each breath comes with more of a struggle. By the time I make it to the final pen and release Apollo, I can barely breathe, my chest so tight and the smoke so thick that it makes it impossible to draw it into my lungs without coughing violently.

Covering my face again, I stumble over a bucket one of the animals sent flying, moving to the corner of the barn farthest from the fire, and the only other possible place he could be if he's in here.

The tack room.

I race toward it and yank the door open. "Davey!"

A tiny sob reaches me over the roar of the flames at my back, and a relieved breath that quickly becomes a violent cough falls from my lips as I stagger inside.

"Davey, where are you, buddy?"

"Dalton?"

His tiny voice carries on a little hiccupped sob from somewhere beneath me.

I squat and duck my head under the table where he's curled up in the corner with his knees tucked against his chest, tears streaming down his face.

"Come on, bud."

The longer we're in here, the harder it's going to be to get back out. Any clear path to the doors will have been almost entirely engulfed by now, and with the heavy, acrid smoke billowing in the small room, I can feel it growing closer.

I reach under the table and try to pull him out, but he resists me, trying to knock away my hand.

"Davey, we have to go."

He shakes his head, lips trembling and coughs, his little body rattling. "I'm going to be in trouble."

"What?" I cough, covering my face with my elbow. "You're not in any trouble."

"I'm not supposed to be out here alone."

"You're not—but I promise you're not in trouble. Come on."

I manage to get both hands under his arms and drag him out from under the table, but when I turn back toward the main barn, a wall of flames blocks the door.

The intense heat immediately makes me twist away, and Davey cries, burying his face against my neck and clinging to me.

Stepping forward, I kick the door closed.

It won't do much to hold off the fire, but we aren't going to be able to go through that. It may just give me a few precious minutes to figure out a way out of his mess.

I scan the tack room for any means of escape.

The small, square window above the table he was under is barely big enough for Davey to squeeze through, and I definitely won't fit. But short of running through fire, it's our only chance of surviving this.

He coughs violently, his terrified sobs mixing with the rush of blood in my ears as I set him on the table.

"Davey, listen to me."

Please, God, let me get him out of here...

The heat grows at my back, but I don't look over my shoulder to see if the fire has made it through the door. If I do, I might panic rather than do what needs to get done.

"I'm going to open this window and help you through it. I'll be right behind you."

He nods, tears streaking down from his red, puffy eyes.

"Cover your mouth and nose with your arm, if you can."

I reach above him, undo the latch, and shove at it, battling the cough that makes me almost double over.

Old paint sticks like glue.

This window probably hasn't been opened in fifty years.

Fuck.

I give another couple of hard whacks up at the top of the frame near the locking mechanism and finally manage to get it to move up a quarter of an inch from the ledge.

Just barely enough for me to get my fingers under the pane.

My eyes and lungs burn as I shove it up with all my strength and get it wide enough for Davey to slip through.

"Come on." I slide my hands under his armpits and lift him. "Quickly."

I help him turn so his legs dangle through the window, which should allow him to come down more safely on the other side after the slight drop. He clings to my arms, and I nudge him out, tightening my grip to lower him as far as I can before my shoulders hit the window.

"I'm going to let go, buddy. You're okay."

His sobs fill my ears, along with the crackling of the fire. A deafening crash comes from the barn behind me—so loud and massive that it can only be the beams that have supported this building for the last hundred years giving way.

I may only have seconds before the roof of this room comes down, too.

Terror grips me tightly, squeezing my already struggling lungs, as I release him, and his cry on the way down makes my heart stop.

But I force myself to turn to assess my exit...that's now fully consumed by the flames.

There's no way I'm getting out.

I quickly scan the room and the various tools and random pieces of equipment we have stored in it.

My eyes land on an old, rusted axe propped against the wall.

It isn't mine that's still up at the house where I like to keep it, but it'll do.

I snag it, immediately run to the exterior wall farthest from the visible flames, and swing.

The blade bites into the wood easily, splintering it and cracking the old board. I pull back and swing again, using every ounce of strength left as the fire and smoke threaten to consume me.

Coughs rattle my chest, but I push through the burn and bear down on the wall over and over again.

Slowly breaking through board after board.

Until muted daylight cuts into the room and I can slip my hand through the mangled edges and tug at them.

The old nails holding them in place pry away easily, and fresh air rushes in at me, but the oxygen causes the fire to surge at my back.

Sparks and ash land on me, searing through my thin shirt and scalding my skin. I shove my shoulder through the opening, trying to get my chest through but meeting resistance that keeps me partially stuck with the inferno advancing.

Please, God...

This can't be the way it ends.

Not after everything we've been through to get here.

Suddenly, the narrow opening I've created gives way, the boards on either side of me collapsing, and I stumble to the hard, icy ground on my hands and knees. My chest heaves, drawing in the cold air, and coughs rattle through me, making me shake so violently that I can't get my legs under me.

Strong arms wrap around me and drag me off the frozen ground and away from the barn.

My eyes water, and I struggle to catch my breath enough to speak. "Davey?"

Pops squeezes his arm around my waist. "He's okay. With Camille."

Blinking away the tears, I search around us through the

blowing snow and smoke that continues to pour from the half-gone barn.

Camille kneels with him in front of her only a few feet away, clutching him as close to her as she can with one hand pressed to that same spot at her side that was bothering her earlier.

She stares up at the barn over his head, and I turn back and watch another massive portion of it collapse inward, sending a burst of sparks and flames shooting higher into the snowy sky.

The animals in the paddock on the side scurry even farther away from their former home, cramming themselves into one corner. But at least they're all safe.

Including Rocky.

Pops helps me move over to Camille and Davey, and I pull Davey up into my arms, gripping him close and running my hands over him to ensure he's really unharmed.

We almost lost him.

If I had been even one minute later in finding him, that tack room would have become our grave instead of the place that held such an amazing memory with Camille.

Pops helps her to her feet, and I wrap one arm around her and tug her against me as all of us cry and stare at what's left of the barn in utter shock.

How the hell did this happen?

We've never had a fire on the property. At least, not during my lifetime. We're so careful never to bring anything with a flame into the barn or any other outbuilding, and any machinery that could get hot and spark something is always kept far away from anything flammable.

Davey whimpers, his hot tears a sharp contrast against my neck to the icy-cold flakes hitting me. "I'm sorry."

He says it over and over again, his sobs becoming more frantic.

I clutch him and Camille tighter. "I already told you, buddy. You're not in trouble. We were just worried about you."

Camille pulls her head back from my chest, and her tear-soaked, panic-clouded gaze meets mine. "How did the fire even start?"

That's a good fucking question.

I share a look with Pops that tells me he's thinking the same thing I am. "Davey, did you see anything or anyone when you came out to the barn?"

He shakes his head. "No...but I heard something."

Pops stiffens, inching closer to us. "What did you hear, kiddo?"

Davey drags his face from my neck, his brow furrowing as he tries to explain. "Like a car."

My back goes ramrod straight.

It wasn't a car.

There's no way a *car* could get up the mountain in this snow when it would be difficult for a well-equipped truck to do so. Plus, we would have seen some sign of tire tracks if someone had used the road.

That only leaves one other possibility.

It was either an ATV, which would have been a *huge* risk, given how quickly the snow is falling and accumulating on the ground, or it was a snowmobile.

Someone was here.

This wasn't a random accident.

It was deliberate.

Those motherfuckers set the goddamn barn on fire to send us a message, and they almost got Davey killed in the process.

I clench my jaw and tighten my grip on him and Camille.

She flinches.

Dipping my head, I try to meet her gaze, but she keeps her focus locked on the snowy ground. "You okay?"

Her mouth falls open slightly, and she takes a step back.

"Camille, what's wrong?"

When she lifts her head, her eyes are filled with a panic that wasn't there only a moment ago, and she wraps her arms around her stomach.

Her lips tremble. "My water just broke."

Chapter Eighteen

DALTON

Pops huffs out an annoyed sigh from his perch on the side of my bed, raising a white brow at me in that condemning way that actually used to bother me as a child but no longer phases me as an adult. "Will you stop pacing? You're making her nervous."

I shove my hands through my hair, annoyed with it falling into my eyes. "Don't tell me to stop pacing when my barn is on fire and she's in labor two weeks early."

Camille scowls at me, her annoyance sharpening her gaze to an icy blue. "*She* is right here and can speak for herself, you know?"

A grin starts to tug at my lips, despite my rising agitation, but it vanishes the second she winces and presses her hand across her belly.

"Contraction?"

She sucks in a long, slow breath, then opens her eyes and nods.

"Shit..."

The little "discomfort" she felt earlier at the table was a warning sign *none* of us caught.

Maybe we would have realized it was more than just her being exhausted and sore if Davey's disappearance and the fire hadn't happened.

Yet Camille remains annoyingly calm.

I resume my pacing, ignoring Pops' objection to it and the withering looks Camille keeps sending my way.

Each time I pass the window, I can't help but look at the still-smoldering remains of the barn that has sat on the property for two generations. It withstood so many storms. Housed countless animals that made this place *work*. And those flames brought it down so fucking quickly.

A blanket of snow several inches thick now covers the ground, helping calm the flames that leaped high into the sky for several hours after we got Camille back into the house and upstairs.

"I still think we should have tried to make it down the mountain to the clinic..."

Pops shakes his head. "You know you never would've made it down the road with it like this even if you left right away. It certainly isn't happening now. Be realistic, Dalton."

Shit.

He's probably right.

And based on the most recent weather report I found on the radio, we're expecting at least half a foot of snow before midnight, which means it's going to be coming down hard and fast the rest of the night.

I'd much rather have her give birth here than stuck in my truck on the slick and winding narrow, gravel road down to James Creek.

"Shit, shit, shit..."

I fist my hands and press them against the cold glass,

dropping my forehead to it, hoping it might cool my heated skin.

"Dalton..."

Camille's voice draws me out of my panic spiral and back to the bed.

I lower myself onto the mattress on the opposite side from Pops and pull her hand into mine.

She squeezes it. "I gave birth to Davey up here; I'll be *okay*."

Every time she reminds me of that, it's meant to ease my fears, but all I can think about are the hundred different complications that could crop up that could put her life or the baby's at risk. We would have no way to get them help. Even if we trust the sheriff right now, the chopper couldn't get up here in a storm like this.

We're completely stranded until the weather improves.

And I have never felt more helpless in my entire life.

I clench my jaw, wanting to argue about all the things I keep obsessing over, but I know it's pointless.

Camille is strong.

She's done this before.

If anyone knows the medical risks, it's *her*.

And she chose to have Davey up here with only Dave to help her, even with all her knowledge and training.

Trust her...

"Besides, Pops is right." She rubs her free hand over her stomach. "The baby has dropped, and my contractions are coming fast. Far faster than they did with Davey. That sometimes happens with a second pregnancy. Things move along quicker. We wouldn't make it to town. We wouldn't have made it even if we'd left two hours ago when my water broke. I've helped deliver dozens of babies in the ER when there wasn't time to get them to L&D, and Dave and I did it on our own..."

"But I don't know what the fuck I'm doing"—I point to Pops—"and he sure as shit doesn't, either."

Pops gives me a dirty look. "You know how many cows and horses I helped give birth before *you* were even born, son?"

Camille scowls at him. "Are you comparing me to livestock?"

A laugh bursts from deep in my chest, joined quickly by her own and Pops huffing. The moment of levity releases a bit of tension from the room, but she still clutches my hand tightly as another contraction hits her.

She grits her teeth, and I let her crush my fingers, wishing I could absorb some of the pain she must be in.

Seeing her like this and being unable to do anything to help must be what she felt like standing outside that barn, knowing Davey was inside.

My lungs still burn from all the smoke I inhaled, and even after a quick shower, the smell permeates the air, a lingering reminder of almost losing him.

Camille finally relaxes and opens her eyes to meet mine.

"I'm worried about the baby and you..."

"I know, but thirty-seven weeks is technically full term. The baby is just fine. She wouldn't be coming if she wasn't ready to be here. Let's not worry about something until we have to."

It shouldn't be so easy for her to say those words when she's the one who is going to have this baby, not me.

"We're really going to do this up here?"

She nods. "It looks like it."

I squeeze her hand and lower my lips to her temple,

breathing her in, letting her warmth seep into me. "Then you better tell us what to do."

She offers me a half smile when I pull back. "I can certainly do that. Is Davey still occupied?"

I nod and glance through the open door into his bedroom across the hall. "I set him up in his room where he'll be close enough for us to keep an eye on him, but hopefully, he won't try too hard to get in here when things get..."

The right word eludes me.

Messy.

Scary.

Utterly terrifying.

"I know he'll be worried about you once it gets louder."

Her lips twist. "Not looking forward to that part."

No matter how tough Camille may be, giving birth isn't a painless experience. She's already in so much discomfort with contractions, so I can't imagine how bad things will be once she starts pushing.

"What can I do to help?"

It doesn't matter what her answer is—I would do *anything* for this woman.

She offers me a soft smile and tightens her grip on my hand. "The same thing I did for you."

A few seconds pass before what she's saying clicks. "The tub?"

She nods. "Water delivery. It's how I had Davey, and the warm water helps with the pain of the contractions until it's time to push."

"But won't the baby—"

Her bark of laughter interrupts me before I can even get the full question out. "No, the baby won't drown. Trust me."

"I do." I kiss her gently, then rise to my feet, releasing her hand. "I'll go draw a bath."

Pops gives me a sharp nod. "I've got her."

By now, the thick, black smoke pouring from the barn will have drawn everyone's attention in James Creek. If it weren't for the snow, half the town would've been up here by now. But as it stands, we're on our own, and that means making use of anything I can find to ensure this delivery goes well for Camille and her daughter.

That means I need to gain control of myself.

My panic isn't good for her.

And I do my best to slow down my breathing as I head into the bathroom, crank on the tap, and sit on the edge.

Water pours into the cast iron, the rushing sound now filling my ears instead of the roaring crackle of the fire that I can't seem to get out of my head.

Today was chaos.

The kind that gets people killed.

We should have heeded Sheriff Wilson's warning, should have anticipated they'd try something like this...

Maybe we were stupid to believe we could remain up here on the mountain, living the way we do, without interference from the outside world forever.

It always manages to find us.

First, it took Mom and Dad.

It almost took Davey today.

And for all we know, Dave could have been an unwitting victim.

I release a heavy sigh as the water starts to fill and reach my hand down to check the temperature.

"What are you doing?" Davey's soft voice drags my focus to the door as he stands there with his new action figures clutched in his hands.

"I'm drawing a bath for your mom."

His pale-blue eyes still rimmed with red from his earlier ordeal widen, instantly filling with worry. "Is she okay?"

The frantic responses from Pops and me when she announced her water broke must have terrified him. We swept him and Camille into the house so quickly that I haven't even had a chance to sit with him and explain what's happening.

I motion for him to come over, and he steps between my legs as I rest my ass on the edge of the tub.

Running my hands through his thick, dark hair, with the same shimmery shade of amber underneath it that's in Camille's, I try to tell him what I would have wanted to hear if I was his age and in this situation.

"She'll be fine, buddy, and your baby sister will be here before too long. You might hear Mama crying a little because having a baby sometimes doesn't feel very good, but I promise she'll be okay. Pops and I will be here with her the whole time, and I know *you'll* do everything you can to help."

He nods vigorously.

"Why don't you go in and sit with her for a few minutes right now?"

"Okay."

I kiss his forehead, and he rushes off, leaving me alone with my thoughts and the running water.

Murmured voices float from the bedroom, but I can't make out what they're saying. Camille's laughter cuts through the air, though, and my shoulders sag slightly at the pleasure that simple sound can bring.

We can do this.

She can do this.

After everything she's been through, this will not be the thing that takes her down.

God, please let her and the baby be okay...

It seems like I've been asking an awful lot of Him recently, especially today, but praying for a miracle seems like the only solid plan at the moment.

The water finally fills high enough to cover her once she climbs in. I flip off the tap and step into the hallway when the sound of the radio from downstairs hits my ears.

Of course, people are calling to check on us after seeing the smoke, and chances are, we're going to need help to get down the mountain once the snow stops, to have both Camille and the baby checked out at the clinic.

Doc already knows what's happening since he was our first call after her water broke—both because of the impending labor and to determine what we should do to address any smoke inhalation issues Davey and I might suffer.

It could be him checking in...

I pop my head into the bedroom quickly. "Water's ready."

Davey sits on the bed next to his mom, holding his hand over her stomach and giggling, apparently as the baby moves.

Camille smiles at him, thankfully in between contractions at the moment.

"I'm going to go make a few radio calls. I'll be back."

Her eyes meet mine. "Don't take too long. I don't think the baby's going to wait."

Is that a good thing or a bad thing?

I'm disgustingly clueless when it comes to human birth, but the confidence in the way she says it assures me that's the nurse in her talking.

All I can do is trust that and her.

———

CAMILLE

Leaning back in the tub, submerged in the warm water Dalton has kept at the perfect temperature for hours as my labor progresses, I watch him pace the small bathroom.

His bare feet barely make any noise as he moves, but the occasional worried sighs that slip from his lips speak volumes—even if he's barely saying a word.

Laser-focused green eyes continuously rake over me, searching for signs of distress, then drift to the window that looks out over the burned barn. He stares at it for far too long, undoubtedly reliving the fiery nightmare he barely survived and the fact that we almost lost Davey.

He tears his gaze away with a huff and instead inspects the items laid out on the counter that we'll need when the baby comes.

"Pops was right..."

Dalton looks over at me, pinching his bottom lip between his thumb and forefinger anxiously as his feet move almost absently across the worn floorboards. "About what?"

"That your pacing is making me nervous."

He freezes instantly and winces. "Shit."

Shoulders slumping, he moves over to the tub and lowers himself onto his knees next to it, where I sat beside him in this exact position not so long ago.

So much has happened so quickly. It's hard to wrap my head around the fact that I didn't even know Dalton James

301

when I got pregnant with this baby he already cares about so much.

His hand slides over mine, the callouses so rough against my skin, despite the tenderness of the touch. "The last thing I want to do is make you nervous right now."

I grin at him through the current discomfort and the intense pain I know is coming with the next contraction.

They've become *strong*.

And given how dilated I was the last time I had Dalton check...this baby isn't waiting much longer.

He searches my face, a mixture of awe and affection filling his gaze. "How can you be so calm right now?"

I draw in a deep breath and release it, trying to formulate an answer he'll understand.

It's hard to explain the sense of calm that always settled over me during the busiest times in the ER, when most people would be frantic. I thrived in that environment. The fast pace. The life-and-death stakes. That's part of what Dave always said made me such a "natural" at homesteading.

Though, I don't know how he would have felt about that assertion had he seen the state of the place when Dalton arrived.

My savior...

I turn my hand to twine our fingers together. "I'm calm because I know there's nothing I can do about the situation, I guess." The water ripples around me with the shrug I offer. "I'm having the baby here whether I want to or not"—I squeeze his hand—"and I *do* want to. This was always the plan, so it doesn't scare me. Neither does the fact that the baby's coming, whether it's two weeks early or not. Nothing is going to stop this. And ultimately, I'm calm because I'm confident that you and Pops will do everything you can to make sure this goes as smoothly as possible. I know you're here, and that makes all the difference in the world."

Because he's *always* here.

By my side.

Since the moment he stared down the barrel of my shotgun.

Tears shimmer across his eyes, and he blinks rapidly to clear them. "I know you wish Dave were here."

The emotions I've been trying to keep at bay since the birthday celebration about the man I thought I'd spend the rest of my life with burst through the wall I created around them, and I fight back a sob that lodges in my throat.

Dalton's hand tightens on mine, and his other palm drifts over my stomach in the water.

"Of course I do..." Hot tears slowly slide down my cheeks. "He's this little girl's father."

"He's the love of your life."

There isn't any resentment or animosity in Dalton's statement—just the level sound of him speaking something he knows is the truth.

I press my lips together to keep from sobbing, not wanting to give in to the utter despair threatening to overwhelm me. "But I love you, too."

His mouth curls up, and he leans in and kisses my temple. "I know you do. I love you, too, and Davey, and I'm going to make sure this baby knows how much her father loved her even before she was here."

The sob finally slips free, but it's cut short when another contraction slams into me.

This time, the pain is so intense that my body demands I push. I grit my teeth and crush Dalton's fingers in my own.

"Don't hold your breath. In. Out. Long and slow."

He repeats the instructions I told him to drill into me

because I remember what it was like last time and how hard it was for me to remember to do something so damn simple.

I open my mouth and force myself to take a long inhale, then exhale. Then again. And again.

Until the contraction finally ebbs.

"How far apart are they now?"

Dalton asks over his shoulder, and Pops steps in from the hallway, where he's been trying to keep an eye on Davey in his room and an ear out for anything we might need.

"Under two minutes."

I sag against the cast iron, releasing a groan. "I'm going to have to start pushing. I'm fully dilated, and the contractions are coming harder and faster. My body feels like it needs to push, like it *wants* to. Exactly how I felt right before I delivered Davey."

Dalton brushes sweaty hair back from my face.

Holding his gaze, I slide my dry hand across his stubbled cheek.

He wraps his fingers around my wrist, holding me in place, and turns in my hold and kisses my palm, letting his lips linger there. "I know what I have to do. You just worry about what you have to, and let us handle everything else."

"Now look who's being the calm and rational one."

He laughs and kisses me hard squarely on my palm before releasing his hold.

Less than two minutes.

The next one will come at any moment.

And it's time to bring this little girl into the world.

I glance over Dalton's shoulder at Pops. "Davey?"

"Occupied. I'll try to keep an eye on him while helping you in here, if you need it."

"Thank you..."

Knowing I don't need to worry about him is a tremendous weight off my already taxed shoulders.

He offers me the kindest smile I may have ever seen from the man who can be so grumpy at times, and I realize how much he has become the father figure I never had.

Just like he was for Dalton when he lost his parents.

"You don't need to thank me, sweetheart. You've done more for us and for *him*"—his gaze drifts to Dalton—"than I could ever put into words. Having you and Davey around keeps me young."

"You won't be saying that when you're changing diapers and there's a baby screaming in the middle of the night..."

He chuckles deeply. "That's probably true."

Another contraction ripples through me, the pain so intense the tears falling from my eyes this time aren't simply from all the hormones and lovey feelings floating around tonight.

It's time.

As soon as it ends, I open my eyes and meet Dalton's concerned gaze. "I'm pushing on the next one."

He nods, then releases my hand to go to the counter and grab the stack of clean towels, the sterilized scissors, and everything else I told them to have ready—just in case.

"I'm sorry there isn't more I can do for you."

I want to tell him that he's done more for me than anyone else in my entire life. That each minute, each hour, each day he spent trying to fix *my* home only reinforced what an incredible, selfless human being he is.

The type of people Dave and I thought didn't exist anymore after what I saw come into that ER every day.

Dalton kisses me again, but it's cut off by the next contraction.

I grit my teeth, hold my breath, grip the sides of the tub to pull myself forward, and *push*.

Pain explodes, blinding me to anything else but the agony and the need to keep going even when I want to stop and end it...

A strong hand presses against my back, helping to hold me up as I struggle to keep bearing down...

The contraction eases, and I sag back into Dalton's hold.

"I can see her head."

Dalton's voice breaks slightly, his fear filling his words.

I open my eyes to see how concerned he looks, staring into the water where his other hand is poised to catch her. "It's okay. It can take a couple of pushes."

My reassurance doesn't change the way the clenched muscles tic in his jaw, but he seems ready.

And I'm as ready as I'll ever be.

When this contraction hits, I bear down as hard as I can, trying to block out the pain. Both the physical and wondering what Dave would think about the fact that Dalton has stepped into his role so quickly after I lost him.

It's the last thing I should be worrying about in this moment.

But when she finally slips out and Dalton lifts my little girl from the water, *everything* else vanishes.

All I can see is her.

He quickly cuts the umbilical cord, and Pops appears at his side with an open towel to dry off her tiny body.

Her little startled cry makes me finally release the sob I've been holding back—overflowing with relief, happiness, and something I never thought I would have again.

Dalton wraps her carefully and cradles her against him, turning her so I can see her face as he settles beside the tub again. "What are you going to name her?"

He's asked before, and I never really had an answer.

Looking at her in Dalton's arms, there's only one name that rings true.

A single word that this man has brought back to my life. "Hope."

Chapter Nineteen

CAMILLE

Davey whimpers slightly where he sleeps along my side in the hospital bed, adjusting his position to snuggle closer, clinging to me the same way he has been for days.

And I can't blame him for wanting to stay close after what he's been through.

I adjust the blanket around him and press a kiss to his disheveled hair Pops never bothered to brush before he brought him back to the hospital from the hotel this morning.

"Is he okay?"

Dalton's concerned question comes from my left, barely a whisper, like he's worried about waking him even though Davey has managed to nap here with the hustle and bustle of the hospital surrounding him with no problem.

I glance over to where Dalton sits in the same chair he has occupied for the past two days, never leaving my side since we got here.

Hope sleeps on his bare chest, the plaid shirt spread open to allow skin-to-skin contact. One large hand cradles her head while the other rests across her back, as if she might fall if he doesn't cling to her so tightly.

"He's fine." I smile at him. "And so is *she*. You can relax a little."

After the emotional upheaval of the fire and Hope's early delivery, then finally managing to get to the hospital once the snow stopped, I would have thought learning that Hope and I were both one hundred percent healthy would have allowed Dalton some space to finally breathe again.

But he's still tense.

Worry constantly creasing his brow.

Sometimes, I have to remind myself of how young he is, how inexperienced he is when it comes to things like babies. But he's a natural with both Davey and Hope, if he can just get over the constant hovering.

He spends too much time worrying about them and not enough about himself. Sleeping in that chair for days must be wrecking his back, but he hasn't complained once, hasn't even hinted that he's in pain when I know he must be.

"How are *you* feeling?"

One of his sandy brows rises. "Me? I'm fine."

"Are you?" I motion toward the chair that's become his permanent residence. "You can honestly sit there and tell me your back isn't jacked up from sitting and sleeping there?"

Dalton presses his lips into a tense thin line. "I'm the last person you should be worrying about."

His selflessness is Dalton's greatest quality and what could be his greatest downfall.

"If you don't take care of yourself first, how are you going to do it for Pops or us?"

He shifts under my assessment. "I am taking care of myself. You know I can handle the discomfort. It's nothing."

The way he so easily dismisses his own pain makes my heart ache for him.

"I need you do do something for me."

His determined green gaze locks with mine. "Anything. You know that."

"When things settle down, when it's safe, I need you to go see a surgeon again, to have your back looked at. There may not be anything else they can do, but medicine in general and surgical options advance so quickly, and it's been a long time since your last operation. They may be able to help you."

Dalton glances down at Hope, gently brushing his hand across her back. The silence that falls between us suggests he's going to argue with me about my request, but when he lifts his head again, I see the resignation in his gaze.

"Okay."

It's my turn to raise a brow at him. "That easy?"

He nods slowly. "That easy. I don't want to not be to lift this little girl or Davey in five years because I let it get so bad. Maybe they can't help, but at least I would know I tried everything to make it easier, right?"

Warmth spreads through my chest. "Right. And it can also be easier if you can trust them to just *grow up* without always anticipating the worst will happen."

He leans back farther in the chair, watching me thread my fingers through Davey's hair. "I know what you think."

I smirk at him. "I doubt that."

"You think that I worry too much and will drive myself crazy with it."

Well, damn.

He sure called me out on that easily.

"Okay. Maybe you're right…"

Dalton grins, gently gliding his hand across Hope's back. "Is it wrong for me to worry about you and them?"

I shake my head. "No, but you can't let it consume you."

He nods slowly, considering the parenting advice. "Right…but it's a little hard not to when we've got mobsters setting fires and doing God only knows what else to try to get us to concede, or worse."

An icy chill as cold as the wind on Davey's birthday returns to my blood at the reminder of what we still face when we return to the mountain.

If what we left is even there when we get back after spending two days at the hospital in Saran Lake…

Anything could be happening up there.

That uncertainty has been weighing on Dalton and Pops, but I've been trying to have faith. Something that's been hard for me the last six months.

Dalton shifts, adjusting his hold on Hope so he can slide his hand on top of mine on the bed, intertwining our fingers. He brings them up and kisses my palm, an unspoken apology for saying it like that and rattling me in the light brush of his lips. "What do you want to do when we get back up there?"

Besides never leave again?

"What do you mean?"

The past few days have been filled with a lot of sleeping. Almost hourly breastfeeding sessions. Changing diapers and teaching Dalton how to do the same. And trying to keep Davey occupied and content in a single small hospital room without any of the comforts of home, save for his teddy bear and blanket.

We haven't even *begun* to discuss what will happen when we go back.

Maybe because we're both afraid to have the conversation.

The way Dalton watches me now, it's apparent that he's worried whatever he's about to say will upset me. "When you get released from here, it might not be safe for all of you to come home, not after what happened with the barn."

Of course.

I should have known that was where he was going with this.

"Don't." The word comes out louder and sharper than I intend, and I glance down at Davey to ensure I haven't woken him before refocusing on Dalton. "Don't try to make that decision for me. I know what the risks are, and that mountain is my home as much as it is yours. I don't want to leave it."

He squeezes my hand again, an appreciative smile pulling at his lips. "That's what I figured, but it still begs the question..."

"What question is that?"

There have been so many over the last few days.

Over the last several weeks.

And the months we've known each other.

Some that I still don't have the answers for and some that are crystal clear.

"Where do you want to live when we go back?" Tension crinkles the corners of his mouth. "Your place or at the big house with Pops and me? I go where *you* go."

God, he's so sweet...

Any woman would be lucky to have a man like Dalton willing to give up so much for her, but that isn't what I want.

I don't want him sacrificing for me—not when he already has in so many ways.

"You can't leave your home. And you can't leave Pops alone."

Dalton snorts a laugh, releasing my hand to settle back in the chair, readjusting Hope on his chest. "He's a grown-ass man. He'll be fine, at least for a while. And when he's not, we'll deal with it then."

I peek down at Davey, then back over to Dalton and my daughter.

It isn't that I haven't thought about this at least a few times over the last few months with as many hours as we spend at their place and them at ours. Early on, it was a very simple decision—I didn't want to leave the homestead or the life Dave and I had built there, the life we had created for Davey.

But now, a different answer seems just as simple.

"We're going to stay with you at your place."

His eyebrows rise.

"You seem surprised."

"I am. We just spent six months fixing your homestead, ensuring you and Davey could stay there. I know how important it is to you, and I'm more than willing—"

"No." I shake my head, trying not to let myself get worked up and have Dalton think it's because I'm not confident in my answer. "I'm not going to let you uproot your life and mess with Pops', making you split your time between helping there and at my place, especially because..."

I can't believe I'm going to say this.

My chest tightens with the words.

"It doesn't *feel* like my place anymore."

Silence fills the room as Dalton stares at me, apparently stunned speechless by my confession.

He waits for me to continue, and when the tears start to

fall down my cheeks, I try to wipe them away, even though there's no hiding them from him.

"When I was there with Dave, it felt like home. Like it was where I was supposed to be. But after he died, before you showed up, I spent those weeks, those months, fighting so hard to keep it going, to keep the dream we had alive for my sake and for Davey's. And..." I bite my lip, glancing down at Davey. "And I think that was a mistake because we're never going to have that life, not without him. Over the last six months, our lives have changed so much. You and Pops and everything you've done for us..." I let out a little sob. "It's just shown me where my *real* home is, and it's wherever *you* are. And that *needs* to be on your homestead with Pops. Rent out my place to someone else looking to build their dream. I have mine on the James property, if that's what you want."

Dalton swallows thickly, shifting forward to the edge of the chair slowly and carefully with Hope in his hold. "Of *course*, that's what I want, Camille. I've never wanted anything more in my life than to have you, Davey, and Hope with me permanently. But I don't want you to feel like you have to do this, like we can't figure something out."

"I don't." I manage to say that without sounding like I'm on the verge of another emotional breakdown. "I promise. This is what I want."

His lips twitch. "And I know how determined you can be to get what you want."

I return his growing smile. "I can be."

His joy and any humor fade quickly, a seriousness settling over his face again. "But it isn't safe to go back there right now. I think you three should stay down here until Pops and I can get something figured out, a way to handle all this more strategically."

"Trying to send us away again... How well did that work last time?"

He releases a shaky breath. "I know."

The *last* time, he ended up bending me over the table in the tack room and fucking me senseless, then demanding I stay instead.

"Last time, I was selfish, and look what it almost cost us."

His gaze drifts down to Davey at my side, then down to Hope, both sleeping so peacefully, oblivious to all the drama that surrounded both of them only a few short days ago.

"I am coming back up the mountain with you, Dalton." I say it with as much finality as I can inject into the statement so he understands there is no room for argument. "I can handle a gun, and I am sure you and Pops will be more than willing to help me get even better with it. We're safest when we're all together, watching each other's backs."

He looks ready to argue, but a knock at the door draws both of our attention toward it and away from the impending fight Dalton seems to want to have.

The door swings open, and Pops steps in from the hallway, scanning over both of us and the sleeping children. "I hope I'm not interrupting, but we need to talk."

———

DALTON

The tone of Pops' voice immediately makes me tense, and Hope shifts where she sleeps against my chest. I rub my hand over her back until she resettles, her tiny hand pressed against my skin.

Camille reaches for Davey beside her, drawing him

closer as Pops enters, followed by a man in an expensive-looking dark suit and equally impressive tie.

Shit, this can't be good.

The entire time we've been down here, Pops has been making calls—something I haven't seen him do in years since he refuses to use a SAT phone up at the cabin. And, of course, true to form, he wouldn't tell me a damn thing about what he was doing.

He just keeps insisting he has been "taking care of things" where the fire was concerned.

It's not like we could report it to Sheriff Wilson and expect anything to come of *that* investigation, considering his connection to the person who likely perpetrated the crime in the first place.

But I can't simply take Pops at his word anymore without some sort of satisfactory explanation and *plan*.

I am not going back up there with my family until I know we can be safe—no matter what Camille says...

Her determination to stick with me and be at my side no matter what gives me faith in our future, even when everything else looks so uncertain, but I'm not about to risk her life or the lives of Davey and Hope just to have her with me when we could be walking into literally anything.

"Camille. Dalton." Pops nods at both of us. "This is Gary Beller, an old friend from James Creek."

I narrow my eyes at him.

He looks to be at least two decades younger than Pops, maybe in his fifties, with graying hair and a stern expression that tells me this isn't a personal visit.

Pops continues, resting his shoulder against the wall near the door. "He's the attorney I told you I've been speaking to."

Oh.

I shift upright in the chair, my interest in the visitor instantly piqued.

Beller offers us a tight smile. "Sorry we're meeting under these circumstances. It's been a long time since I've been back to the mountain." His gaze moves to mine. "It was your parents' funeral. I knew them both well, and I'm sorry to hear about what's happened up there lately." He releases a sigh, glancing toward Pops before offering a smile that seems more genuine this time. "But I come bearing good news."

A flicker of hope lights in my chest, below where the baby named after that unreliable emotion sleeps. "What kind of news?"

Pops crosses his arms over his chest, watching Beller with a look that tells me the old man has been privy to whatever information we're about to receive for a while.

"Your grandfather and I have been speaking for about a year regarding a certain man who showed up in town, asking around about purchasing your land on the mountain..."

A fucking year?

So, Pops wasn't full of shit when he said he was taking care of things even when it felt like nothing was happening and we had nothing to show for his efforts.

"Unfortunately, I know Attorney Gallo all too well... and his clients. And Marciano Ermilio is not a man you want to fuck with unless you're me."

Camille leans forward, her eyes narrowed on him. "Who the hell *are* you?"

All the secrets Pops has been keeping seem about to unravel, and this man appears to be at the center of them.

Beller squares his shoulders slightly, then smiles. "I'm the Attorney General for the State of New York."

I jerk my gaze to Pops, who just gives me a smug smirk.

"And as of"—Beller glances at his watch—"an hour ago, Ermilio and eight members of his organized crime family—were arrested under the New York State Racketeer Influenced and Corrupt Organizations Act, charged with multiple felonies that, hopefully, are going to keep them in prison for a very long time."

My mouth gapes, and I glance at Camille, who seems to be having the same reaction. "You're serious."

He nods and steps farther into the room. "When Pops contacted me saying that Attorney Gallo showed up and was making threats to force the sale of the land, he had no way of knowing we had already initiated an investigation that had been going on for years regarding him and his representation of the Ermilio family. He isn't just a mob lawyer. He's an active participant in many of their schemes, this one included.

"Whether they planned to use the land as their own sort of secret hideout, or the plan was to try to sell it at a massive profit to some resort builder—which seems to make sense, given what Pops saw at the lake that day—they needed to get rid of you. The arson is what pushed us to act immediately and ultimately gave us the final nail for the coffin. The cameras you placed caught a known member of his crew entering your homestead and leaving around the time the fire started. They won't be able to get out of this one."

Stunned silence fills the room, the only sounds the soft beeping of the machines monitoring Camille's vitals and occasional little snore from Davey as he shifts and clings to her.

All of this has been happening under our noses.

For a year.

And Pops never let on.

He never clued me in on the fact that he had been in contact with this man or that there was a legal case being built against the very people who were threatening us.

Beller shifts his gaze between Camille and me. "This is a violent crew, willing to do whatever they have to in order to get what they want. I'm sorry you were pulled into it, but rest assured, I'm going to do everything in my power to keep them locked behind bars for as long as possible. That includes Sheriff Wilson, who was surprisingly cooperative when he was taken into custody. I think he felt guilty for his involvement, especially after the fire."

Camille clears her throat. "And what about the rest of his organization? Aren't they going to be a little pissed off and potentially come after the people who caused all this— which is *us*?"

Everyone looks at her.

She asked exactly what I was thinking, voiced precisely the same fear starting to grow in my own head.

"I've already discussed this with Pops." He glances back at him, where he still leans against the wall. "Additional security measures are going to be installed on the mountain. Dozens of trail cameras and motion sensors, all hooked up to the state-of-the-art system in your cabin. You'll be able to monitor the property far better than what's possible now. We've cut the head off the snake, but I can't guarantee someone won't slither around and try the same thing again. At least you'll know they're coming. And if you need help, you know who to call."

Camille nods slowly, then allows her gaze to shift to me, and I know what she's going to ask. "What about my husband. Did Gallo or Ermilio have anything to with—"

She can't get the rest out, and if the baby wasn't fast

asleep on me right now, I would climb from this chair and tug her into my arms.

Beller offers a sympathetic look. "As far as we know, your husband's death *was* an accident, like everyone thought. Of course, we'll always keep our ears open for any information to the contrary."

But we may never really know.

The final part goes unspoken, but it's the very truth I've feared since Camille first had that dream—that we will have to live with never being one hundred percent certain.

Pops pushes off the wall and slaps Beller on the shoulder. "Thanks again. I'll be in touch…"

I'm speechless as Beller slips out of the room, closing the door behind him and sealing us in with the old man who apparently never forgot how to keep secrets, even when he wasn't fully in his right mind.

Pops turns to us and raises a brow. "You don't have to look so surprised. I know you thought I was a stupid old man who didn't know what he was doing or saying for a long time there—"

"Pops, I never thought that. You were sick and—"

He holds up a hand. "And I wouldn't be back to my normal self if it wasn't for both of you. So, if I haven't said it, thank you for pushing me, for jabbing me with those damn needles." An amused look gets tossed at Camille, who laughs. "We're going to have to stay vigilant, but when I told you I wasn't going to let anything happen to the mountain and wasn't going to let it be taken from us, I was serious. It's your legacy, your birthright. It's all going to be yours soon, kid." Affectionate eyes roam over Davey and Hope. "And one day, it will be theirs."

No…

The way he's talking, it's like he is expecting to keel over at any moment, and I refuse to even *consider* that possibility after what's happened.

"Not soon." I shake my head. "You're not going anywhere, old man."

"But I will be *eventually*." He releases a long sigh, moving to the end of the bed. "It's time I bring you in on the business and teach you everything you need to know to keep it running."

I've waited years for him to say those words, for him to open up and invite me in fully. And hearing them now, it's like a giant weight being lifted off my shoulders.

He throws a thumb toward the door. "I'm going to head back to the hotel, take a shower, and have a long nap like these two here." A finger swings between Davey and Hope. "I hear they're discharging you tomorrow."

Camille nods. "Yes. We should all be able to leave in the morning."

"Good." A smile brightens his face more than I've seen it for months. Finally having all this be *over* has taken its toll on him as well. "It'll be nice having everyone together on the mountain again without always having to be looking over our shoulder."

He slips out the door without another word, pulling it closed behind him.

Davey shifts in Camille's arms and pops his head up, blinking sleepy eyes. "Did Pops leave?"

I guess he heard some of that conversation.

Camille pushes his hair back from his face. "Yeah, Bub."

He releases his grip on his blanket to rub his eyes, then looks over at me and Hope. "She's still sleeping."

Camille offers him a kind smile. "Babies sleep a lot, Davey. Even more than you. And when they're not asleep, they're usually pretty hungry. For the first couple of months, that's all they really do—eat and sleep. But when she gets older, you're going to have a great playmate."

That draws his mouth into the happiest grin, and he slides off the bed and makes his way over to me.

I move over as far as I can on the chair to give him room to climb up, and he snuggles against my side, resting his cheek on the side of my chest not currently occupied by his baby sister.

He touches Hope's dark hair with his tiny fingers, then leans in and kisses her softly on the forehead.

I don't know if I'll ever get used to seeing how beautiful they are together or the sheer love he holds in his gaze for her.

"Let her sleep, okay?"

Davey nods and snuggles against me again, a peaceful quiet settling over everyone in the room.

And for the first time since I met them, it feels like it might last.

Camille slides down in the bed on her side, resting her head on the pillow facing us, and releases a contented sigh. Her blue gaze stays locked on mine, and the longer we stare at each other, the harder the question knocks at my brain.

The thing I've been wanting to ask her since I first realized I had feelings for the beautiful widow Bower.

"Did you ever think we'd end up here after we made that bargain?"

The corners of her lips twitch up. "No." She shakes her head. "Definitely not. But I'm glad we did. It would have been a much different outcome if I had pulled that trigger."

Epilogue

Four Years Later

CAMILLE

Dalton tightens his grip on my hand, leading me through the trees on the narrow, barely defined path. Sunlight filters through the canopy, bright spots illuminating what would otherwise be dark due to the lush spring cover the leaves provide.

Birds chirp from their perches above, and a light warm breeze occasionally flows between the trunks, lifting the loose strands of my hair that always seem to fall out of the bun at the back of my head.

As much as I love this little hike and time alone with Dalton, away from the kids, the fact that he's being so secretive about today has been annoying me since we left them at the lake with Pops. "Are you going to tell me what we're doing?"

He gives me that playful, boyish grin that always makes him look *exactly* his age. "You'll see."

I huff, allowing him to keep moving us forward. "You know I'm not the biggest fan of surprises..."

He pauses mid-step and turns back, tugging me up against him. His hard, lean body aligns perfectly with mine, and I press my hands to his bare chest and let them drift down over his rippling abs.

No matter how irritated I might be, I will *never* pass up an opportunity to touch him when he's like this—open shirt, jeans that hang dangerously off his hips, and that sexy smirk that always promises something incredible is coming.

I know that look all too well.

Dalton kisses my neck, sending a shiver through me, despite the unseasonably warm spring day. His breath tickles my skin, and I shift restlessly against him. "You liked the surprise I had for you last night."

Hell...

I sure did.

A wicked rush of heat floods my body, and my pussy clenches at the memory of how he showed up while I was soaking in the tub...

And then made me *very* dirty before he cleaned me up again.

The little needy sigh that slips from my lips as I tilt my head, giving him better access, is downright embarrassing. This man can so easily turn me into putty with a simple word, look, or touch.

There isn't any use trying to deny it.

Or how much I enjoyed last night.

Four times...

"That I did, but that's beside the point..."

He nips at my ear, then pulls back, and I instantly miss the press of his body against mine. His hand closes around mine again, and he tugs, leading me farther down the path that's become so familiar over the years.

"Are we going to the meadow?"

Dalton peers over his shoulder, fighting a grin, but the way his green eyes dance with mischief might as well be confirmation. "Maybe."

It's a long walk. At least forty-five minutes. If I had known this was where we were heading when he led me away from the lake, I might have warned the old man.

"Should we have left the kids with Pops?"

He scoffs at my concern. "You know they'll be fine. Now that Pops has his little ATV to get around the property, if he really wants to leave with them and head back to the cabin, he easily can." His gaze meets mine over his shoulder. "Weren't you the one who always used to tell me to stop worrying about them and not to 'helicopter' so much?"

Shit, he got me there.

And he's become such an incredible father to them.

A natural.

Patient.

Kind.

Protective.

Loving.

Exactly who I knew he was once I let him onto my property that fateful day.

He even underwent another painful surgery to better correct his back so he could ensure he would be able to do all the fun things with them without restriction or having to endure the pain he would have otherwise.

The sheer number of sacrifices he has made for us only make me love him more each day. And further confirm what I began to suspect years ago, that Dave is looking down on us and sent Dalton to be our guardian angel.

He certainly has been that.

So, I don't bother pushing the issue of leaving the kids

with Pops anymore, just allow him to lead me through the trees, stepping over several fallen logs on the familiar hike—though, I have no idea why we're going to the meadow *now*.

It's too early in the spring for it to be anything but an empty green space.

Or...it *should* be.

When the trees finally start to thin, Dalton pulls me up next to him and presses a hand at my lower back, urging me through them ahead of him.

We step out of the tree line, and my breath catches.

Thousands of wildflowers cover the clearing, swaying gently in the warm breeze.

Reds...

Yellows...

Pale blues...

Indigos...

Violets...

An entire rainbow spread out before me.

"Oh, my God, they bloomed early."

He rests his chin on my shoulder and nods, wrapping his arms around me and tugging me back against him fully. "Yep. The unseasonably warm weather the last couple of weeks did the job."

"How did you know?"

Dalton grins against my neck. "There's nothing that happens on this mountain that I don't know about, Camille."

That's probably true at this point.

Over the last several years since Hope was born, he and Pops have spent countless hours and hundreds of thousands of dollars ensuring our safety, making sure we have electronic eyes and ears covering as much of the property as possible.

He's made sure it's safe for me and the kids to relax here, to live, and to just *be* in a way I could never find anywhere else.

"I wanted you to see this because it's so rare that it happens this early in the year, and I know things have been a little rough lately..."

I let out a huffed laugh.

They definitely have been that, though. It has absolutely nothing to do with Dalton or the kids or this beautiful life we've built together.

His hands settle splayed across my still-flat stomach protectively.

"I'm too old to be having another baby, Dalton."

He laughs, the sound making his chest vibrate against my back. "You are not too old. You don't even turn forty for another few weeks."

I turn my head and scowl at him. "Thanks for the reminder."

"I knew I was getting myself a beautiful cougar when I locked you down..."

The humor and love in his voice help melt away those concerns that have been plaguing me as much as the morning sickness has.

I relax into him, and he kisses my cheek.

"This isn't the full surprise."

He releases me, slips out from behind, takes my hand, and leads me farther into the meadow and the wildflowers. "How long do you think Pops can manage those two alone?"

My laugh floats across the open space, the mountain accepting the sound as part of what just naturally belongs here. "Two hours tops."

It took us forty-five minutes to hike over here, and it will be the same going back, which means we don't have a lot of time for whatever Dalton has planned.

That playful grin pulls at his lips as he leads me toward the center, where some of the flowers are depressed to the ground. "That gives us time."

"Time for what?"

I look down to find a plaid blanket spread with a small picnic basket settled on the corner. "How did you..."

Dalton smirks. "This morning."

"You weren't out in the barn?"

He shakes his head. "No, I was not."

My gaze drifts to the basket. "What exactly do you have in there?"

The morning sickness has finally calmed down for the day—and hopefully won't be returning later—and I'm actually hungry for the first time in what feels like months.

He grins. "Well..."

Slowly kneeling on the blanket, he pulls me down, facing him, his chest brushing mine. He takes my face between his palms and kisses me deeply.

The sweet, reverent brush of his lips draws a groan from my throat, and I tug at the sides of his open shirt to keep him close.

My body responds instantly.

The goddamn pregnancy hormones again.

I love to hate them and what they do to me, but I could never hate what this man does.

The way he owns me—mind, body, and soul.

By the time he finishes devouring my mouth and pulls back, the evidence of how *I* affect him presses into my thigh.

He shifts against me, ensuring I feel *all* of him. "I have all sorts of delicious snacks I thought you'd enjoy, but first, I thought I'd feast on you."

DALTON

The little shiver of anticipation that races through her as I press her down onto the soft blanket makes my cock throb between us.

Camille is the most beautiful woman I've ever seen. The most beautiful thing in my life, along with the kids. And now, knowing we have another one on the way, seeing how glowy she is pregnant, I can't keep my fucking hands off her.

Or my mouth.

I raise a brow at her, grinding my hard length against her thigh. "How does that sound? I eat lunch, and then you do..."

She grins and loops her arms around my neck, tugging me down until her mouth brushes mine. "I wouldn't want you to go hungry."

Fuck yes.

I waste no time sliding down her body and dragging her jeans and underwear with me. But I don't even bother removing them fully, leaving them stretched across her ankles.

Her eyes flare, the blue blazing the heat of need and confusion. "What are you doing?"

Lifting her legs, I drape her thighs over my shoulders. "We're short on time, and I don't want to waste a single second fighting with your fucking jeans."

Not when her pussy already glistens with her arousal in the bright sunshine.

Not when my mouth literally waters to taste her.

I dip my head and drag my tongue through her slick core.

She arches into me, groaning, her fingers digging into my hair, nails scoring my scalp.

All thought of anything else melts away at the feel of her response to me.

So secure in her sexuality.

So willing to tell me what she needs.

I grasp her ass in my left hand, keeping her exactly where I want her, and glide the other between us to slip two fingers inside her.

She whimpers and clenches around me, her body pulsing in time with my tongue and ministrations. "Have I ever told you...how fucking *good* you are at this?"

Yes.

Hundreds of times.

But it doesn't mean I don't enjoy hearing it each and every time I put my mouth on her.

I chuckle against her warm flesh, then probe my tongue around her clit, not giving her the direct contact I know she so desperately seeks.

It's so much better to watch her squirm.

To build her into a frenzy before I finally let her have it.

I always worried that I wouldn't be enough for Camille, that my inexperience and naivety when it came to relationships and sex would disappoint her. But she's grabbed that bull by the horns and used them to direct me and mold me into what she calls her "perfect weapon."

And that's what I have become.

After four years of learning every inch of this woman's body, I *know* exactly what to do to get her off—whether it be slow or fast. A long, drawn-out night of sex that leaves us exhausted and sated or a fast release up against the back of the new barn when we manage to sneak away for a few moments.

No matter how...it's *always* like this.

The desperate, thrumming need that consumes both of us.

I curl my fingers into that spot deep inside of her, swirling them in a circle and gliding back and forth as I suck her clit between my lips, and *pulse.* Her hips do the same, rolling against my face, and my cock strains against my jeans, eager to be where my fingers are now.

Patience is a virtue, but not when what we both seek is so easily attainable.

I graze my teeth across that tiny, sensitive nub, and Camille goes completely rigid.

Her thighs tightening around my head.

Her body twists violently, like she's trying to break my neck as she comes.

I continue to suck and lick and drag those fingers in that spot she loves so much, drinking down her release as my body begs for my own.

By the time she starts coming down, I'm already swinging her legs up over my head and unbuttoning my fly. Her hands brush against mine, frantic in the same scramble I am to free my cock. The warm breeze hits my bare ass as I shove the fabric down enough to get the job done.

I lean over her, bracing myself on one hand, as I align the throbbing head of my cock with her heat and sink into my favorite place in the world.

"Fucking hell, Camille."

The words come out on a low growl, and she mewls and clenches around me, trying to lift her hips. But pinned in place, restricted by the fabric still at her ankles, she's stuck under me, completely at my mercy.

There was a time I would have worried that I was going to hurt her or the baby, but I learned my lesson quickly never to underestimate this woman.

I drag my hips back and thrust into her again, bottoming out deep enough to draw a gasp from her parted pink lips. She arches to meet the next one, frantic to move, to find that perfect position.

Unlike the orgasm I just gave her, I want to savor this one slowly, watch her build again, absorb the pleasure, and relish the way ecstasy flickers across her face until it finally brings her to that place where the world disappears.

The place only *I* can take her.

She squeezes around me with each retreat, her body clinging and trying to keep me inside, and I lean back slightly, altering the angle so that the head of my cock catches on that spot deep inside of her.

Her throaty moan confirms I've found it.

Soft hands and sharp nails claw at the back of my neck.

Her hips roll, trying to get the friction she needs.

And her eyes flutter open and meet mine—a carnal need shimmering across them.

"We don't have much time, Dalton. Stop toying with me."

I grin at her, stilling my movements. "But I love to do that so much."

She digs her nails into my skin and pulls me down to her, brushing her mouth to mine. "You're not going to love it if Pops and the kids come looking for us because we've been gone for too long."

"Shit."

I mutter the word against her mouth and redouble my efforts, grinding down and pressing my pelvis against her already engorged clit. Her hips rock against mine, and a frustrated whimper slips from her lips.

No more waiting.

I slide my free hand between us to give her the direct stimulation she needs.

"Oh, God..." She gasps, her head dropping back, neck straining. "That. Right. There."

"I know, baby. I got you."

A sharp pinch and twist later, her body trembles beneath me, her pussy clamping down and rippling along my cock as she comes again, which allows me finally to unleash what I've been holding back.

I increase my tempo, driving into her, needing it, needing this more today than I could have ever anticipated. When I finally come deep inside her and sag onto her warm, pliant body, she cradles me against her, kissing me gently on the temple.

"Well, that was a great lunch."

Chuckling, I brush my lips over any skin I can get them on.

She shivers. "But we need to go back to the lake."

I nod. "We do."

As much as I would love to lie here with her, soaking in the first *truly* spring day we've had this year in this beautiful meadow, real life is calling.

And Pops doesn't deserve to be left to wrangle *those* two alone for long.

I reluctantly climb off her, groaning as my cock slips out, and I tug my pants back up.

She does the same, wincing slightly. "Didn't exactly think this through."

I smirk. "I did." Kissing her again, I cup her pussy through the stiff fabric. "And I love the thought of you walking around with my cum inside you until we can get back to the cabin and you can shower."

"Jesus, Dalton..." She shakes her head, but the grin she offers tells me she isn't offended in the least. "Keep talking like that and we're never getting back to the lake."

I slide back and get to my feet, then hold out a hand and tug her up. "Don't tempt me."

The walk back is quiet, peaceful, both of us content in a way that makes the beauty of the mountain explode tenfold. And by the time we step out into the clearing the lake sits in, I've almost forgotten how rough the last couple of weeks have been with her morning sickness and exhaustion because she seems more full of energy and life than I've seen her in a long time.

Pops' voice carries to us as we approach him from behind. "Will you two knock it off?"

I drop my head closer to Camille's, squeezing her hand. "Is he talking to us?"

She laughs. "I don't think so. Probably the little terrors."

Davey runs around the edge of the lake, with Hope chasing after him, trying to grab the string of fishes he holds high.

"Daveeeeeeey! Let me have them!"

She's no match for his speed or agility at her age, and he's taking full advantage.

We approach, and Pops glances over his shoulder. "Oh, thank God. These two are full of piss and vinegar today."

I raise a brow, watching Davey continue to taunt his little sister. "When are they not?"

He smirks. "Good point, but at least we have dinner."

"Excellent."

Hope runs up to me, her bottom lip quivering the way I

know is about to spell tears, and I scoop her up. "What's wrong, Princess?"

"Daddy...he won't give me the fish."

Davey offers an annoyed raise of his brows, as if to ask if he was *supposed* to. "I'm the one who caught them."

Camille fights a grin but doesn't move to intervene.

I motion toward the catches of the day. "That may be, but maybe you could let her carry them back to the house."

He issues a reluctant sigh, then stalks over and holds up the string. "*Fine.* Here."

The attitude of a nine-year-old...

We haven't even hit the hormonal teenage years yet, and already, I'm dreading it.

Hope smiles. "Thank you, Daddy."

I let her back down to her feet, and she accepts the string from Davey and immediately starts racing back toward the path that will lead her to the cabin.

Pops pushes up from his spot on the rock and slowly lumbers toward his new toy—the ATV that helps him get around the property and actually be able to keep up with the kids. "I'll meet you guys up there. Seems she doesn't want to wait."

He turns the machine and takes off after her, leaving Camille, Davey, and me on the shore.

I squat in front of him. "Thanks, buddy. That was a very nice thing to do, letting your sister help."

He scowls slightly in a way that's so much like his mother that I have to glance up at her.

She hides her smirk behind her hand, but she gives me a nod.

Confirmation that it's time to do the *thing* we've been holding off on for the last few months.

"I know being a big brother is tough sometimes." I reach

out and squeeze Davey's shoulder. "But you're the best one there is, and you're going to be with a new baby, too."

His eyes widen. "New baby?"

He looks to his mom, and she drops her hand to her stomach and nods.

"Yes."

Instead of being upset like I thought he might be, he grins. "It better be a boy this time. I can't handle another sister."

————

I hope you enjoyed *Billionaire Lumberjack's Bargain*.

Meet the McBride brothers in The McBride Brother Lumberjacks Series and find love *Beneath the Mountain Sky* with the first book in this exciting series that promises more grumpy mountain men and the women who bring them to their knees and give them their happily ever afters: books2read.com/BeneathTheMountainSky

If you haven't met the rest of the Lumberjacks in Love, snag their stories now:

Beau in *Billionaire Lumberjack* - available now at all retailers! books2read.com/BillionaireLumberjack

Wells in *Billionaire Lumberjack's Baby* - available now at all retailers! books2read.com/BillionaireLumberjacksBaby

Silas in *Billionaire Lumberjack's Bride* - available now at all retailers! books2read.com/BillionaireLumberjacksBride

Weston "The Beast" in *Billionaire Lumberjack's Beauty* - available now at all retailers! books2read.com/ BillionaireLumberjacksBeauty

To stay up to date on news, releases, and sales from Gwyn, sign up for her newsletter here: www.gwynmcnamee.com/ newsletter

About the Author

Gwyn McNamee is an attorney, writer, wife, and mother (to one human baby and two fur babies). Originally from the Midwest, Gwyn relocated to her husband's home town of Las Vegas in 2015 and is enjoying her respite from the cold and snow. Gwyn has been writing down her crazy stories and ideas for years and finally decided to share them with the world. She loves to write stories with a bit of suspense and action mingled with romance and heat.

When she isn't either writing or voraciously devouring any books she can get her hands on, Gwyn is busy adding to her tattoo collection, golfing, and stirring up trouble with her perfect mix of sweetness and sarcasm (usually while wearing heels).

Gwyn loves to hear from her readers. Here is where you can find her:

FB Reader Group: https://www.facebook.com/groups/1667380963540655/

Facebook: https://www.facebook.com/AuthorGwynMcNamee/

Newsletter: www.gwynmcnamee.com/newsletter

Website: http://www.gwynmcnamcc.com/ Twitter: https://twitter.com/GwynMcNamee

Instagram: https://www.instagram.com/gwynmcnamee

Bookbub: https://www.bookbub.com/authors/gwynmcnamee

Acknowledgments

Thank you to my incredible team. Renee, Patricia, Stephie, and Caoimhe - you are my rocks. I couldn't ever do this without any of you.

OTHER WORKS BY GWYN MCNAMEE

The Hawke Family Series

Savage Collision **(The Hawke Family - Book One)**

He's everything she didn't know she wanted. She's everything he thought he could never have.

The last thing I expect when I walk into The Hawkeye Club is to fall head over heels in lust. It's supposed to be a rescue mission. I have to get my baby sister off the pole, into some clothes, and out of the grasp of the pussy peddler who somehow manipulated her into stripping. But the moment I see Savage Hawke and verbally spar with him, my ability to remain rational flies out the window and my libido takes center stage. I've never wanted a relationship —my time is better spent focusing on taking down the scum running this city—but what I want and what I need are apparently two different things.

Danika Eriksson storms into my office in her high heels and on her high horse. Her holier-than-thou attitude and accusations should offend me, but instead, I can't get her out of my head or my heart. Her incomparable drive, take-no prisoners attitude, and blatant honesty captivate me and hold me prisoner. I should steer clear, but my self-preservation instinct is apparently dead—which is exactly what our relationship will be once she knows everything. It's only a matter of time.

The truth doesn't always set you free. Sometimes, it just royally screws you.

Tortured Skye (**The Hawke Family - Book Two**)

She's always been off-limits. He's always just out of reach.

Falling in love with Gabe Anderson was as easy as breathing. Fighting my feelings for my brother's best friend was agonizingly hard. I never imagined giving in to my desire for him would cause such a destructive ripple effect. That kiss was my grasp at a lifeline—something, anything to hold me steady in my crumbling life. Now, I have to suffer with the fallout while trying to convince him it's all worth the consequences.

Guilt overwhelms me—over what I've done, the lives I've taken, and more than anything, over my feelings for Skye Hawke. Craving my best friend's little sister is insanely self-destructive. It never should have happened, but since the moment she kissed me, I haven't been able to get her out of my mind. If I take what I want, I risk losing everything. If I don't, I'll lose her and a piece of myself. The raging storm threatening to rain down on the city is nothing compared to the one that will come from my decision.

Love can be torture, but sometimes, love is the only thing that can save you.

Stone Sober (**The Hawke Family - Book Three**)

She's innocent and sweet. He's dark and depraved.

Stone Hawke is precisely the kind of man women are warned about— handsome, intelligent, arrogant, and intricately entangled with some dangerous people. I should stay away, but he manages to strip my soul bare with just a look and dominates my thoughts. Bad decisions are in my past. My life is (mostly) on track, even if it is no longer the one to medical school. I can't allow myself to cave to the fierce pull and ardent attraction I feel toward the youngest Hawke.

Nora Eriksson is off-limits, and not just because she's my brother's employee and sister-in-law. Despite the fact she's stripping at The Hawkeye Club, she has an innocent and pure heart. Normally, the only thing that appeals to me about innocence is the opportunity to taint it. But not when it comes to Nora. I can't expose her to the filth permeating my life. There are too many things I can't control, things completely out of my hands. She doesn't deserve any of it, but the power she holds over me is stronger than any addiction.

The hardest battles we fight are often with ourselves, but only through defeating our own demons can we find true peace.

AVAILABLE AT ALL RETAILERS:

books2read.com/StoneSober

Building Storm (The Hawke Family - Book Four)

She hasn't been living. He's looking for a way to forget it all.

My life went up in flames. All I'm left with is my daughter and ashes. The simple act of breathing is so excruciating, there are days I wish I could stop altogether. So I have no business being at the party, and I definitely shouldn't be in the arms of the handsome stranger. When his lips meet mine, he breathes life into me for the first time since the day the inferno disintegrated my world. But loving again isn't in the cards, and there are even greater dangers to face than trying to keep Landon McCabe out of my heart.

Running is my only option. I have to get away from Chicago and the betrayal that shattered my world. I need a new life-one without attachments. The vibrancy of New Orleans convinces me it's possible to start over. Yet in all the excitement of a new city, it's Storm Hawke's dark, sad beauty that draws me in. She isn't looking for love, and we both need a hot, sweaty release without feelings getting involved. But even the best laid plans fail, and life can leave you burned.

Love can build, and love can destroy. But in the end, love is what raises you from the ashes.

AVAILABLE AT ALL RETAILERS:

books2read.com/BuildingStorm

Tainted Saint (The Hawke Family - Book Five)

He's searching for absolution. She wants her happily ever after.

Solomon Clarke goes by Saint, though he's anything but. After lusting for him from afar, the masquerade party affords me the anonymity to pursue that attraction without worrying about the fall-out of hooking-up with the bouncer from the Hawkeye Club. From the second he lays his eyes and hands on me, I'm helpless to resist him. Even burying myself in a dangerous investigation can't erase the memory of our combustible connection and one night together. The only problem... he has no idea who I am.

Caroline Brooks thinks I don't see her watching me, the way her eyes rake over me with appreciation. But I've noticed, and the party is the perfect opportunity to unleash the desire I've kept reined in for so damn long. It also sets off a series of events no one sees coming. Events that leave those I love hurting because of my failures. While the guilt eats away at my soul, Caroline continues to weigh on my heart. That woman may be the death of me, but oh, what a way to go.

Life isn't always clean, and sometimes, it takes a saint to do the dirty work.

Steele Resolve (The Hawke Family - Book Six)

For one man, power is king. For the other, loyalty reigns.

Mob boss Luca "Steele" Abello isn't just dangerous—he's lethal. A master manipulator, liar, and user, no one should trust a word that comes out of his mouth. Yet, I can't get him out of my head. The time we spent together before I knew his true identity is seared into my brain. His touch. His voice. They haunt my every waking hour and occupy my dreams. So does my guilt. I'm literally sleeping with the enemy and betraying the only family I've ever had. When I come clean, it will be the end of me.

Byron Harris is a distraction I can't afford. I never should have let it go beyond that first night, but I couldn't stay away. Even when I learned who he was, when the *only* option was to end things, I kept going back, risking his life and mine to continue our indiscretion. The truth of what I am could get us both killed, but being with the man who's such an integral part of the Hawke family is even more terrifying. The only people I've ever cared about are on opposing sides, and I'm the rift that could end their friendship forever.

Love is a battlefield isn't just a saying. For some, it's a reality.

AVAILABLE AT ALL RETAILERS:

books2read.com/SteeleResolve

You can find information on the rest of Gwyn's books on her website:

www.gwynmcnamee.com